MW01592641

EBANDTE, INC

P R E S E N T S

UNFALLEN ROSES

PETALS & THORNS

A Novel Anthony Walker

UNFALLEN ROSES
PETALS & THORNS

Anthony Walker

Available
EVERYWHERE
Books Are Sold

A BOOK BY
EBANDTE
GOTTA BE
GOOD!

EBANDTE. INC
The Hood

EBANDTE.INC
The Game
Chose Me

Ebandte, Inc.
P.O. Box 341147
Jamaica, NY 11434
www.ebandte.com

w w w . e b a n d t e . c o m

Ebandte Inc. Presents...   Anthony Walker

UNFALLEN ROSES:
PETALS & THORNS

An *Anthony Walker* Fable

PUBLISHED BY
EBANDTE INC. PUBLISHING

"A BOOK BY EBANDTE GOTTA BE GOOD!"

Sale of this book without a front cover may be unauthorized. If this book was purchased without a cover, it may have been reported to the publisher as "unsold or destroyed." Neither the author nor the publisher may have received payment for the sale of this book.

This book is a work of fiction. Names, characters, places and incidents are products of the author's imagination or are used fictitiously. Any resemblance to actual events or locales or persons, living or dead, is entirely coincidental and is intended to give the fiction a sense of reality and authenticity.

Published by:
Ebandte Inc. Publishing
P.O. Box 341147
Jamaica, New York 11434
WWW.EBANDTE.COM

Library of Congress Control Number: 2006925274
ISBN-10: 0-9749298-2-4
ISBN-13: 978-0-9749298-2-8

© Copyright 2006 by Anthony Walker

UNFALLEN ROSES: PETALS & THORNS CREDITS
Written by Anthony Walker
Revised by Crystal Gamble-Nolden & Ebony Stroman-Clarke
Edited by Crystal Gamble-Nolden & Ebony Stroman-Clarke
Cover Concept by Ebony Stroman-Clarke
Cover graphics & design by www.mariondesigns.com
Text layout and formation by Ebony Stroman-Clarke

All rights reserved, including the right to reproduce this book or portions thereof in any form whatsoever.

Printed in Canada.

THANK YOUS

Most of all I want to thank God for putting me in a situation in the dark that I could only find the light. Thanks to the Ebandte Inc. Publishing Company; Ebony Stroman-Clarke and Danté Clarke for believing in me; ya'll got a friend for life! Thanks again for letting me ride in your car! Shout out to the whole Ebandte Inc. Publishing staff. Jacquline Walker, your son finally did something positive and made a name for himself. I finally turned my dreams into reality with a positive mentality. To my kids; Antoniette, Brandon and Quemoni; don't ever give up! Thanks to my brothers; Mellow and Johnny Walker. Thanks to my sisters Paris and Crystal. To the woman in my life; Adrienne Carroll, thank you for being there for me when so called friends turned their back on me, what's up Gavaughn? A special thanks to Tonya Clark Gillyard and Marilyn Girillo for all of your support by helping me with your input. Diane, Michelle and Monique; thank you for being a part of my life at one time – I still love you. Shout out to Keith Burton and his family. Also shouts out to the Hasty, Pierce, Avery, Jones and Mack families. Shout out to my block; 123rd and 7the Avenue, ya'll know I had to represent. Thanks to my peoples; you know who you are; Best Kept Secret! RIP my brother Jimmy Lee Hasty; there is a lot unsaid that needed to be talked about, I'll meet you at the crossroads. My father Eddie Walker; I hope it's clear enough for you. Sandman Simms; thank you for teaching me how to tap dance! The world famous Apollo Theater will miss you like everyone else will. Thanks to Eddie Jones, Kenny and Ronnie Hall. Damn! I still remember all the fun times we had together. Wayne Harris, thank you for rushing me to the hospital when you did! I'm sorry I left Queens when I did; I might've been able to return the favor… Darryl Wright 119th Street, Evelyn Hasty, April Banks and Ivannia Brack – gone but never forgotten! I'll love you always! Thanks to Mable Patterson and Alma Cambell. To all my brothers and sisters that read my book when it was just loose papers; thank you! It is too many to name but you know who you are. HOLLA AT YA BOY!

Ebandte Inc. Presents...   Anthony Walker

UNFALLEN ROSES:
PETALS & THORNS

An Anthony Walker Fable

PUBLISHED BY
EBANDTE INC. PUBLISHING

"A BOOK BY EBANDTE GOTTA BE GOOD!"

Ebandte Inc. Presents...   *Anthony Walker*

SISTERS

BOOM! BOOM! BOOM! Ava banged on the door.

"Get up! You know it's your weekend to go shopping!" she shouted.

"Ava, what the fuck is on your mind banging on my door like that!?"

"Mommy left a list for you, so get up now and go shopping!" Ava replied.

Ava and Kia are sisters with two different outlooks about life. Kia is a straight 'A' High School senior. She's very pretty, 5-foot-3, One-Hundred-and-Nineteen pounds with green eyes and a caramel complexion. She kept her hair in a low cut Halle Berry style. Girlfriend has a bad attitude and will fight or cut anyone bigger or smaller than her. She loves basketball. She even plays point guard for her school team. She's convinced she can play the sport better than any WNBA player and is willing to bet her life on it. There's hardly anything that Kia doesn't know about basketball teams or players from the sixties on up.

Now, Ava is way different from her little sister. She works in Chase Manhattan Bank. Ava has a bachelor degree in math. She's single by choice with no kids. Everyone always says Ava looks more like her father than her mother. She's dark skin, 5-foot-6, and One-Hundred-and-Thirty pounds. Ava has dark shoulder length hair; she's a real cutie, not as cute as Kia though.

Kia has a habit of always telling Ava she acts and talks like she's white. That statement always made the two of them fight. When it's all over, both of them would sit in front of the television eating ice cream together.

"Where is mommy?" Kia asked.

"She had to work overtime,"

"So why are you rushing me to go shopping if she's not here?"

"Because, it's twelve noon," Ava replied in an aggravated tone.

Kia got out the bed. She walked over to her window. In the middle of March it was still cold in New York City. The neighborhood drug dealers and dopefiends were the only ones fool enough to stand outside in the cold. Kia headed to the bathroom to wash. When she came out, Ava was on the phone talking to her girlfriend; Pam. Kia rolled her eyes then walked into the kitchen for something to drink.

Ava sucked her teeth, "Pam, let me call you back. I'm about to split somebody's head open in this house today." When she hung up the phone, Kia walked pass her.

"What's your fucking problem?" Ava yelled. Kia didn't respond. She just kept walking back into her room, then slammed her door closed.

Kia sat on her bed. She picked up the phone to call her girlfriend, Melody. Then she pressed the CD remote for R. Kelly to come on, the phone rung twice.

"Hola?" Melody's mother spoke.

"Good afternoon, may I speak to Melody please?" Melody's mother yelled something in Spanish. Then Melody picked up the phone.

"What's up?" Melody answered.

"Melody, your mother lived in Harlem all her life you might as well say. She still can't speak English?"

"Watch your mouth," Melody responded.

Kia laughed, "You know I love her boo-boo!"

Melody is Kia's best friend. It's been that way since they

were kids. Melody lived on the sixth floor of the same building Kia lived in. She lived with her mother and her brother John. John's had a drug problem since his teenage years. Now twenty-five years old, his drug problem only got worst. He used about two bundles a day now. Melody's mother, Mira Cruz has been living in Harlem since she moved from Puerto Rico twenty years ago. She's a short woman with a heart of gold.

Melody's the only Puerto Rican girl on the block. She's a straight 'A' student in her computer class. She even attends after school computer classes in Hunter College. Her dream is to one day run the world by computers with her great ideas. She always says "HI-SURF will rule!" She's about one-hundred-and-thirty-two pounds with brown hair down her back. But she always wears her hair in a ponytail. She could pass for a young Selena or Gloria Estefan.

"Melody, I need your help. Will you please go shopping with me?" Kia asked.

"Only if you pay for the grapes,"

"No doubt," Kia assured her

"I'll be down there in five minutes."

"Cool, I'll be waiting," Kia shot back. Both girls hung up the phone.

Kia put on her old Guess jeans, black Timberland boots and her Fubu sweater. She turned up her song, *I Wish* by R. Kelly. She started dancing in front of the mirror. "Damn! I still look good on my worst days," she mumbled to herself. Ava was calling her name. Kia opened her door then yelled, "What?"

"Your rice and bean eating friend is here," Ava yelled over Kia's music.

Melody looked at Ava, "If you wasn't my homegirl

11

sister I would whip your black ass in this house."

"Melody, when did you ever hear a Puerto Rican whipping a black's ass?"

"If you keep talking shit, March Fourth, Two-Thousand-and-One will change history forever because your black ass will get whipped."

Kia burst out laughing, "I'll whip both of you together!" Ava said.

"Don't play yourself," Kia stated. "Melody come in my room please before we catch a case." The girls walked into the room.

"Kia, why she so disrespectful towards me? She keep running her mouth, I'm gonna put the blows on her."

"And I'll help you," Kia replied. They both laughed. Melody sat on Kia's bed. "Why every time I come here you always playing R. Kelly or that fucking Nelly CD?"

"They both mines, I paid for them," Kia answered. Melody picked up Kia's remote control then pressed hot 97.

"It's time for us to go, I hate Blu Cantrell," Kia stated. Melody smiled at her then turned the music up louder. Kia walked into the living-room. Ava was back on the phone. "Where's the list?" Kia asked. Ava pointed to the white envelope on the kitchen table. When Kia opened the list she yelled. "This is the whole fucking supermarket!"

Ava continued talking on the phone. Kia walked back into her room. Melody had both remotes in her hand. She had the television on BET, and the radio on hot 97. Kia put on her Northface coat. She pulled her red hat over her head. When she was finished, she walked over to Melody and clapped both hands together to get her attention. When Melody looked up, she saw Kia was ready to leave. Melody clicked off both remotes. The girls left the house.

Walking down the stairs Melody held her nose, "Damn! This hallway smell like piss! The super ain't worth shit! If I was my mother I wouldn't even pay rent, I'll make his ass pay us for living like this."

"Don't worry about it, one day we'll be living in a big house with a fence around it," Kia stated. Both girls smiled at each other.

When they got to the stoop, there were dopefiends lined up to buy that get high for a day. There were all kinds of different names the dope was called. Some of the names were Seal-A-Meal, NBA Slam, Sting Ray, and American Dream just to name a few. The line of dopefiends waiting to be served was so long, you would've thought Kenny and his crew was giving free money away.

"Look at them fools lined up to buy that shit. They making a lot of money over here," stated Melody.

Kia replied, "You right about that." She pulled her hat over her ears. Melody stood on the stoop looking dead at Kenny. She knew if she had his money, she would have ten times more in a month's time. The two girls stepped of the stoop. They started walking towards the supermarket on Eighth Avenue.

Melody grabbed the shopping cart. Her and Kia walked up one aisle. Melody put a bag of grapes in the cart, while Kia was picking up food items. Melody's face was glued to a magazine. She was reading PC magazine and Black Enterprise, still managing to eat her grapes. She was so much into the magazine that she crashed into the bread stand.

"Girl, watch where you going. Please," Kia yelled.

"Yeah, yeah whatever," said Melody as she kept

reading her magazine. When she finally looked up she noticed all the food in the cart.

"Kia, how the hell was you going to get all this food home?"

"If there's a will, there's a way," Kia smiled. Her and Melody headed to the register.

While they were on line, Kia tapped Melody. She looked up. They both noticed Vevook on the cash register. Vevook winked at Melody. Melody winked back, she knew what that meant. Kia started putting food on the counter. When Vevook finished ringing up the food, the total only came out to twenty-seven dollars. It was well over one-hundred dollars worth of food on the counter.

"Kia, have twenty dollars for me in school tomorrow," Vevook stated.

"You got it," Kia smiled.

A young kid was packing the food into the bags. He took a look at all the food, then looked at Melody and Kia, "Miss, do you need help?"

Kia looked at all the bags, she counted about nine and the kid wasn't done packing. There was no way her and Melody was going to carry all those bags by themselves.

"How much?" Kia asked.

"Five dollars Miss."

"Okay, let's do it," Kia told the kid.

The young kid ran off to get a shopping cart. He put nine bags in the cart, Kia and Melody carried a bag a piece. Kia zipped up her coat as they headed out the door. Melody walked out without paying for the Black Enterprise or the PC Magazine.

When they got outside, Melody noticed her brother, John walking across the street by himself. She called out to him. He looked in her direction. She waved for him to come to her. John walked up to Melody, she knew right away, he was high off dope. She hated him for his habit, but she would still do anything for him.

Melody grabbed Kia's bag then handed both bags to John.

"Now, let's go," she said to John. John was walking in front of them. Melody kicked him in his ass, he turned around.

"You know what that's for!" Melody said. John knew better than letting his little sister catching him high in the street. Plus Melody always thought she was the oldest anyway, at least that's how she acted. All four of them walked back towards Seventh Avenue. This is when a tall, dark skinned guy with a bold head called Melody's name. She turned around, it was Mike, a guy from school that had been sweating her. It was four years ago when they first met. The first day of school five black girls wanted to jump Melody in her homeroom class. Mike stood up for her then walked her home after school. He wanted to make sure she got home safe. Since then, they've been friends. Mike really liked Melody since day one. Only now was Melody starting to feel the same way about him. But she still wanted to make him sweat.

"Mike, what are you doing around here?" she asked

"I just stopped by to see my man Kenny about something," Mike replied. Melody knew right away it must've been about drugs or money. She knew Mike was slinging on one-hundred-Eighteenth Street himself.

Kia, John and the young kid from the supermarket stood waiting for Melody.

"Miss, I have to get back to work, time is money. I'm

wasting time so I'm losing money." Kia smiled at the young kid.

"I'll give you seven dollars for a few more minutes of your time," Melody replied.

"Okay, as long as you're paying. You're the boss," the kid replied. Kia respected what the kid just told Melody. She knew there was a lot of truth in that statement, but coming from a kid, Kia was shocked. Harlem breeds money makers young.

"Melody it's time to go. Time is money," Kia said. The little kid laughed at her.

"Miss, why you biting my lines?" the kid joked.

Melody told Mike she had to go. Then she smiled at him.

"If you stay out of trouble, I'll give you my number."

"That's what I'm talking about!" replied Mike. He walked up to Melody then kissed her on her mouth.

"That's not fair," Melody stated.

"It's fair in my ball park," replied Mike while walking away from her. Melody stood there smiling from ear to ear.

"Melody, you're not old enough to date guys," John yelled.

"Fuck you!" she responded. Then she stared at her brother with daggers in her eyes.

"What floor Miss?" asked the young kid once they were in front of the building.

"Third floor," Kia revealed. John took five bags out of the cart. The kid took four. Kia and Melody carried the remaining two up the stairs. When they reached the top, Kia gave the kid a ten dollar bill.

"I don't have any change Miss."

Kia smiled, "Keep it. Time is money right?"

The kid smiled back, "Thank you!" He ran down the stairs.

Kia banged on her door. When Ava opened it she started pulling bags inside the apartment.

"I'll be back down later," Melody told Kia.

"Cool," Kia replied. She took a ten dollar bill from her pocket then handed it to John.

"Give it back before I split your head open in this hallway!" Melody told her brother. She grabbed him by his jacket.

"Kia, don't forget about Vevook tomorrow."

"I got that for her," Kia replied.

"Let's go John!" Melody demanded.

Kia knew Melody was going to chew his ass out for being high and taking money from her. But she had her own problems dealing with Ava. Kia took off her coat.

"Did mommy call yet?"

"No," Ava answered, and then added, "She'll be home around eight."

Kia grabbed her coat then walked in her room. She went through her DVD selection. She pulled out *Sugar Hill*. Kia loved that movie. It's about two brothers getting money together in Harlem. She wondered if Ava was a boy would things be different. "One day I'll be rich, then I'll move far away from Harlem. I'll only come back to visit," Kia mumbled to herself.

Kia went into the kitchen. Ava was putting the food away. She grabbed some cookies and a glass of milk. Then she headed back to her room.

"Ava what are you cooking?"

"Chicken, corn and rice."

"Please don't fuck up the rice," Kia stated.

Ava paused, "If you so worried about it, why don't you cook?"

The next thing Ava heard was the sound of Kia's bedroom door slamming.

"Damn! That bitch gets me sick!" Ava mumbled to herself. She continued mumbling to herself, "I'll be glad when I move out and get my own place, it's time. I'm twenty-four, no man, no kids, working in a bank for twenty-seven-thousand dollars a year, counting other people's money, and risking my life for it."

Ava knew it was time to make some changes in her life, for the best before shit got worst. She walked over to the living-room window. It was about eight nice trucks and cars parked in front of her building. She remembered when she first moved to One Hundred Twenty Third Street and Seventh Avenue, it was known as "The Dust Block" of Harlem. Ava remembered hearing names like "Red Devil, C-Girl, He-Man, and Pac Man" just to name a few. She remembered days when it use to be crowded in front of her building as she made her way home from school. People use to wait for Tone and his brother James just to buy "Dust" from them. Those were the good ol' days. Nowadays theirs a new drug called "Heroin" that rules the streets. They got young punks controlling it who will kill for short money, or a reputation. That's so sad. Now, with the help of Mellow and Mannie one-hundred-twenty-Third Street is controlled by a guy named Kenny. Ava couldn't stand Kenny. She walked away from the window contemplating her next move.

Melody was in her room telling John the way he looks when he's high on that shit. She kept asking him, why was he making the next man rich. John said nothing as Melody continued.

"John, you know the streets in and out. So why risk your life being broke? You just don't know, you killing me and ma. You supposed to be the man of the house, but all you do is get high all night then sleep for two days. You don't give ma no money, but cry to her when you're dope sick."

John was standing in Melody's doorway with his head down to the floor. He still didn't say a word. Melody continued.

"I'll respect you more if you had a nice girlfriend, a job of any kind or something! But, being a fucking twenty-five year old junkie, still living at home, with a habit out of this world...!" Melody frowned. She was getting even more upset by the minutes.

"John, when I get your age, I'll be rich living in a big house somewhere, not in this piece of shit smelling building!"

John couldn't say a word. Melody became vexed. She hopped off her bed.

"Get the hell out of the doorway!" she pushed him.

"You make me sick!" Melody yelled as she slammed her door.

Turning on her Dell Computer, she typed in her password. Nextel.com was the first website she went to on the internet. She wanted to check the week's projections. Every Sunday she did the same thing with other companies as well. Her dream was to design a website that was worth millions of dollars, or a computer chip worth hundreds of millions of dollars. Melody knew it would take a lifetime for a young Puerto Rican girl from a small ghetto in Harlem to be noticed. This is why she stayed on her computer, educating herself. She went to seminars, attended Hunter

College, and read PC Magazine for the same reasons. Melody was well known by her fellow classmates at Hunter College. And she had every reason to be. She was just a High School senior who was at the head of the college computers courses she was taking. The white students hated her. The Black and Hispanic students said she was too ghetto. But Melody didn't care about what any of them said. She often laughed at her fellow classmate because she knew she might be interviewing them one day for a job at "HI-SURF," her very own company. Melody loved knowing a little Puerto Rican girl from Harlem was head of the class. She planned on ruling the world with her profession, just like Bill Gates had done.

Looking at her computer, she noticed only two of the companies lost a few points. That wasn't anything to panic about, she thought to herself. Other companies gained five to seven points. If she had money to invest, she would've gained twelve-thousand dollars in her pockets. Melody knew the ins and outs about investing in companies. She wanted someone to invest in her own ideas, but at eighteen years old, who would take the chance investing in her? This is why she wanted to design her own website to show the world her ideas. But Melody's problem was money. That was the only thing holding her back from her dreams. Sometimes she felt like crying. She even felt as if God didn't love her or he wouldn't have put her in such a horrible situation. But no matter what, Melody was determined! She was going to turn her dream into a reality no matter what it took. Even if that meant having a fucked mentality, Melody was down for the cause if she knew her dreams could come true. What hurt her the most was knowing her own brother couldn't help her in any kind of way. He was a sorry piece of shit in her eyes. That didn't stop her from loving him though. She would still kill anyone who ever tried to hurt him.

Melody got up from her computer. She opened her window. She was mad and offended. She didn't like the idea of being broke and poor. Melody was so upset, she didn't even feel the cold air coming through her window. "Look at them dumb fucks," she mumbled to herself. "They drive around in fifty-thousand dollar cars and trucks without a job the first, acting like they don't have a worry in the world. If I had that kind of money to waste on a car, I'll be rich for sure. Just wait until they hear about Melody Cruz, CEO and founder of HI-SURF."

Melody wanted to do something, what, she didn't know. She walked into her mother's room, but she was sleep. John was in the kitchen warming some leftovers from the night before.

Melody picked up her phone to call Kia. On the first ring Kia picked up.

"What are you doing?" asked Melody.

"Watching Sugar Hill again," Kia replied.

"Kia, listen. We got to put something together. We need some money, real money, about fifty-thousand cash. I got big plans, real big plans. Kia you my best friend in this world, you must understand after graduation our lives are going to change. Which way will our lives change, I don't know, but something gotta give. Are you ready for change?" Melody asked Kia.

"Hell yeah!" Kia responded.

"Kia, go to the window, I want to show you something."

Kia got off her bed then walked to the window. She had the phone to her ear.

"Are you there yet?" Melody asked.

"Yeah."

"Tell me what you see."

"I see four nice cars, Kenny and his workers," Kia paused, squinted her eyes then continued, "dopefiends, people walking fast trying to get out the cold..."

Melody interrupted, "Open your fucking eyes Kia!" she yelled. "That's what society wants us to see! Let me explain to you what I see, it's called opportunity! We all get that opportunity at least once in our lives. The problem is when it comes most people don't see it, even if it hits them dead in the face! Now, theirs others that see it, but take too long to react to it. Some people are scared to change. They get use to this life of hell, they're happy with it. It's sad Kia. That's why so many of our people are still in the ghetto for fifty and sixty years. We as Roses are going to change that cycle, because when our opportunity comes, and it will come. Trust me. Good or bad, you and I are going to ride that wave to success, understand? All I see is a big picture with big things in it. We don't have time to waste on small things in life! You watch my back, I'll watch yours. We both keep our eyes open for opportunity, together."

Kia was still at the window with the phone to her ear. She was in a zone listening to Melody speaking. Kia wanted to say something, but chose to listen instead. All the things Melody spoke about were so true, but now they needed a way to make that opportunity become a reality. Some people wait a lifetime for that opportunity. Melody and Kia knew that was too long to wait for them. Melody heard her mother go into the bathroom.

"Kia let me call you back in about an hour. I got to talk to my mother about something."

"Aight."

The girls hung up the phone. Kia started Sugar Hill over again. She hated when somebody interrupted her while she watched that movie. But then she decided against watching the movie. She turned to the Knicks and Lakers game instead. Kia kept thinking about the conversation she had with Melody. The word opportunity kept banging in her head. She began wondering what Melody had on her mind. Kia kicked off her boots then laid on her bed, one hand was behind her head as she looked up at the ceiling. Her mind started to race.

When Kia woke up it was eight o'clock in the evening. She missed the entire basketball game, but that word opportunity was still in her head. That was the word of the week. She walked into the bathroom to brush her teeth, and wash her face. When she was finished she walked into the kitchen to make herself something to eat. This is when she heard the locks click open. Kia looked at the clock on the wall, it read eight-twenty. It was her mother. When the door opened Kia was standing there. Jacquline jumped back, Kia scared her. She had two shopping bags in her hands. Kia grabbed the bags from her.

"Mommy, you look tired."

"After being on your feet for sixteen hours, you'll feel the same way," her mother replied.

Jacquline Wilson's been working as head nurse in Kings County Hospital for twenty-one years. She worked long hours just to keep her daughters on the right track. Ever since her husband died saving Ava in a fire seventeen years ago, Jacquline has never been the same. She never turned to another man for support or comfort because Edward still had her heart. Jacquline felt in her heart that even though

Edward Wilson was gone, he was not forgotten. He made her the strong woman she is today. Her goal was to show her daughters the same thing in life. She didn't want them to depend on nobody. Jacquline provided her daughters with the best of everything from clothes to schools. She paid for Ava to finish college at Colombia University. Plus she still managed to save up enough money for Kia to attend John Jay College next year. And although Jacquline wanted to retire, she felt her duties as a mother wasn't done yet.

"Where's Ava?" Jacquline inquired.

"She must be in her room. Mommy, give me your coat, have a seat." Kia sat on the floor to unlace Jacquline's boots. Jacquline took a seat on the couch. Kia could see the struggle all over her mother's face. The hurt. The pain. The long hours of standing on her feet just to make sure someone else's life is saved. Kia always told people her mother is her hero. It made Kia cry sometimes to see her mother work so hard and still live in the ghetto. She took off her mother's shoes and socks then started rubbing her feet. That word *opportunity* started bouncing around in Kia's head again. She wondered did her mother ever get her opportunity or was she still waiting. Thinking about how hard her mother worked, Kia understood what Melody was talking about. Kia looked up to say something to her mother, but Jacquline had her head back and her mouth open. She was sleeping. Kia got up from off the floor. She headed to the kitchen to warm some food up for her mother as she took a nap.

At 10pm Kia finally woke her mother up. She had a hot plate on the table with a glass of grape soda waiting for her. Helping her mother from the couch, Kia held her hand until she sat down at the table. Sitting across from her mother, she ate a bowl of ice cream as she stared into her mother's eyes.

"Kia, how are you doing in school?"

"I'm passing all of my classes and I'm head of my math class."

Jacquline smiled, "What about basketball?"

"My team is number five with a 10-4 record. We have a game at City College against Norman Thomas high school. They're the top school in Manhattan."

"Kia, if I never told you, I'm proud of you. I'm proud of you and Ava.

Kia smiled, "Thank you mommy! Can I get you some more soda?"

"Please," Jacquline replied handing Kia her glass.

"Sure mommy." Kia picked up Jacquline's empty plate. She stood to her feet then got her mother the soda she asked for.

"Mommy, do you need anything else before I go to sleep?"

"No baby."

Kia went back into her room. She started picking out her clothes for school the next day. Then she wrapped her hair and headed to the bathroom to shower.

Ava got up about 6:15am like she did every morning. She took her morning shower, pulled out her black two piece business suit with a pair of matching leather boots. After she got dressed she headed to the kitchen. Eggs and grits is what she made herself for breakfast. She thought about making herself a cup of hot cocoa, but she quickly erased the thought from her mind. Ava hated the cold weather, but even more, she hated the thought of what would happen if she was late to work. She hated working at Chase Manhattan Bank. She knew those fake ass people smiling in her face didn't really care about her. It's been plenty of days when Ava just wanted to quit. The only thing stopping her was her bills. She knew they had to be paid. So until something better came along she was forced to stay. Pam, who was Ava's co-worker and only friend on the job, recently took the police exam. She tried to convince Ava to take the exam with her but she refused. Ava felt like her life was more important than chasing criminals with guns, especially since they didn't have a problem killing a cop. *It's not worth it* Ava told herself.

Picking up her coat and bag, Ava checked for her keys, CD player, money and metro card. Then she exited her apartment making her way to the train station. When she stepped outside of her building, the first thing she saw was dopefiends, lined up trying to buy that bag or two to kill that morning sickness. Kenny and Mellow was on the stoop. Mellow noticed Ava, he greeted her.

"Good morning Ava."

"Same to you Mellow."

Kenny knew Ava couldn't stand him, but he decided to try his luck anyway. "How you doing Ava?"

Ava turned around then looked at Kenny. She stared at him with a grill face. "Get a life motherfucker!" then she proceeded to walk down the steps.

Mellow started laughing at Ava's comment towards Kenny. "She don't like you big homie!"

Kenny kept his eyes glued to Ava's back as Mellow continued to laugh.

"I hate that black bitch!"

Mellow finally stopped laughing. "What? Ava. She's that bitch! She got it going on foreal, a good job, pretty and smart. I'd wife her."

"Fuck her! Kia looks much better than her anyway."

"Hell no!" yelled Mellow. "Ava is all woman!"

"Whatever."

Ava got on the number two train. She put on her Koss headphones. Her Aaliyah CD started flooding her ears. It had been two weeks since she bought the CD. Ever since, she's been trying to listen to the entire thing. Ava was in a zone enjoying the sweet voice of Aaliyah, but before she knew it, the iron horse pulled into Seventy-Second Street station. It was time for her to get off. Ava sucked her teeth then placed her CD player back in her bag. She still didn't get a chance to listen to the whole thing.

Exiting the station, Ava made her way to the Coffee Shop.

"Good morning Miss Lady," said the man behind the counter.

Ava smiled, "Good morning Wayne."

The Coffee Shop was only a block away from Ava's job. She stopped there every morning for her bagel and tea. She never understood how a big man like Wayne could be so friendly. He had to be about 6-foot-5, three-hundred pounds. Wayne looked like he was supposed to be some rich person's bodyguard. Secretly, Ava liked Wayne. That's why she stopped at the Coffee Shop every morning, just to see his smile.

When Ava left the Coffee Shop, she walked into Chase Manhattan Bank. The first person she saw was Pam, who was busy counting her money for the morning rush. Ava only had ten minutes to do the same thing before the bank officially opened up at eight. She hung up her coat and bag then grabbed her money drawer. When the bank opened, Ava was ready.

Kia called Melody to inform her that she was ready for school.

"Okay," Melody told her. "I'm on my way down."

Melody picked up her coat and bookbag. Opening her bookbag, Melody checked to make sure her notes and homework was inside. Since it was Monday Melody knew she had classes at Hunter College as well. She made sure all of her work was in order for those classes as well. Melody kissed her mother goodbye then headed out the door.

By the time Melody got downstairs Kia was waiting for her on the stoop. Melody saw Kia's attention was directed toward whatever was going on across the street. Melody turned her attention toward the opposite side of the street as well. What both girls had their attention on was Kenny and Mannie. The two of them were whipping some dopefiend's ass. Kenny pulled out a small gun then hit the man with it. Mannie kept kicking the man all over his body.

"Kia, let's go. We got better things to do with our time."

Melody and Kia began walking away from the stoop shaking their head.

"Let's stop at JAPS," Kia suggested.

Melody looked at Kia like she was crazy, "Hell no! I don't eat out of their! You just went shopping yesterday."

"That was yesterday. Today is a new day," Kia retorted.

The girls didn't make any stops. But on their way to school Kia told Melody the word *opportunity* stayed on her mind all night.

"Melody, you know what? I wanted to ask my mother did her opportunity come. I talked to her last night and, I can see the struggle and the hurt all in her eyes. I felt her pain. I don't want that. Ever."

Melody remained silent, but she listened very attentively to Kia.

"You know what? I'm ready to rob Kenny ass!" Kia stated.

Melody busted out laughing. "It's not worth it. Like I said, our opportunity will come. Watch."

"Opportunity!" Kia repeated the word like it was her first time hearing and understanding what it meant. "That's the word of the week." She looked at Melody then winked and smiled. When Melody didn't smile back she knew something wasn't right.

"What's wrong?" Kia asked.

"Opportunity," Melody stated, "Is not the word of the week. It's something that can happen at any moment in our lives."

"So what are you saying?" Kia asked.

"Let me explain something to you Kia. We're both young with strong powerful minds, but how far can we go without opportunity? It might come, it might not. So in the meantime we still live our lives, understand?"

After a few minutes the girls noticed they walked about ten blocks, talking about opportunity.

Kia put her arm around Melody's neck, "Don't worry. We are the roses, we can't be faded.

Both girls walked into Watley High School on One Hundred Fourteenth Street. Mostly all downtown Harlem's drug lords went to that school. It's a very large school. It covered One Hundred Thirty Second Street, all the way down to One Hundred and Tenth Street. Watley has a reputation for being a very good school. And over the years things have changed for the better. Watley is now ranked number one in academics throughout the entire Manhattan. The boys basketball team is number one and, the girls team is ranked number five. The best thing about Watley is the teachers really care. Instead of just giving the kids work and having them do it, the teachers will take time to explain, show and teach the kids what they need to learn.

As Kia and Melody entered the building they turned towards one another to talk one last time before they parted.

"Remember what I said Kia. We'll talk some more when I get home from my computer classes tonight."

"I got basketball practice all this week," Kia revealed.

"We'll find time," Melody assured her. The two girls winked at each other then headed in separate directions.

"**W**hat's wrong Kathy?"

"Jacquline, it's my husband, he's been missing for five days now," Kathy sobbed.

Jacquline raised an eyebrow, "Five days? Did you put in a missing persons report with the police?"

"The second day I went to the police station and filled out all the papers I needed to."

Jacquline only met Kathy's husband once. Off top she knew he was into all the wrong things in life, she wasn't a person to judge but his lifestyle spoke for itself. Peter was a handsome Italian man with a bronze complexion, and jet black hair. He stood 5-foot-8 and weighed about One Hundred Eighty Nine pounds. He talked real loud about what they had, where they lived and the cars he drove. What turned Jacquline off about him was every other word out of his mouth was "Don't worry about it."

Jacquline knew after five days without calling, Peter wasn't coming back. She didn't want to be the one to tell Kathy her opinion, but her husband was dead.

"How do I pay for the house we live in if he doesn't return?"

Jacquline tried to comfort Kathy with some soothing words. "Don't think of the worst. Leave it in God's hands, he'll handle it for you."

Kathy looked defeated, "Jacquline, between me and you, my husband is dead."

"Don't say that Kathy because it might not be true."

Kathy looked into Jacquline's eyes, "With the lifestyle he lives, he's dead. Trust me, I know.

Jacquline grabbed Kathy's hand, "If you need help, feel free to call me at home any time. Please keep me informed Kathy."

"I will."

Jacquline smiled then rubbed Kathy on her cheek. She was trying to comfort her friend, but she really didn't know what to say anymore. Some times silence is the best way to help people out.

Jacquline got up from her table, it was time to start her sixteen hour shift. Jacquline felt Kathy's pain. When she lost Edward in a fire she also lost part of her soul, faith and confidence. It took years for her to restores parts of herself that she lost back. She almost wanted to cry for Kathy. When she looked back, Kathy was wiping the tears from her face. Jacquline remembered being in that same situation years ago.

Love hurts.

"**Don't** leave without me Ava."

Ava had her shoulder bag and coat in her hand. "I'm right her waiting for you Pam."

Five minutes later Pam walked up to Ava, "Are you ready to go?"

"Hell yeah!" Ava replied. Both women shared a brief laugh then Pam became serious.

"Listen Ava, in a few weeks I'm quitting this job."

Ava was surprised, "Why, what's up?"

"I passed the police exam. In a few weeks they'll be calling me for the physical. It's time for me to move on. Ava, there's days I count so much money on this job it makes me dizzy. The bad part about it is none of it belongs to me." Pam started laughing to herself, "Sometimes I have to go into the bathroom just to get my composure back. It's so tempting to just walk out of here with three large duffel bags filled with money."

"It's not worth it," Ava assured her friend.

Pam was shaking her head, "Some days my hand hurts so bad from counting money that I don't even want my man to touch me."

Although Ava was happy Pam was moving on, she was upset at the fact that her only real friend on the job was leaving. Plus Ava understood everything Pam was saying regarding working at the bank. Everything she said was true. Ava often felt the same way. What Ava couldn't understand was why Pam wanted to be NYPD. Pam was fine enough to sell her beauty to any model agency. Cindy Crawford, Jessica Simpson or Demi Moore didn't have a thing on her. Pam's ocean blue eyes and tall, slim, hourglass frame demanded attention from the time walked into any room. Any man would love to have Pam in their arms. In Ava's eyes, Pam becoming NYPD was a waste of beauty.

Snapping out of her thoughts, Ava spoke.

"Pam, let me know before you quit."

"You'll be the first to know," Pam assured her.

The two women walked out the door. Before they went their separate ways, they greeted each other with a hug.

Ava sat on the train as her body jerked with each turn or stop the iron horse made. After her conversation with Pam, she started contemplating on what she should do with her own life. *Start looking for a higher paying job, or stick it out for another year?* Is what Ava came up with. If she stayed she was convinced she would become even crazier than she already was. Ava already felt like the money had a tendency to talk to her. In her mind the dead old white men on those green pieces of paper were saying *take me, I'm yours, go have fun with me.* Ava had to laugh at herself remembering one day she'd caught herself talking to the money. That day she was convinced she was going crazy foreal. Deep in Ava's heart, she knew if she had a few million dollars of her own, it was on! She smiled to herself thinking of the possibilities. *Daydreaming isn't a crime. But for a few million dollars I'll do a crime,* Ava thought to herself.

"Fuck that! I only live once," Ava mumbled to herself as she exited the trains closing doors. Walking up the train station's steps, Ava had a taste for fish. When she finally reached One Hundred Twenty Fifth Street, she started walking towards Madison Avenue. *Tasty Seafood* was her destination. Ava ordered fish and chips with two coke sodas. The guy behind the counter was trying to get her number, but Ava wasn't paying him any attention.

After basketball practice, Kia and her teammate,

Regeane walked home together. Regeane lived around the corner from Kia, whenever Melody wasn't around Regeane was Kia's second choice. But all three of them have been hanging out since fourth grade.

Regeane was the biggest out of the crew. Not only did she have a big butt and big chest, she was 5-foot-11 and weighed One Hundred Ninety Five pounds. Any time she was mad, her light brown eyes would turn green. Everyone in the school knows Regeane. Some people say she plays basketball better than some guy's on their school's team. Her brother gave her the name "Big Rage." It didn't take long for everyone to start calling her the same thing. Regeane hated that name, but no one stopped calling her Big Rage so it stuck to her like glue. Another thing Regeane loved doing was playing chess. She's been in countless teen tournaments. She's even appeared in the newspaper twice since Two Thousand and One.

"Kia, walk with me to A Hundred Twenty Fifth Street."

Kia looked at Regeane, "For what?" she asked.

"It's that time of the month," Regeane said almost in a whispered tone.

"Say no more," Kia stated.

Regeane picked up four things from Shop Rite drug store. When her and Kia got to the register, the guy behind the counter looked at both ladies.

"You two ladies have some pretty eyes."

"Thank you," both ladies replied.

"Excuse me Miss," the guy said while pointing at Regeane, "You're a pretty young lady, may I ask your name?"

Regeane laughed in the guys face, "I'm Regeane, and

you are...?"

The guy was confused about what she was laughing at, but he managed to smile anyway, "Mine is Lindell."

"That's nice," said Regeane as she totally ignored the rest of what he was saying then walked out the store.

"Regeane, why were you so rude to that guy in the store?"

Regeane sucked her teeth, "He always see me, now he wanna speak. Fuck him," Regeane held her middle finger up to emphasize her point. Kia laughed. As both girls turned on Seventh Avenue, they bumped into Ava coming out of No Pork on My Fork.

"What's up Ava?" Regeane asked.

"Just coming from work, that's all," Ava replied.

"What's in the bag for us big sis," Regeane asked with a smile on her face.

"Fish and chips for me and me only," Ava answered.

The ladies walked until they reached Ava and Kia's building. Regeane lived four buildings down from them. Once in front of the building, Regeane turned to both ladies, "I'm going upstairs before my mother starts acting up y'all." Kia and Ava laughed at Regeane. They knew her mother could cause quit a scene when she wanted to.

"You don't wanna get that ass whipped, huh?" Kia laughed.

"Fuck you Kia!" Regeane spat.

Kenny was sitting in his Yukon, talking to Mannie who was standing outside of his truck. As Mannie moved slightly to the side, Kenny noticed Kia, Regeane and Ava. He rolled down his window to speak to Kia.

"Hello Kia."

Kia waved at Kenny. Mellow was sitting in the

passenger seat looking at the trio as well. Ava was nice enough to greet him, but she didn't say a word to Kenny. But Kenny didn't care, he turned his head soon as she spoke. Regeane said what's up to everyone then stepped.

Inside the building Ava told Kia she couldn't stand Kenny.

"He's a bitch! I look right through his ass. If I was smoking, I'd take his shit."

Kia didn't say a word, "Ava, just open the door please."

Ava passed the bags she was carrying to Kia. Then she placed her keys in the lock and opened the door. Kia put all the bags on the table then went into her room. Kia took off all her clothes then headed for the shower.

Ava picked up the remote, the eight o'clock news was just coming on.

"The top story of the day, a man was found dead in the trunk of his car with five bullets in his head. This looks like it could've been a Mob hit, however the chief of police has not yet confirmed this as a hit. The Thirty Nine year old man has been identified as Peter Taurasi. As more details come in regarding this story we will keep you posted..."

Ava clicked the remote to a different station, "Oh well, he must've fucked up," she mumbled to herself. She didn't know the dead guy so it didn't matter to her. She walked over to the kitchen table and ripped open her bag of fish.

"Kia, come and get some of this food," Ava yelled.

"Ava, I'm still in the bathroom. Put it to the side please."

When Kia finally walked into the kitchen, Ava was just finishing her food.

"Your plate is in the oven," Ava told Kia.

Kia opened the refrigerator to get herself a glass of grape soda. She sat down next to her sister then started eating.

"What's good, Ava?"

At work the next morning, Jacquline walked to her office. She noticed Kathy standing by her door with tears in her eyes, waiting for her. Jacquline knew something was very wrong. The look in her eyes wasn't the same look she had yesterday. Kathy noticed Jacquline approaching her.

"Jacquline, do you have a few minutes?"

"Sure Kathy, let's go into my office." Both women entered Jacquline's office. Kathy took a seat on the leather couch, Jacquline sat beside her.

"They found Peter. He's dead," Kathy paused to let the news sink in.

Jacquline took a deep breath then grabbed her friend's hand, "Oh, Kathy. I'm so sorry."

Kathy tried blinking real hard to hold back the tears, "It was all over the news last night. They found him dead in the trunk of his car with five bullets in his head. They said it was a 'Mob hit.'"

Jacquline didn't know what to say. What do you say to someone who has just found out their husband is dead?

"I'm so sorry Kathy," were the only words Jacquline managed to get out.

Kathy cried harder, "Jacquline, that's not even the half. I just got an eviction notice on my door this morning. Peter hasn't paid the mortgage on the house for the past six months. He hasn't even paid for Antoinette's school," Kathy sobbed.

Jacquline did her best to hold herself back from crying. "You haven't noticed or checked the bills Kathy?"

"No, Peter always took care of it."

Shaking her head, Jacquline spoke softly, "It's your job as a woman of the house to make sure all the bills are paid on time."

"I know. I know," Kathy kept repeating.

There was a brief moment of silence between the two women. Shortly after, Jacquline began weeping harder.

Jacquline put her arm around Kathy's neck. She whispered into her ear, "You must stay strong for your daughter. Don't give up now."

Jacquline really felt Kathy's pain. It took all the strength she had not to break down herself.

"Listen," Jacquline continued, "You can move into my building. It's a two bedroom apartment vacant."

"Where? In Harlem?" Kathy asked as if she were surprised. "I don't know about that."

"Listen," Jacquline said. "The rent is cheap and the building is clean."

Kathy looked at her with tears in her eyes, "Let me think about it."

"What, you too good to live around black people? Remember, I'm black and I sign your check, and I'm your friend," Jacquline stated with much defense in her tone.

Kathy got up off the couch. "I have thirty days to move. When can you have the apartment ready for me?"

Jacquline smiled, "I'll make sure you're there in time. Don't worry about a thing, I'll handle everything. Just take care of your business with your husband."

"Thank you so much."

Once Kathy left, Jacquline picked up her office phone. She dialed Jake's number, he was the Super of the building. Jake's been the Super since Jacquline moved there fourteen years ago. When he answered the phone, Jacquline asked about apartment 3-A.

"Jake, I need a favor from you."

"What is it?"

"I've got this friend," Jacquline explained. "She needs a two bedroom apartment. Since 3-A has been vacant for almost a year, I was hoping she could have it."

"Only because she's your friend Jacquline, have her call me today."

"Thank you Jake."

"No problem."

Jacquline hung up the phone. She called the front desk and had Kathy paged. Ten minutes later, Kathy showed up knocking on her office door.

Jacquline passed Kathy the phone and Jake's number. "He's waiting for you to call," she said with a smile on her face.

Kathy was surprised, "You work fast."

"Only for people who pay me or for people I really care about," Jacquline added.

"You really have been a real friend to me in these hard times Jacquline."

"That's what friends are for, right? I've been in your situation and trust me, I know what you're going through."

Jacquline got up from her desk, "Handle your business. You'll be my next door neighbor in a few weeks." Jacquline closed the door behind her. She had to make her rounds and make sure everything was running right.

Kathy knew it was going to be shocking to her daughter Toni, about them moving to Harlem. She was hoping Toni could adapt around black people. Kathy wasn't worried about herself. She was a fifth degree black belt in karate, with the heart of a tiger.

Sometimes people have to make sacrifices she thought to herself. Now it was her turn. Kathy took a deep breath then dialed the number Jacquline gave her.

Kathy and Jake spoke for about a half an hour. He informed her that the apartment would be ready April 19th. After hanging up the phone with Jake, Kathy thought about how she was going to break the news to her daughter. She already figured out what she would do with her husband's body. Kathy was going to have him cremated. She didn't want fake people, or possible even the killer amongst his remains, smiling in her face.

When got Kathy got home, Toni was watching television in her room. Kathy sat on the bed next to her.

"Toni, I need to talk to you about a few things."

"What is it mother?"

Kathy rubbed the side of her daughter's face, "Honey, in a few weeks, we'll be moving out of Brooklyn."

Toni just sat there, listening. She already knew about the eviction notice.

"So where are we moving to," she asked her mother.

"Harlem," her mother answered.

Toni smiled, "You mean Manhattan?"

"Yes," Kathy shook her head.

Toni jumped up, "When are we moving? I hate Brooklyn. Mommy, it's time for a change since daddy got killed. None of his so-called friends even called or came to see if we needed anything. In my eyes, they the ones who put them five bullets in his head."

Kathy was shocked to hear her daughter talk like that. She was also shocked about how excited Toni was about moving.

"You know you'll be changing schools to, right?"

"So, I don't care. Mother, do we know anybody over there?"

"My co-worker got the apartment for us." Kathy paused, "She's black."

Toni hunched her shoulders, "So, it don't matter to me. I'm color blind, people are people."

Toni continued to surprise Kathy. She never knew her daughter was into black people. She knew Toni even had a few black friends, but Kathy would've never guessed she would be this excited about moving to Harlem.

A few of Toni's Italian friends even called her a 'nigger lover' behind her back. None of them were bold enough to say it in her face. They knew Toni wouldn't hesitate about whipping their ass.

Just from looking at Toni, you wouldn't think she was a fighter. Toni stood 5-foot-2 with a petite frame. Her pretty brown eyes were the same color as her hair. With Toni's cream complexion and the right clothes on, she could almost pass for being Spanish.

Toni couldn't wait to get to Harlem, USA. All she kept thinking about was the Apollo. She was excited to be leaving Brooklyn, so she could go do the things her friends wouldn't dare do. That was one of the things that made Toni so unique. Her friends would talk about it, but Toni would do it.

When Kathy walked out of her room, Toni started thinking about her best friend, Marilyn. In her heart, she knew Marilyn was the only person she was gonna miss. That was her girl foreal! Down for whatever, like Outlaws. "Yes, I am my sister's keeper," Toni mumbled to herself.

When Jacquline got home, Ava was sitting in the living-room by herself. She explained to her mother, after the fifteenth, her and three of her co-workers were being let go. Then she broke down crying in front of her mother.

Jacquline yelled, "What the hell are you crying for!? People get hired and fired everyday! Guess what, today it's your day to get fired! Now pick up the pieces and keep it moving!"

Ava wiped the tears from her face then thought about her dad. She mumbled something he always said to her, "I will survive all the let downs. I will fight in the dark when trouble sparks." Ava's mother was a trooper, and so was her father, all the way to his last days on earth. So Ava knew she had the strength in her to survive. But at that very moment, she felt as if her world came crumbling down.

"Thank you daddy," Ava mumbled once more.

Jacquline looked into her daughter's eyes. She knew she was up to something. What? She didn't know. Jacquline just hoped Ava didn't do something crazy, like go postal.

Kia and Melody interrupted Jacquline's thoughts as they came racing through the door.

"Where have you two Hoodrats been?" Jacquline asked.

"Shoe shopping, Mrs. Wilson," Melody replied, holding up the bag of shoes she'd purchased.

"Why are you looking like you dun gone crazy?" Kia asked Ava.

Ava shot Kia a look that could kill, but she remained

silent. The way Ava felt, she knew if she would've touched Kia, she'd be sitting up in Central Bookings on charges of first degree murder. She chose to remain silent 'cause she knew if she said what she really wanted to, her mother would've slapped the shit out of her.

"Melody, Kia, have a seat," Jacquline told them. "I wanna talk to all of you."

"Is everything alright, ma?" Kia asked.

"Everything is fine," Jacquline assured her. "I would just like to speak with you all about one of my co-workers. Her name is Kathy and she has an eighteen year old daughter named Toni. Their white, and next month they'll be moving next door."

Kia and Melody looked at each other at the same time.

"You're telling us that we're going to have some white neighbors? What are they, white trash," Ava asked.

Jacquline got up off the couch then walked over to where Ava sat. When she was within close range, she slapped the shit out of Ava.

Kia and Melody sat there laughing, while Ava sat there holding her face. Jacquline raised her hand again and they both covered up. Jacquline done slapped Melody plenty of times before, her house was Melody's second home. Whenever she was having problems with her mother, she'd run downstairs to Jacquline's house.

"Listen," said Jacquline. "Her husband got killed about a week ago. Now they want a change."

"They sure picked a fine place," said Melody, "paradise, on One Hundred Twenty Third Street."

"Melody, don't make me get back up, it's going to be real ugly," Jacquline warned.

"Sorry Mrs. Wilson, what's their last name?"

"Antoinette and Kathy Taurasi."

Ava knew she heard the name before, where, she couldn't figure out."

"Mommy, is her daughter going to go to Watley with us?"

"So far, it looks that way Kia."

Melody just sat there listening, while Ava kept trying to figure out where she knew the name Taurasi from. After a few minutes passed, Ava shouted like she was crazy.

"Oh shit!" Jacquline looked at her. Ava put her hand over her mouth. "Mommy, is that the same person who was found in the trunk of his car with five bullets in his head?"

Kia and Melody sat there waiting for a response. Ava continued, "It was all over the news, right?"

Kia and Melody was shocked to hear what Ava just revealed. Jacquline finally answered the question, "Yes," was all she said.

"Word?" Melody asked with an eyebrow raised.

"Listen all of you. Do not repeat that. Kathy has been a good friend of mine for a lot of years now."

"When will they be here?" Melody asked.

"Next month, on the nineteenth."

"Don't worry mommy, we will show them some love," Kia stated. "And her daughter, Toni, we'll show her the Harlem shake."

Everyone started laughing. Kia and Melody went to the center of the living-room floor, then started dancing. Jacquline cracked a smile. When both girls finished clowning around, Melody picked up her shoes.

"Let me go upstairs. I have to deal with my mother and my crazy brother."

"Melody, how is your mother doing?" Jacquline asked.

"She's fine. Thanks for asking Mrs. Wilson."

"And your brother?"

Melody shrugged her shoulders, "He was okay, the last time I seen him."

Jacquline shook her head. Kia walked toward the door to let her friend out. Melody said goodbye to everyone. Ava smiled at her then stuck her middle finger up. Melody did the same thing back to her, but she also stuck her tongue out her mouth. Then she winked as Kia closed the door behind her.

"Ava, why are you so mean to Melody?" Jacquline asked. Kia sat back down next to her mother.

Ava smiled, "Mommy, you know that's my arros havichuela y chuletas little sister. You know I love that girl."

"Yeah right," Kia replied.

The next day, Jacquline left work early, she wasn't feeling well. While on the train, she noticed two guys watching her. When Jacquline got off the train on One Hundred Twenty Fifth Street, those same two guys were behind her. Jacquline walked over to an empty phone booth, she was hoping someone was home. On the first ring, Kia answered the phone.

"Kia, listen. I'm at One Hundred Twenty Fifth Street train station. I think two men may be following me..."

Before Jacquline could say another word, Kia dropped the phone and ran into her room. She grabbed her coat and orange box cutter. Ava didn't notice her running out the door, her eyes were glued to the television. When Kia got outside, Kenny, Mellow and Mannie were standing on the stoop talking. At the speed of light, Kia took off running towards One Hundred Twenty Fifth Street. All three guys paused then looked at each other. Kenny slowly began walking behind Kia, but then he started running trying to keep up with her. Mellow and Mannie looked at each other, then they started running behind Kenny. They didn't know what they were running for, but they wanted to make sure Kenny was alright. Kenny wanted to make sure Kia was safe. Kia wanted to make sure her mother was safe. When Kia ran into the train station, she pushed the blade out on her box cutter. She was ready to cut anyone near her mother. When Kia got to the platform, Jacquline was standing by the token booth with Regeane. Kia smiled at her mother. She knew she was safe with Big Rage.

"Who's following mommy?" Kia asked, with her box cutter in her hand.

"They walked away when Regeane came to my aide," Jacquline answered. All three ladies started walking up the stairs. Kenny, Mellow and Mannie were on their way downstairs.

"Is everything alright?" Kenny asked.

"Everything is cool for now. Thank you," Kia replied. The fellas turned around and started walking towards One Hundred Twenty Third Street. Mellow spoke first.

"Kenny, you feeling Kia?"

Kenny smiled, "That's My Boo! She can have anything I got."

Mellow started laughing, "You trick-ass-nigga! Look at you, open off that pretty young thing!"

Kenny got upset at Mellow's statement. Mannie remained silent 'cause on the low, he was feeling Kia too.

Mellow stepped in the street, then looked Kenny up

and down. "What nigga? If you don't like what I said then you need to handle your business."

"Yeah, aight," Kenny stated.

"Kenny, what you need to do is get your priorities straight! Understand this, we out here to get money, not to play Superman."

Kenny ignored Mellow as he and Mannie kept walking down the block.

"How many bundles you got left out of the Two Hundred I gave you this morning?" Kenny asked.

"About ten," Mannie answered.

"Aight. Finish the rest. I got something important to take care of." Kenny started walking towards his X5 BMW. Mannie and Mellow continued walking up Seventh Avenue.

Kenny couldn't stop thinking about Kia. As he walked to his BMW, he thought about how he was going to get her. He knew Ava was standing between them, but he was determined to find a way. Kenny thought about buying her a three caret diamond ring, some flowers and a card. But it would make him feel like a sucker if she rejected him, or he might've even felt soft doing those things. Finally reaching his car, he sat behind the wheel then pulled out the blunt he rolled this morning. He lit it and then took a long pull. No one knew Kenny got high. To him, any drug was a sign of weakness. He put his X5 in drive then pulled into traffic with the blunt in his mouth.

Jacquline, Kia and Regeane was on One Hundred Twenty Fifth Street, window shopping. Regeane stopped at a book stand. She was holding three different chess books in her hand, but only had enough money for one. After contemplating which one she should get, she finally purchased *Completely Krushing* by Irina Krush. Since the age of nine Regeane has been playing chess, she played in all the tournaments at the YMCA, PAL and in the summertime, she plays in Washington Square Park located in downtown Manhattan. Regeane has a reputation for being the youngest female in charge in the park. People bet big money on her, she wins more than she loses.

Regeane handed the man ten dollars for the book. He was about to put it in a bag, but Regeane insisted on carrying it.

"What book did you buy," Kia asked.

"Another chess book," Regeane answered, "Something you don't know nothing about.

"That game is wack!"

"No it's not Kia. It's the game of everyday life, one false move, life is over. Don't knock it until you try it. Just respect it."

"Come on ladies. It's cold out here," Jacquline told both girls. Kia and Regeane started walking behind her. The two of them were still talking. Suddenly, Jacquline stopped in the middle of the street.

"What's wrong mommy?"

Jacquline crossed her arms, one into the other. Then she looked at Kia, "Where do you know those guys from?"

"They're from the neighborhood ma." Kia did not want to go into details.

"Yeah, they're friends of ours," Regeane added.

Jacquline looked at both of them, "I hope so."

When the trio got to One Hundred Twenty Fourth Street, Jacquline noticed one of the guy's from the train station. He was walking out of the store drinking a soda, he waved and kept walking. Regeane stopped in front of her building.

"It's time for me to depart Mrs. Wilson."

"Have a good not Regeane."

Moments later, Kia and Jacquline walked into their home. Ava didn't even hear them walk through the door. Kia had to yell her name three times before she answered. Ava turned around and noticed her mother standing there.

"Turn down that damn TV!" Jacquline yelled.

Ava picked up the remote then flicked the television off. She stood up from the couch, "What's wrong mommy?"

"It's too late now. If you didn't have that TV up so loud, you would know," Kia said.

Ava was puzzled by her comment. Jacquline took a seat on the couch. Kia sat on the floor to unlace her mother's shoes. Jacquline explained to Ava, she thought two men were following her. Then she called home and Kia answered the phone. By the time Kia got there, however, Regeane was already there, they were on the same train together.

Ava walked over to Kia then started pulling a hand full of her hair. Kia hopped to her feet, Jacquline told her to sit back down and unlace her shoes.

"It's not over," Kia yelled.

"Shut up, will you?" her mother told her.

Ava walked into her room then slammed the door.

"Don't be slamming no doors in my house," Jacquline yelled. "You two are going to be the cause of my death.

TONI

A blue and white moving truck parked in front of 2010 West One Hundred Twenty Third Street and Seventh Avenue. Two white men and three black men got out of the truck. A blue Honda Accord pulled up right behind it, two white women were inside. Kathy called Jacquline to inform her that she was downstairs with the moving men. Jacquline headed downstairs to meet her friend.

Kathy smiled at the sight of Jacquline exiting the building.

"Jacquline, I'd like you to meet my daughter, Toni. Toni, this is Mrs. Wilson."

Toni shook Jacquline's hand, which was already extended, "Nice to meet you Mrs. Wilson."

"Same to you Toni."

Jacquline looked around. She noticed dopefiends buying dope from the neighborhood dealers across the street. Jacquline was always the type of person to mind her own business, but when she stared a little longer, she noticed one of the guys from the train station the other night. Kenny had a crowd around him. When he noticed Jacquline watching him, he walked away from the crowd. Jacquline was embarrassed at the sight of the Harlem street, but she still loved Harlem and wouldn't dare hesitate telling anyone that's where she was from.

One of the moving men interrupted her thoughts.

"What floor ma'am?"

"Oh, I'm sorry," Jacquline replied. "Apartment 3-A." She reached into her pockets then removed a set of keys. She passed the keys to Kathy then headed in the building.

"Follow me to your new apartment."

All three ladies walked slowly up the stairs. When the

ladies reached the third floor, Toni brushed pass her mother to enter the apartment.

"Mommy, can I have this room?" Toni asked. She was standing in the room facing the avenue.

"Sure, why not," Kathy answered.

Kathy turned to face Jacquline, "Thank you so much for everything."

Jacquline waved her hand, "Don't worry about it. I'm always willing to help a friend out."

The moving men were working fast. Within one hour the entire apartment was filled with boxes. Kathy paid them, plus gave each man a twenty five dollar tip.

Toni was standing by her bedroom window. She was amazed how things looked so different from where she'd just came from. Toni wanted to go to One Hundred Twenty Fifth Street bad. All she kept dreaming about was the Apollo, she wanted to see it up close and personal for herself. However, Toni knew her mother would not let her leave with so much work needing to done. Toni's concentration was broken once her mother called her.

"Yes mother," Toni answered.

"Could you come in the living-room," Kathy yelled back.

When Toni entered the living-room Jacquline and Kathy were in the middle of a conversation. When Jacquline noticed Toni she smiled.

"Toni, would you like to meet my daughter, Ava?"

"Sure," Toni answered.

A few seconds later, all three women were heading next door, Kathy clicked her locks, then they entered Jacquline's home.

"Ava!" Jacquline yelled.

Ava came racing out of her room. She didn't know the two white ladies standing in the middle of the living-room floor with her mother, but she assumed it was the new neighbors Jacquline's been telling them about. Jacquline confirmed what Ava was thinking.

"Ava, I'd like you to meet Mrs. Taurasi and her daughter, Toni."

Ava smiled and shook both of their hands, "Nice to meet you. Toni, you could come with me to my room?"

Toni didn't say a word, she just followed Ava's lead. Once the two girls entered the room, Ava took a seat on her bed.

"How old are you Toni?"

"I'm eighteen years old," Toni replied dryly.

"Will you be going to school in Harlem?"

"I guess so. My school is too far from here."

"Well, if you are going to school around here, you'll probably go to Watley. My little sister Kia goes to that school, she's in the twelfth grade."

"Oh yeah," Toni stated. "Maybe we'll have the same classes. I'm in the twelfth grade too."

Ava heard what sounded like two men arguing outside of her window. She sucked her teeth then turned to Toni.

"Don't worry about the neighborhood. You'll get use to it."

Toni just looked at Ava. *If you only knew...*Toni thought to herself.

"So, do you have a boyfriend?" Ava asked.

"No. My father use to chase 'em away."

Ava paused for a moment. "I'm sorry about your father."

"Thank you," Toni answered. "But my life must go on now. To me that's yesterday's news."

Ava remained silent. She didn't know if she said the wrong thing, or was this little white girl in front of her just cold and heartless. Toni changed the subject.

"So, when is your sister coming home?"

"Kia might not be home until later. Once her, Melody and Regeane get together, theirs no telling what they could be up to or where they are."

"Do they all go to the same school with your sister?"

"Yeah, they do," Ava replied. "Kia and Regeane play basketball for their school team. Melody is a computer whiz. She's like a little sister to me. And Regeane, or *Big Rage* as we call her, plays chess all over the city. She's a real freak at it.

Toni raised her brow while shaking her head, "Your sister seems to have some interesting friends. I must meet them?"

Ava laughed and threw her head back, "Trust me, you will. They are a trip."

Walking into the hallway, Kia and Melody noticed boxes all over the third floor.

"Your new neighbors are here," Melody smirked. Kia didn't respond.

"What the hell is wrong with you," Melody asked.

"What did you say," Kia's mind was someplace else.

"Just forget it," Melody shot back, heading up the stairs.

When Melody got upstairs, her mother had just finished cooking dinner. She kissed her mother on the cheek then sat down.

"Are you hungry," Melody's mother asked in Spanish.

Melody didn't even have to answer that question. She gave her mother the look and both of them knew exactly what that meant. Melody loved eating her mother's cooking. Although her mother never cooked pork, Mel and the girls would sometimes sneak and eat pork chops or pork skins from One-Sixteenth Street and Second Avenue.

Melody went into the bathroom to wash up for dinner. When she finished eating, she walked pass John's room. He was sleep with his shoes still on. That meant one thing; he was high off that shit.

Melody turned on her computer to check the weekly projection of the companies' she wanted to invest in. She started with Nextel. Next was Dell then came Wendy's. After checking a few more companies she cleared her computer screen then started making graphics for her own website. She used the mouse to make colors, shapes, designs and more colors. Finally, she made a list of things she wanted to offer the public; mail orders, locations of stores and five star restaurants around the world.

Melody knew it would take years before her dreams became a reality. But, she always kept a positive thought.

Looking at her Mickey Mouse watch; it read 3:10am. Melody didn't realize she spent almost four hours on her computer. In her heart she knew it would pay off one day.

The annoying sound of a ringing telephone woke Melody out of her sleep.

"Hello," Melody spoke into the phone.

"Are you still coming with the crew to watch me play chess," Regeane asked.

It took Melody a moment to realize she'd fallen asleep

in her chair. Her computer was still on from the night before.

"Are you going or what," Regeane yelled into the phone.

"What time is it," asked Melody while wiping sleep from her eyes.

"It's twelve noon."

"Gimme 'til 1:00."

"I'll meet you downstairs," Regeane responded.

"Okay. One."

When Melody got in front of the building she noticed Kia and Regeane talking to some funny looking white girl on the stoop. Melody introduced herself then stuck her hand out.

"So you the new girl that moved into this rathole."

They all started laughing.

"Are you coming with us to watch Regeane play chess," Kia asked.

"I don't care if you ladies don't mind," she responded.

They all started laughing at Toni's last remark.

"Girl, you got to change your way of talking in the hood. People gon' be teasing you all the time around here."

Toni just looked at her.

When the ladies got on the train Regeane explained the plot to Toni. Kia and Melody already knew the routine. They did this every weekend last summer. Toni was shaking her head listening to Regeane talk.

"What's wrong," Regeane asked.

"It's all wrong," Toni started to explain. "Why take a piece of steak from the farm when we can take all the cows from the farm?"

They all started smiling at Toni's idea. She continued, "Listen, we're not here to stand around all day for short money. If Regeane feels she's losing, give us the sign and we'll start a fight over the table and knock the pieces over, that's all."

The three amigos agreed to Toni's idea.

Within no time the train was pulling into West Fourth Street. All four ladies exited then walked to Washington Square Park.

Regeane spotted two white men playing chess, the way the men were dressed made Regeane smile.

"I think we've found our first two herbs ladies."

Kia, Melody and Toni followed Regeane's lead as she headed towards the two white dudes.

"Can I play next," Regeane asked in her most innocent voice.

"Sure," the white guy said, "for only twenty dollars a game."

"Why so much, I'm a woman," Regeane protested.

"The price just went up to fifty," the white guy replied in a real nonchalant way.

"Fifty dollars a game," Regeane asked with that fake innocent voice that she does so well.

"Yep," the man smiled. Just then his opponent got up from the table.

"Okay," Regeane sighed as she took the seat the other guy left vacant. She looked at Kia and winked. Kia knew exactly what to do from there.

Kia started placing side bets on Regeane. Altogether Kia had at least one hundred dollars in bets. But, before Regeane could make a first move, Toni yelled.

"BITCH WHERE'S MY MONEY!?"

Regeane didn't know what the hell Toni was doing 'cause it wasn't part of the plan. Toni continued.

"Don't move any of them chess pieces!" Toni looked at the nerdy looking white guy, "I'm sorry sir. She won't be betting any of my money with you today." She looked at Regeane, "now let's go," she winked.

When the foursome got out of the park, Regeane started spazzing.

"What the hell is wrong with you Toni!?"

Toni started shaking her head the same way she did on the train.

"Listen, all of you," she looked around to make sure no one was following them, "y'all gotta learn to pay attention. Both of those guys back there were undercover cops, waiting for you to show your money so they could arrest you for promoting gambling."

"How you know they was Jake?" asked Kia.

Toni took a deep breath, then started to explain, "The first guy that got up from the table, his gun was sticking out from under his shirt," Toni turned to face Regeane.

"Regeane, you've been playing chess for a long time, right?"

"Yeah," Regeane answered.

"Okay," Toni continued, "when did you ever see someone get up from the middle of a chess game to let someone else play?"

Regeane started to think about what Toni was saying to her and everything suddenly made sense.

"And the guy you were about to play, he had a wire hanging behind his neck. The reason you couldn't see the wire is because his hair was too long. The entire conversation was being recorded."

"Damn girl! You good," Melody shouted.

Toni put her hand on her hip. "Let me explain something to all three of you. Don't think 'cause I'm white I'm not hip to the streets of New York City. I did things with my father that none of you would ever believe and trust me, it's not pretty. What we're doing is bullshitting. If y'all really want to get some money let's rob a bank for nine or ten million dollars, 'cause what we doing now is not worth none of our time. I was always told that if a person wants money, you gotta be willing to take it, and willing to die to keep it."

They all stood outside the park looking and listening to Toni.

After a few moments of absolute silence, the peace was finally disrupted.

"Now what the fuck are we going to do?" Regeane wanted to know.

They all stood in the street looking at each other.

"Let's go to the movies," Toni stated.

"And see what," Kia asked.

Toni started walking, "Come on, we can see Blade 2, it just came out yesterday, it's on me."

Melody finally came to life, "Let's go! We don't turn down anything free. You know we po' black people," she joked.

Kia put her arm around Toni's neck, "You'll be alright hanging with us."

All four ladies headed in the direction of the train station.

At the movies Toni bought four tickets to Blade 2. While standing on the concession line, getting ready to be served, three black girls with gold teeth in their mouths jumped in front of Toni. One of the girls laughed while looking at Toni.

"Is there a problem," the black girl asked.

Before Toni got a chance to reply, the girls' friend was putting her two cents in.

"White bitch, what the fuck are you looking at?"

Regeane and Kia couldn't have walked up at a better time. Regeane stared the girls down then looked at Toni.

"Is there a problem Muffin?" Muffin was Regeane's nickname for Toni.

"Yeah theirs a problem," one of the other girls answered, "this white bitch looking at us like she crazy."

Toni looked at all three girls like she was disgusted. Then she looked at Regeane and Kia, "Don't worry about Larry, Curly and Moe..." before Toni could finish her statement Kia busted out laughing.

On the sneak tip, the smallest one out of the three girls who were standing in front of them tried to sucker punch Toni from the right side. Toni backed away then swung her left arm, hitting the girl in the nose. One swift kick to her abdomen caused the girl to fall on the floor. Without hesitation Toni started kicking the girl over and over in her ribcage. The other two girls tried to rush Toni but Regeane snatched one of them by their ponytail weave. The girl tried to fight back but Big Rage was too strong for her. Regeane hit the girl in the face once. All that broads gold teeth flew out of her mouth. Regeane didn't even give the poor girl a chance to defend herself. It was over before it started.

Kia and Melody had the other girl by her jacket.

"Bitch if you move I'll blast your ass," Kia warned her.

When the girl looked down she noticed Melody and Kia were holding orange box cutters in theirs hands. Melody pressed her box cutter in the girl's face.

"I should cut your ass for fronting on us, what you think Kia?"

"Cut 'er," Kia answered.

Melody smiled then cut the girl from her right ear to the corner of her mouth. When Kia let the girl go she took off running out the theater, in the middle of the street she was screaming for help.

Out of nowhere about six security guards came running toward the big rumble. Toni backed away from the girl she was fighting, or rather the girl's ass who she was kicking. The girls nose kept spilling out blood, Toni knew it was broken. That chick needed medical attention – fast!

Two security guards had to help the other girl Regeane had by the hair. Regeane had a firm grip on her hair, and she wasn't letting go. She kept punching her in the face and body.

"Please get her off of me!" the girl screamed.

Kia, Melody, Regeane and Toni gave the girls a real uptown ass kicking. Security escorted Kia and Melody out first, then Regeane and Toni.

"Don't ever come back to this theater! You're banned for life!" one of the guards yelled.

"Fuck you!" Regeane shot right back, "We been thrown out of better places!"

All four ladies were standing on Forty-Second Street the same way they did on Fourteenth Street just an hour earlier. Regeane was huffing and puffing, "That was fun," she stated. All of them busted out laughing, except Toni.

"What are we gonna do now," Toni asked. "I gave

away forty dollars to give other people a show! The first day hanging out with you three, in one hour tops, we almost end up in jail, then we fighting in the movies, what's next!?" Toni paused then continued, "You know what, fuck this shit! I'm going home!"

She proceeded to walk towards the train station. Regeane waved for Kia and Melody to follow behind her. When they were close enough, Regeane grabbed Toni by the arm.

"Listen Muffin, we all sorry about the money. We're willing to pay you back. We'll give you ten dollars apiece right now."

Toni smiled, "Don't worry about the money, it can be replaced."

There was a brief moment of silence before all the girls smiled at one another then headed toward the train station once more.

On the train, heading back uptown, Kia sat next to Toni.

"Are you still mad at us," she asked with her bottom lip poked out.

Toni took one look at Kia then started laughing at the funny face she was making.

"Kia why did you cut that girl," Toni managed to ask.

Kia shook her head, "That was Melody's work, not mine."

Toni spoke as if she felt the girls' pain, "Her whole cheek bone was showing."

"Fuck her!" Kia responded.

Melody and Regeane sat across from them smiling. Within no time the train was pulling up into One Hundred Twenty Fifth Street station.

Toni stopped on the platform then turned to Regeane, "You know how all of you can pay me back?"

"Anything," replied Melody.

"Take me to the world famous Apollo Theater!"

They all looked at Toni as if she lost her mind. To them, the Apollo was just another building on One Hundred Twenty Fifth Street. Living in Harlem all their lives, the Apollo wasn't really a big deal to them. But, people who weren't from around the way seemed to love it. On any given night, the Apollo would be surrounded by tour buses from all over. In fact, the Apollo would be so packed with people from out of town; there'd rarely be room for people who lived in the neighborhood to get a ticket, if by chance there were any tickets left.

To most of the people around the way, the best part about the Apollo was the end. Anytime a show ended there the people would stand around, hanging out. The Apollo was the place to be on a Friday or Saturday night. And after 11pm, that's when the real Ballas', Pimps, Players' and Hustlers' would come out. You could get a sneak preview of the hottest cars that year, and find out who's who and who's doing what.

Harlem.

No place in the world like it.

While Regeane, Kia and Melody stood laughing at Toni, she cut their laughs short.

"Fuck all that shit y'all saying! I want to go to the Apollo!"

All Toni wanted to do was see the Apollo Theater for herself; she desperately wanted to tell her best friend, Marilyn in Brooklyn what it really looked like.

One Hundred Twenty Fifth Street was crowded with

Sunday afternoon shoppers, the sun beaming down on all of them. At that moment Toni didn't care how hot is was. The only thing that was on her mind was the Apollo.

When all four ladies finally reached the Apollo, Toni was looking at all the pictures of black performers that lined the walls. There were pictures of Redd Fox, Nat King Cole, James Brown, Billie Holiday and the list goes on. Regeane and the crew didn't know Toni grew up listening to black music groups like; Four tops, Dells, O'Jays and The Manhattans. For some odd reason, Toni never understood. Her father would always cry whenever he listened to Phyillis Hyman sing. When the singer committed suicide, Toni's father played her music for a month straight. Toni could still hear her voice like it was yesterday.

When Toni turned around she noticed Kia talking to some guy and his friends. Kia smiled then grabbed Toni's wrist.

"This is my girl Toni, she's not to be fucked with," Kia smiled.

Everyone exchanged pleasantries, but one guy was more outspoken than the rest. He stepped closer toward Toni then extended his hand, "I'm Harvey," he bit his lip and winked his eye, "but you can call me tonight."

Everyone laughed at Harvey, including Toni. Toni took a step back then looked Harvey up and down.

Brown Sean John jean suit.

Six inch Timbs unlaced.

A Colgate smile.

Harvey was fly. Toni threw a million dollar smile of her own right back at him.

A few minutes passed and Harvey and Toni seemed to be talking nonstop, rather Harvey was talking nonstop while Toni couldn't stop laughing and smiling at him.

"So Toni, with an *I* right," Toni laughed, so did Harvey. Then he continued, "Are you seeing anyone?"

"I see you. I see my homegirls over there talking to your boys," Toni nodded. Harvey laughed again.

"Toni, cut it out. You know what I'm asking. Are you seeing anyone, dating 'em, who wining and dining you *exclusively*?"

"You ask a lot of questions, you know that?"

Harvey smiled, "I want a lot of answers. If I don't ask, I won't know."

"Well Harvey *the Hustler'*," Harvey laughed at Toni then shook his head. "Since you've been asking me all these questions, I got a question of my own to ask you."

"Knock ya self out."

"What is it to you if I'm seeing someone or not?"

"It's a lot to me since I wanna see you again, if that's possible."

Toni looked at Harvey again; he was a handsome black brother and fly! Plus, he kept her laughing. Her brain sent the signal to her mouth. The words rolled off her tongue.

"It can happen," she smiled.

Harvey pulled out a pen and a piece of paper. He wrote his cell phone number down then handed the piece of paper to Toni.

"Call me if you wanna go to the movies or get a bite to eat or something like that. Or you could call if you just looking for someone to talk to."

Toni took the paper and smiled, "Thank you. I'll keep that in mind." She turned around and spotted Regeane. And whatever some guy was whispering in her ear must've been good 'cause Regeane was smiling from ear to ear. Kia and Melody didn't look like they were interested in the other guys. Toni directed her attention back towards Harvey.

"Come closer to me Harvey."

Harvey did as Toni said without hesitation. When he was close enough, Toni whispered in his ear.

"Why are you talking to me? You want some of this Italian pussy, right?"

The statement caught Harvey totally off guard. He tried stepping away from Toni but she grabbed him by his hand.

"Harvey, don't be scared of little ol' me," Toni smiled. Harvey stood there with the stone face. Toni continued, "Don't worry, it's not that easy. But, if you play your cards right something just might happen."

While Harvey was still trying to figure out who was this bold ass white girl whispering in his ear, Toni put her right hand down his pants.

"You holding big down there. I'll give you a call one day soon. Just make sure you keep your phone line open."

Harvey couldn't believe what this white girl just did to him on One Hundred Twenty Fifth Street! He stood there with a hard dick and an open mouth.

Toni started walking toward Seventh Avenue. Kia and Melody was right behind her. Kia turned around then yelled.

"Regeane, bring your hot ass on!"

Melody turned to Toni, "I didn't know you were into black men."

"I don't judge any man by his race. If I'm interested in him that's all that really counts to me, fuck what people say! This is my life and I plan on living it to the fullest."

"You go girl," Kia shouted!

"Well you know the saying...," Melody stated.

Toni cut her off, "*Once you go black, you never go back. I've been there and done that. You're late my dear.*"

Melody was shocked to hear this white girl standing in front of her, sounding blacker than any other black girl she knew from the 'hood.

It was their first day hanging out. Already, all of them were getting along just fine.

It was Toni's first day at Watley High. The school was predominately black, but for some reason she felt like that is where she belonged. As Toni walked down the hallway she'd hear the other students calling her names. None of this bothered her. She always told herself that was just the ignorance of some people.

Toni just wanted to finish the two months of school she had left, so she could graduate and go about her business.

It was a little after 11:30 when the bell started to ring. Toni started walking, she noticed a girl walking toward her.

"Excuse me, which way is the lunchroom located," Toni asked.

"Follow me. I'm going that way," the girl replied.

Toni wanted to sit down. Plus the books she was carrying started to hurt her arms.

The girl she was walking with introduced herself, "I'm Kandie."

Toni introduced herself as well while the two of them headed toward the lunchroom.

When Kandie opened the lunchroom door, the first thing Toni heard was Jay-Z's *Give It To Me* coming out of the large radio some guy had sitting on top of a lunchroom table. When she looked the other way, there were about ten guys shooting dice against the wall. On another side of the lunchroom, it was crystal clear how the light skin girl with the box braids was bopping her head and moving her hands, she was caught up in a rap battle with some other guys and girls.

One thing Toni missed at that very moment was her girlfriend Marilyn. She missed her so much! As Toni looked around, she began wondering did Hannibal the Carthaginian General and his black army rape her great, great, great grandmother in Sicily back in 183bc. If he did, things would make so much sense to Toni. That would be the only way she could explain the love she had for black people. She loved their food, music, way of living, but most of all their men! That's what made Toni so different from the rest of her friends in Brooklyn, even Marilyn. Toni always felt like God must've made a mistake because she was meant to be black. She felt like a black girl trapped in a white girl's body.

Yeah.

God must've made a mistake. Toni thought.

Out of nowhere, a girl bumped Toni, knocking her books out her hands. Toni bent down to pick up her books. Suddenly the two girls, Monica and Judy, leaned a little closer to Toni.

"Don't pick up your books until we tell you to!"

Just in time, Kia and Melody walked around the corner talking to each other. Kia noticed Toni bending down while Monica and Judy stood over her. They walked faster until they were close enough for Monica and Judy to hear them.

"What the fuck is y'all problem," Melody asked.

"Get out my way," Judy replied.

Kia whispered something in Toni's ear. Before Judy could say another word, Toni was punching Monica in the face. Judy tried to help but Melody and Kia had their box cutters open, ready for war!

"Don't make me cut your ass too short to shit, Puerto Rican style," Melody warned.

"That's not fair," Kia wined! "This one is mine!"

Melody and Kia both stood there, blades in hand.

"Okay Kia. You can have her."

Kia smiled, "Now move bitch. I dear you!"

Toni was beating Monica so bad that Melody had to pull her off of the girl.

By now, the entire lunchroom was looking and laughing at Monica. She just couldn't win. Toni was all over her like white on rice. People started whispering and wondering, who was this white girl beating up on the school bully?

When Melody pulled Toni away, Kia pushed Judy away from her as well.

"Next time I'll cut your ass!"

Judy and Monica took off, speed-walking. Kia bent down to pick up Toni's books. The trio walked out of the lunchroom together. They couldn't stop laughing.

Later that night, Melody got a phone call from Mike. Although Mike's been sweating her for the past three years, she never gave in and Mike never gave up. But tonight Mike was changing all of that. Something inside of him just made him call Melody and tell her how things would be from that point on.

"Melody, as of today, you're my girl, understand?"

Melody paused then smiled. She always liked Mike because he never gave up. And for the first time, Melody gave in, "Okay, Mike. If that's the way you want it, you got it. Now, you better treat me right, like a lady, understand Mr. Green?"

"How do you know my last name?"

"I've been doing my homework," she spoke into the phone. "Hold on for a minute Mike while I turn on my computer.

Melody retrieved her school bag for the notes she copied down earlier that day, then she turned on her computer. She waited for her it to boost before checking the daily progressions of all the companies she wanted to invest in, as usual. Then she put the phone back to her ear.

"Mike, what kind of phone do you have?"

"Nextel, the best! Why, you want one?"

"No," Melody answered. "Do you know Nextel service over fifteen million people in the good ol' USA?"

Mike was surprised at both, the answer and the person it was coming from, "How did you get that type of information yo?"

Melody laughed. She was used to people wondering how she knew the things she knew.

"It's simple really," Melody explained, "I watch the company's projection and how many people invest into the company. I would like to invest a few dollars myself, but the minimum rate is five thousand dollars."

"Let me see what I can do. We might be one of the thousands of stock holders they have."

Melody laughed at the statement Mike just made.

"What's wrong," Mike asked.

"You trust me with that type of money?"

"Melody, listen. If I can't trust you then I don't need to be with you."

Melody liked his answer. She shook her head up and down while holding the phone to her ear.

"Mike," Melody changed the subject, "I'm taking you out to eat this week."

Mike laughed.

"Now what's wrong with you," Melody asked.

"Nah, I'm good. I just never had a female take me out to eat."

"That's the problem. I ain't them hookers you used to dealing with, I'm Melody Cruz!"

Kia walked into her apartment.

"Where have you been," Ava asked.

"I'm a grown woman. Don't be sweatin' me. Find yourself some business please and stay out of mine," Kia answered as she continued walking into her bedroom. Once she reached her bedroom she slammed the door.

Kia started pulling out her basketball gear for tomorrow's game. She picked up the remote for her CD player then pressed track ten. Biggie Smalls *Dead Wrong* started pumping out of her speakers. Walking over to her window, she went into a trance wondering why those people across the street never went home. Kia wondered how many lives they ruined. How many mothers' put their child in the oven or some crazy shit like that just so the kid wouldn't fuck up their high, or how many children killed his or her parent because they wouldn't give them ten dollars to get high. Kia tried to stop thinking about the pain, agony, anguish and suffering each of those dealers caused the next person, but it was hard.

She looked at all the nice cars on the block. They all belonged to drug dealers.

"They stand around all day selling drugs to the homeless, crazies and addicts. Get a fucking life," Kia mumbled to herself while shaking her head.

The next morning Kia stood outside of her school talking to Regeane.

"You ready for tonight's game Kia 'cause…"

"Hell yeah!" Kia answered before Regeane could finish her sentence.

"You know what time it starts right?"

Kia looked at Regeane like she was stupid, "Come on now. Who you talking to," Kia asked. "Why wouldn't I know the game starts at six?"

"Yeah Kia, but we gotta be there at five."

Kia turned her head away from Regeane as if she was insulted. Then Melody and Toni walked up on the scene.

"What's popping," Melody asked.

"Ain't shit," Regeane answered. "Muffin, you coming to tonight's game?"

Nobody knew why Regeane called Toni Muffin, but Toni didn't get upset so no one else said anything about it. And for some odd reason, those two became real tight.

"I don't have anything else to do. I guess I could go to the game," Toni answered.

"Well that's what's up," Melody cut in.

"Look, we gon' meet y'all in front of the building at 4:30. Don't be late," Kia informed Toni and Melody.

"Why so early," Melody asked.

Kia laughed then folded her arms across her chest,

"Oh, you ain't know? You talking to a star! We gotta get there early so we could warm up and all that good stuff."

Melody rolled her eyes up in her head while Toni and Regeane laughed at Kia's little ass.

"Alright, then 4:30 it is," Toni answered.

"Hello ladies," Mike walked up on the scene, interrupting their conversation.

"Hey Mike," they all replied, except Melody. She walked up to her man then put her arms around his neck as she gave him a kiss.

Kia looked shocked!

"Uh oh," Regeane managed to get out.

"Mind your business," Melody stated with her arms still around Mike's neck.

"You are my business," Kia replied.

Melody ignored all of them.

"Mike, are you coming to the school game tonight?"

"If you want me to," he answered.

Melody smiled, "Nah, it's going to be some cuties there and you'll just be cock-blocking."

Melody started laughing, but Mike didn't find any humor in her joke. Melody peeped it.

"Don't worry Mike, I'll be good for you tonight, and bad in the bed for you another night."

Melody gave him another kiss. This kiss was longer than the first one.

"Not in school," Toni shouted. "My mother won't be home until late tonight, so you two can do the nasty at my place if you want."

Melody raised her eyebrow then laughed, "We don't need your room. My man can pay for any hotel!" She put her hand into Mike's pocket then pulled out a knot of money. Melody waived it in their faces.

"See, my man is holding."

They all looked at Melody, shaking their head.

When Mike finally left, Kia was curious about what just went down.

"When did that start happening Mel?"

Melody looked at Kia, "It's a long story," she replied.

Later that afternoon, Melody kissed her mother goodbye then headed downstairs to Toni's apartment. Just as Melody got to Toni's apartment, she noticed Regeane standing on the steps.

"What's up Big Rage? You knocked on Toni or Kia's door already?"

"Kia said she'll be out in a minute, I ain't knock on Toni's door yet," Regeane answered.

Melody knocked on Toni's door. She figured by the time Toni came out locking her door, Kia should be ready to come out and lock her door as well.

Toni opened the door.

"Are you ready," Melody asked.

"Hold up, let me get something," Toni replied. She ran into her bedroom.

When Toni reappeared, she was kneeling down on one knee, pulling her Old Navy jeans over her black Timberland boots. Melody stood next to her.

By now, Kia was in the hallway with everyone else.

"What's taking you two so long," Kia asked.

Melody pointed to Toni who was still kneeling down, fixing her pants over her boots.

Regeane was still on the steps with her hands on her hips, "Let's go please!"

Toni finally got up, "I'm ready now, but I wanna walk. We can take a cab back."

"Well then the two of you must be carrying me and Kia's bag," Regeane stated.

"Okay, deal," Toni replied.

Toni took Regeane's bag while Kia passed hers to Melody.

"Toni, next time you make arrangements involving me, please make sure it's okay with me first."

Toni ignored Melody.

The sun started to set low when they started walking up One Hundred Twenty Fifth Street. The streets were crowded with people, it was a Friday night – show your ass night in Harlem. Last minute shoppers were racing in and out of the stores in fast motion. It would still be a while before the ladies got to One Hundred Thirty Eighth Street and Convent Avenue.

"Let's walk up Convent Avenue," Melody stated. "It's faster and a lot less people."

Turning the corner of A Hundred-Thirty-Fourth Street, Kia and Regeane couldn't stop beefing about who's a better rapper: Jay-Z or Nas.

Toni looked around then spoke to Melody. "It sure is dead around…"

BOOM! BOOM! BOOM! BOOM! Gunshots rangout stopping Toni mid-sentence.

The sound of gunshots was loud enough to capture anyone's attention. But not Kia and Regeane, they were so caught up in their heated debate that they hadn't even noticed the two cars that zoomed past them in full speed. Stepping off the sidewalk onto the pavement, Toni and Melody stopped short as they noticed a man lying in between two parked cars bleeding.

"Yo come here," the man cried out. Melody was ready to run off, Toni grabbed her by the arm. Finally, Kia and Regeane were silent as they realized what was going on. "Don't move!" Kia warned Melody who still looked like she was ready to run.

"What's the problem mister?" Toni asked as she stooped down between the two parked cars.

"It's... it's a la la lot of mo money in this bag," the man struggled to get his words out.

Toni looked at the bag then back at the bleeding man. "How much?" she daringly asked.

"Maybe a lifetime worth." Dude said as blood started leaking from his mouth.

Kia looked down at him, "He's dying!"

"Hel hel helpppp me puh puh--leeease and half of everything is ya ya yours."

Melody looked at the man as if she were a deer stuck in headlights, while Kia and Regeane looked around nervously.

"Fuck this shit!" Toni said as she whipped out her butterfly knife. Toni swung it so smoothly that none of them noticed it, and when they did realize what she was doing it was too late. Toni turned the blade in the injured man's chest.

"Holy Shit!" Melody yelled.

"Hurry up Muffin!" Regeane yelled while Kia bent down to help Toni unhook the bag from the dead man's shoulder. Kia grabbed the bag and tossed it to Melody as she continued removing the dead man's solid gold chains.

"Put that shit back!" Toni said. "That's not part of the plan, it will cost us later." Toni wiped off the handle of the knife dropping it in the sewer on 130th street. That was something her father taught her; never leave evidence around.

"Let's go into the Manhattanville Projects," Melody said pointing over to building number 1431. She was leading the pack with Kia, Rage, and Toni right behind her. Kia began vomiting in the middle of the street, Rage went back to check on her.

"Kia look we don't have time for you to be sick now."

By the time they walked inside the building Melody was holding the elevator door. There were some guys in the lobby shooting dice and smoking blunts. One of the guys spoke calling them cuties. They all waved and kept it moving. When the elevator door closed Rage pressed the button for the 20th floor. Stepping off of the elevator, all the girls looked around to make sure the cost was clear. When Melody opened the bag all she saw was stacks of hundred dollar bills wrapped in rubber bands. But that wasn't all the contents.

"Holy Shit!"

"What's wrong Melody?" Kia asked.

Melody pulled out a white powdered shaped brick. "It's about 8 or 9 more of these in here." They all looked at one another.

"Let's switch these bags." Rage said.

Toni opened her bag and they put the money inside of it. By the time Kia had put all of the white powder bricks inside of her bag the elevator door was back on their floor opening again. All the ladies stepped inside. Before the door had a chance to close, Melody stepped off the elevator and tossed the bag with the dead man's blood on it towards the roof's landing. On the elevator ride down Toni suggested that they all count the money later at her house and find out what the white powder substance was.

"Yeah, but right now we gotta go to the game and act like nothing happened." Kia stated.

"Of course," Toni cosigned leaning against the elevator wall, heart racing a mile a minute.

Kia and Regeane played their best while Toni and Melody sat in the bleachers cheering. Watley won by 10 points, Kia scored a total of 19 points, and Rage scored 26 points with 13 boards. When the game was over Melody was up and insisting that they leave. Kia and Regeane stood in the cold wearing only their warm up suits, March night air ain't no joke. Toni carried the bag with the bricks, and Melody held tight to the one with the money as she flagged down a cab. Kia stood next to Toni.

"Toni, how much money you think we…"

"Shhh!" Toni stated without even looking Kia's way.

Finally, a cab stopped. Rage opened the door and all the ladies hopped in.

"One-Eighteenth Street and Eighth Avenue please," Toni said.

"Where we going?" Kia asked.

Toni shushed her again. Finally reaching their destination the cab driver looked back at all the ladies.

"That will be eight dollard please."

"Here," Melody said, tossing the driver a ten, "keep the change.

The driver smiled, "God bless you young ladies."

The ladies couldn't get out of the cab soon enough. Walking towards 123rd street without missing a beat, Toni pulled Kia closer to her then started talking, "Look, Kia. I told the driver to drop us off where he did 'cause we don't know for sure if someone saw us. By doing things this way we're covering our tracks." Toni said as they continued on foot. "Now look we're all in this together, so if one of us goes down then we all go down. So we need to keep it tight like fish pussy," Toni said.

"She's right, if we don't stick together there is going to be problems." Regeane said.

"Anybody got a problem with this, 'cause I don't not when it comes to money." Kia said.

Everyone remained silent.

When they reached the building Kenny and Mellow were standing out on the stoop, "Girl where your clothes?" Kenny asked.

"I'm not cold," Kia said.

"How ya'll doing?" Kenny asked.

"Fine." They all replied trying to get out of the cold.

When Melody stepped in the hallway she noticed John standing there with some girl she didn't know. "What the fuck are you doing?" She yelled keeping war.

Melody loved her brother to death it was the two hundred dollar a day habit she disliked about him. The worst thing about it was shit was so bad that he started acting just like Pookie from New Jack City. The only difference was Pookie loved that crack, and John loved fucking with that dope. There's even been a few times when Melody had to save his ass from OD'ing in their bathroom or his bedroom. And in the streets, people was talking 'bout how this nigga even started main-lining, shooting that shit all up in his veins. This news made Melody pay attention to him even more, he was her only brother and she loved him deeply. She said a silent prayer as she walked past her brother. He was only 25 and destroying his life. And even Melody had to admit; when he wasn't on that shit he was handsome, but when he was… that was another story.

John spoke as the girls past him, and none of them bothered to reply.

They all headed to Toni's house since her mother was still at work. Once they got in Toni's room she turned the bag upside down on her bed. Rolls of Hundred dollar bills fell all over the place! After they all finished counting they calculated that the 40 rows of money laying on the bed was two-hundred-dollars.

"WE RICH!" Kia yelled. Toni looked at her.

"Kia relax, that's not shit compared to what we got over there," she said as she pointed at the bricks. Regeane and Melody both agreed.

"Get me a knife," Melody said as Kia walked into the kitchen. Melody picked up one of the bricks examining its contents. Kia passed her the knife.

"What are you going to do?" Regeane asked. Melody stuck the knife inside of the brick with everyone focusing on her. She placed the tip of the knife on her tongue causing her to run into the bathroom where vomit immediately spilled from her catching the sink, floor and walls. Melody yelled out for water as her friends stood by afraid.

Toni rushed into the kitchen grabbing a bottle of water. As Melody was able to catch her breath she looked at each of her friends circling her, "this is dope!" She said with remnants of tears still dripping from her eyes and spit on the sides of her mouth. Now sitting on the floor she used the bottle of water to rinse her mouth.

"Opportunity," she said as she began to smile. Her and Kia's eyes met, "This is it Kia!" Melody said enthusiastically as Big Rage and Toni looked on.

"Opportunity," she said as she made her way back towards Toni's bedroom. She sat on the floor with the plastic bag in between her legs. "We have to organize now." They all nodded their heads in agreement. "So here it is if anyone here isn't feeling this then bounce, take your cut and get up outta here and there won't be any hard feelings." They all looked around staring intensely at one another. "Look choosing to stay means that our lives will drastically change. At this moment it's unclear whether this will be for the better or worse, but we all know that there are hefty risks associated with the drug game. What we witnessed tonight is something that we have to prepare for. We might have to kill people to get what we want or even be killed. As Roses we have to vow to watch over one another just to stay alive. Now, like I said; if anyone don't want no parts of this then just take your cut and bounce."

No one stood to leave the room Melody smiled proudly.

"Well it's going to be hot up in Harlem this summer, we about to blow the fuck up!"

Melody stood up then walked to the window, she pointed outside. "So all them motherfuckers out there are either going to roll with the Roses or, get rolled over by them, there is no turning back."

Kia smiled at Melody. She knew her friend was dead serious and the fact that she called them The Roses made it even clearer that she wasn't playing. The only time Melody reffered to the clique as Roses was when she was talking 'bout some serious shit.

"We ain't got no time to bullshit y'all," Rage announced.

"No mistakes, no slip-ups, no falling," Toni added.

Kia smiled then said out loud, "UNFALLEN ROSES!"

Melody shook her head and winked, "Unfallen Roses, I like that! From now on, that's who we be, and this paper is what we be 'bout! Anything or anybody else who comes along will just be petals and thorns.

"Wait," Kia cut in. "Ya'll we have to include Ava in this."

"No doubt," Regeane said as Toni tossed Kia the phone. Ava picked up on the first ring.

"Come next door."

"For what," Ava asked snidely.

"Bitch, bring your black ass next door!" Kia yelled as she slammed down the phone. "Damn that bitch gets under my skin!" Everyone laughed fully aware of Ava and her ways. Kia however was not amused.

"That shit ain't funny, ya'll don't have to live with her, I do."

"That's exactly why we assigned her ass to be the black rose." Melody said. "No one likes her, but we all love the shit out of her mean ass."

Kia stood thinking to herself, *why the hell did I even bother putting her down*. Just that quick she remembered she loved Ava just as much as she hated her.

"Mel, can you please open the door for that girl? I don't want to ring her neck."

Everybody laughed and Melody walked out of the room to open the door for Ava. Ava was in the hall locking the door to their apartment.

"What's wrong?" Ava asked genuinely concerned. Melody raised her index finger to quiet her.

"Melody I am not in the mood for no damn rice and beans today," Ava sarcastically said as she walked towards her.

"One of these days I'm going to whip your ass something good."

"Girl please!" Ava said while rolling her eyes.

Melody shook her head and sucked her teeth, "Shut up and follow me."

They went back inside Toni's apartment to join the others. Before anyone got the chance to say anything Toni raised the volume of the television for a channel 9 breaking news report.

Gunshots erupted roughly four hours earlier here on 134th Street; right now its being reported that there are two fatalities. Wait a minute, it's also being reported that another victim is on 129th street. Police at this time aren't certain if the two crimes are connected. They are asking for anyone who might have seen anything to please call the number listed on the screen.

They all looked at one another knowing now that they hadn't been seen.

"Turn that off," Kia said as she faced Ava.

"Ava I love you, but before we can explain what's happened we all need to know that we can trust you?"

Ava took note of the serious faces surrounding her.

"Kia if you're involved then y'all know that I can be trusted. Now tell me what's going on?"

Toni reached under her bed pulling out the two gym bags allowing the contents of both bags to fall on the bed. Ava's eyes stretched wide as she examined the contents and then looked at each girl intensely.

"What the fuck have y'all done?"

"Opportunity," Melody said coolly.

"We just so happen to be in the right place, at the right time." Toni said.

That's when Ava remembered the news flash, "So that's y'all they talking about on the news?" Ava pointed toward the televison which was now off.

"Hell no!" Rage yelled.

"If anything we completed the job," Toni boasted with a devilish grin. Everyone was laughing except Ava.

"Well Ava now you're officially involved!"said Melody.

It was at that moment that Ava realized her life would forever change. Though she didn't love her job finding out about the downsizing had hurt, but things seemed to be looking brighter. A life of crime hadn't been in her original plans, yet she found herself intrigued by the thoughts. She wasn't a fool she knew the downside that came with the drug game; murder; kidnapping, murder, money, murder and more money but her mind was already made up. Fuck all the problems and fuck jail! It was time to make it happen!

"Listen, Ava, as equal partners we are going to split the money. Your cut is Forty-Thousand dollars. Now we're not touching the drugs until we find out what we really got and what its worth." Kia stated.

Melody looked at Ava and spoke with a deep seriousness in her tone, "Ava, you're officially down with the Unfallen Roses. And you, you the black rose." Melody paused before speaking again. "You do know what that means, right?"

Ava wasn't stupid; she knew exactly what Melody was trying to say! The black rose is the death rose. Ava knew exactly what she had to do.

"Damn!" Ava thought out loud. "What the fuck am I going to do with Forty-Thousand dollars?"

"Well I already plan to invest 10 g's of mine, and I'd suggest that each of you did the same." Melody said.

Ava raised an eyebrow, "Into what?" she asked Melody.

"I have a list of companies that I've been watching for a long time. The only thing that held me back from investing into these companies was capital, now that that's fixed I'm ready to make that move. It is my strong beliefe that this will be a sound investment for us. We also need to do what we can to get all of our mothers' out of this building, and invest in a steel door for downstairs. 'Cause we can't forget to protect our main investment Roses. After all we're about to seize Harlem."

Ava and Regeane were standing at the window. Ava had been watching Kenny. Her tapping on the window captured everyone's attention. "We need to start with him first," she said.

Kia didn't have to look out the window to know that it was Kenny she was speaking about. For some unexplainable reason Ava hated him.

"Whoa, we're going to need a lot of help," Toni interrupted. She looked directly at Ava, "Meaning man power, guns, a place to break all of this stuff down. I know some people who are into the gun play and the cleaning business."

"What in the hell does cleaning have to do with guns?" Kia asked innocently.

Regeane smirked as she looked over at Kia. "No, what she means is these people are paid to kill. Do you understand now?"

Kia nodded her head.

"I may be able to assist in that department as well," Ava said as Wayne instantly popped into her mind. Hell she didn't know much about him but figured for the right price he'd be willing to help, he was definitely big enough.

After equally splitting up the money Toni suggested that they keep the drugs over at Ava and Kia's house. Kia eyed Melody as she counted out Ten-Thousand dollars.

"It's finally time for you to put all of that computer knowledge to use." She said as she and the rest of the Roses passed her their money.

"Ladies trust me this is a wise choice." Melody said as she and Kia both started chanting the word opportunity over and over again out loud, soon the others joined in. Melody Cruz was proud she knew now that HI SURF was well on its way to becoming a reality.

"Okay so tomorrow meet me upstairs at my crib," Melody said.

"What's at your apartment?" Regeane asked.

"John can show us what to do with that dope."

"OH hell no," Ava said while shaking her head in protest.

"Well do you have a better idea Ava?" Melody asked with an attitude.

"I sure do, why not give his ass a taste of it. That's a lot of shit to be handing him. I'm not trying to be funny but we need to be on point with the securing of our investments and that's by any and all means."

"Yeah Melody, she's right," Regeane cosigned.

"Just bring John over to our place tomorrow to test it." Ava said as everyone agreed.

Melody looked at Ava then at the rest of the Roses, "Yeah, aight." She stated.

Melody left feeling good about the money that she was carrying inside of her coat pockets. She opened the door and her mother was sitting on the sofa watching a Spanish station eating fried plantains laughing hysterically. Melody kissed her cheek the same way she'd always done. She loved her mother deeply. Mira Cruz hadn't been the same since her divorce five years prior. It was time that her mother got her life back. All she ever did was go to the supermarket and watch television. She'd already decided that by this time next month her mother would be moving back to Puerto Rico.

Melody walked in her room and like always she turned on her computer typing in her password and checking on the daily projections on the companies she was about to invest in. Each company was still gaining. She counted out the Roses Forty-Thousand and then another Twenty-Thousand dollars of her own money. She picked up Ten-Thousand dollars then walked into the living room and placed it in her mother's hands.

"C`ono! Where do you get thee money from?" Her mother asked in a heavy Spanish accent.

"I got it all from the help of my computer." Melody knew that the truth would break her mothers' heart. She about faced and walked back into her room.

"Kia did ya'll kill those people tonight?" Kia looked at Ava as she smirked inwardly.

"Don't worry about that you just make sure that you do your fucking part! If you really wanted to know then you would've been there." She took the gym bag into her bedroom.

Ava picked up the phone and dialed Pam.

"What's up girl?"

"Fucking bitch! Why haven't you called in a few days?" Pam wanted to know. Ava laughed it off. Pam was excited to hear from her good friend, and she couldn't wait to share her even better news, "I already have a post; I'm going to be at 124th and 7th for the year." Pam said.

"That's good, Pam, I'm really happy for you. I still don't know why you'd wanna be a cop instead of America's Next Top model, but it's all good I guess."

"Well, at least now I have a license to kill! What's better than that?" Pam joked.

Ava became serious as she got to the bottom of what she really called for, "Can we meet tomorrow for lunch I really need to talk to you, it'll be my treat."

"Of course, but what about work?"

"We'll discuss all of that tomorrow."

"Okay then what about meeting at Under The Stairs on West 94th about 1pm?"

"That sounds like a plan," Ava agreed.

Next, Ava wanted to call Wayne but at the moment she couldn't remember what she'd done with his number. It was already clear that tomorrow would be her last day at Chase Manhattan. From here on out they would be counting her millions.

Ava dressed in a black and gray 2-piece Prada business suit with a pair of matching open toe Fendi shoes. She admired herself in the mirror then cracked a smile.

"Fuck, I might as well go out in style."

She caught the number two train feeling good about the Eight-Thousand dollars inside her Fendi shoulder bag. As usual Ava stopped inside the coffee shop. She and Wayne exchanged friendly smiles.

"Good morning Wayne," Ava said as she slowly walked towards him.

"Yes it is!" Wayne assured as he admired her looking stunning in her suit.

"Look I really need to talk with you about something important I just don't have the time." She smiled again as she looked up in his eyes.

"Today is my last day at my job," she slid him a piece of paper, "Call me tonight."

Wayne opened his mouth to say something as Ava turned to leave. When she got to the door she winked, "I'll be waiting to hear from you."

Once inside of Chase Manhattan she held her head up high and walked over to the bank president who was wearing a blue silk suit, with a white crisp shirt adorned with a polka dot tie. He was always dressed very sharply.

"Mr. Ortman, might I have a moment of your time?"

"Certainly," he said as he led the way to his office.

"Have a seat Ava." Mr. Ortman sat and waited patiently for Ava to speak. He knew that hearing of the downsizing had been hard on them, but he had a feeling that Ava was going to be okay.

"Mr. Ortman, I'm here to personally tell you that I quit." With that Ava stood up to leave. Outside she flagged a cab and to Macy's she went. A shopping spree was definitely an order and this time money was not an object. There'd be no need to check sales tags because she could afford whatever it was she wanted. She grabbed dresses, pant suits, boots, and every fragranced body spray, oil and soap she could. Ava was loaded down with shopping bags as she exited the store. As her cab pulled up Pam was standing outside waiting on her and assisted with her new purchases.

"So, you went shopping for the family?" Pam joked. Both ladies laughed.

"Jeeze, I was beginning to wonder if you'd make it."

Ava frowned, "Girl please, I lost track of time."

Inside the restaurant the waiter helped the ladies with their bags. After getting situated in at a window booth Pam looked over at Ava.

"So let's have it, what's on your mind?"

Ava took a deep breath and as she leaned forward she placed her hands under her chin with her elbows on the table.

"Pam we've been friends a long time, what I'm about to share with you may change the respect that you have for me, and if so then I'll completely understand that."

"What the hell are you talking about Ava, you're scaring me."

"Pam out of respect for you and our friendship I'm here, and despite what the outcome is, I'm going to still follow through with my plans."

"Enough with the warnings, what the hell is it?" Pam asked with urgency in her voice.

"Your new post is directly in the place where my new associates, The Roses will be conducting business."

Pam looked at Ava not fully comprehending what her long time friend was saying.

"Business, what exactly are we talking about and who in the hell are the Roses, is this some street gang?"

"It's Unfallen Roses actually, and no, it's nothing like that," Ava said.

"I'm no longer an employee of Chase Manhattan. My new business partners and I are joining the drug trade."

Pam folded her arms across her chest then tilted her head to the side. "So what exactly is this meeting about Ava? Am I supposed to turn my head to your corruption?" Pam asked shocked.

Ava took a deep long sigh. She hoped she wasn't in over her head, even more than that; she hoped Pam was willing to accept the proposition. She leaned in even closer to Pam.

"We're just looking for someone who can help us orchestrate our plan by concentrating on the competition. This position pays Five-Thousand dollars weekly."

"Whoa," Pam said as she sat back to let Ava's words marinade. "You're asking me to risk everything including my freedom for you and some people I don't even know. Who in the hell else did you tell that you were meeting me today?" Pam demanded.

This is not going good Ava thought. "No one knows Pam." She paused as she allowed Pam to sort through everything they'd said.

Pam knew that what she was thinking was wrong. When she decided to become a cop it was to work against people who were diligently breaking the laws. However, the appeal of having all that tax free cash was slowly sinking in and soon her smile couldn't be denied. Ava passed a bank envelope across the table.

"If you accept this envelope then that means you're in, and if you don't, I'll be disappointed but I'll understand. I'll push it to the side for now and at the end of our meal if it's still there, I'll know that you don't want anything to do with it. But if it's gone then that means you're in."

Both ladies remained silent for a minute. Pam's eyes remained locked on the envelope.

"You don't have to worry Pam; this conversation is between us and won't be repeated. We'll only meet so I can pass you these envelopes. Now that's enough of this, let's eat," Ava said as she summoned the waiter to their area.

After dining on lobsters, crab legs, tossed salads and champagne Ava remembered she had to meet the Roses.

"Pam I'm sorry, but we'll have to finish lunch some other time," she said as she stood and peeled off a $100 bill placing it on the table. She kissed Pam's cheeks and as she gathered her packages Pam cleared her throat.

"What about this envelope?"

"What envelope?" Ava asked as she walked away from the table.

Pam kept her eyes glued to the envelope. $5,000 cash money meant that she could afford to do a lot of things. "Fuck it," she said as she picked the envelope up and slid it deep down into her coat pocket. The devil had purchased her soul for a mere $5,000.

Melody was heading out to computer class. John came walking from his room wearing only his boxers.

"Motherfucker show some damn respect in here!" She yelled as she sucked her teeth in disgust. "Give me $10?" She said as she opened her hand.

"Melody all I got is $5, but you can have it, it's yours." John reached inside his pocket and grabbed a crumbled up worn looking bill, he handed it to his sister.

Despite it all Melody couldn't deny that her brother was a good person. He'd willingly give her his last and she just wished he'd let go of his habits.

"Keep it John; just meet me here later please. It's very important."

"I'll be here Melody."

Toni and Kia were waiting for Regeane. They'd planned to go on a shopping spree of their own.

"So what do you know about this guy over here?" Toni asked directing her attention to Kenny.

"Not too much," Kia admitted. "I know he's big time though."

Toni laughed snidely, "He ain't shit! I bet if I placed a gun in his damn mouth he'd bitch up and beg for his damn life. I've been watching him and his weak ass crew the last two nights and I'm not at all impressed. His crew beat down the very people who are putting money in their pockets."

It was obvious to Kia that Ava's dislike for Kenny had spread to Toni as well.

"Why don't you wait before we start laying down our gangsta," Kia said.

Regeane walked up. "Yo ya'll ready to go? My pockets fat and I'm ready to spend this money."

"Hell yes, let's hit 125th street," Kia suggested.

Regeane and Toni looked at her like she was crazy. "Check this out baby girl," Toni said. "125th street is over for us from here on out. It's that good shit, Prada. Gucci. Fendi. That's the only shit we'll be rockin' from now on. We're not going in reverse we're elevating our status."

"That's what I'm saying," Regeane cosigned. "And I already called a cab, please we outta here!"

"So Big Rage," Toni said. "What you think of Kenny?"

"Shit fuck him, and just like everyone else his ass can get it too. If he knows what's good for him he'll roll with us, and if not like others he'll have to learn the hard way." They all laughed aloud not caring who heard them.

A black Chevy Tahoe with tinted windows pulled up on them, "That's us right there," Big Rage said. All three ladies jumped in filled with joy! The first stop was the Fendi store on Madison. Kia and Toni easily found plenty of items. Regeane was upset because the selections weren't for her size.

"Ya'll let's hit Saks."

There cab was sitting there waiting.
Inside Saks Regeane and Kia lost their minds running out of money, while Toni took her time making her selections.

"Muffin let me hold 3 stacks."

"Wait, I want to see if I can find something in here."

After finally deciding on some outfits Toni was able to give Regeane what she needed and offered Kia what she had left.

"Nah I'm good," Kia said. The Tahoe took them back uptown where they each remembered that they had a meeting. Toni paid the driver $400 and reminded Regeane not to forget the meeting.

After putting her things up Kia made her way back downstairs where she found Toni standing alone, watching the dealers and dopefiends exchange money and drugs, the steady flow seemed to be non-stop and done with ease. Toni couldn't help but wonder how much money a block like this one made in a day.

"What's up?"

"Man we have to figure out a way to take this block over," Toni said. "Maybe we should just offer him a better price than what he's paying now for his product."

"Wait hold up, I thought that he either rolled with the Roses or we rolled over him? Don't tell me that your tough ass is scared now Toni."

"SCARED?" Toni looked hard into Kia. "I've killed three men connected to the mafia, each one of them were aiming to kill my father. So do you really think some two-dollar-ass street hustler scares me?" She huffed, "I'll do his ass for free. This shit ain't new to me, hell you could never understand what my life consisted of before they got to my father. So don't you ever accuse me of being scared! If anything ya'll better be the ones bringing the heart to the table because as soon as they figure out that we're all women then you better believe they all coming at us and hard!" Toni didn't need to tell Kia that who didn't know that Harlem bred killers.

As agreed Unfallen Roses met at Kia and Ava's and began talking about the arrangements they'd need.

"We're going to need some help with this," Melody said.

"We should all get one person that we trust, and who's willing to go all out with us."

"WHAT!?" Regeane yelled. "Fuck we might as well put an ad in the newspaper."

"No Regeane, listen we're going to need help," Melody said.

"Melody's right," Kia agreed.

"I know I can trust my friend in Brooklyn, Marilyn, she's my heart."

"Oh really," Melody said.

"I trust her with my life in any situation."

"We've all heard the stories about the two of them from her Brooklyn tales," Kia said. "It sounds good to me." They all agreed.

Ava stood up, "Listen everybody, I got a girlfriend she's a beat walker..." before she could explain further.

"She's the police!?" Regeane yelled out.

Ava nodded her head. "Whoa, how do you know that she won't flip out, or start getting greedy when the money start coming in?" Regeane demanded to know.

"Because she won't that's how!" Ava snapped.

"Well what if she does?" Regeane asked. "You do realize it's your duty as a Rose to get rid of her friends or not. I don't trust the police, and don't have a problem killing one or two, especially if they are interfering with what we're trying to accomplish here."

Ava looked at Toni, "Yeah I get that, as long as it's agreed that Toni and her friend will abide by the same code."

Toni nodded her head as she and Ava exchanged devilish grins.

"None of you probably will agree with my choice, but at least hear me out completely." Melody started, "I want my brother as my partner."

"There goes the neighborhood," Ava said. Melody looked over at her.

"This is not the time Ava," Melody stated. "He's the only one we really know that has the street connections we'll need."

Regeane cut in, "Melody, I love you like a sister, but we all know that he uses that stuff. That makes him a weak link to all of this. I feel what you're saying but what if he fucks up or jeopardizes us are you prepared to do what must be done? Could you kill your own brother?" Melody sat on the bed obviously considering what had been said.

"If the situation arises I'll deal with it."

"Okay so that goes for you Ava and you too Muffin; I don't have time to be babysitting anybody friends it's too much money to be made."

"Who are you putting down with you?" Toni asked.

"No one," Regeane replied quickly. "Like Melody said this is our opportunity, I'm running with mines, I'm with the Roses and that's it!"

"Kia?" Toni said.

"I feel the same way."

"Kia, you brought Ava in, remember?" Regeane remined her.

There was an awkward silence that filled the room for about thirty seconds before Toni spoke. "Are you prepared to do what has to be done if the situation arises?"

Kia looked at her sister with tears in her eyes. She and Ava's eyes locked then a tear fell as Kia spoke, "Yes!"

"Ava, don't worry, as long as you play by the rules of the game then theirs nothing to fear," Melody winked.

The way Ava looked at Melody, if looks could kill then Mel would definitely be dead.

"Bring that open brick from yesterday," Melody said. Kia got up from Ava's bed and went into her bedroom. When she returned she passed it to Melody, who opened it and took some of the powder out placing it on a piece of paper.

Melody picked up the phone. John answered on the very first ring, "Come down to Ava and Kia's apartment."

"For what?"

"Just bring your ass down the stairs!" She yelled before hanging up. John knew that it must be something important by the tone of her voice.

When John reached the third floor, Regeane was standing in the hallway with her hands on her hips, "follow me."

John walked into Ava's bedroom. Toni and Ava were sitting on the bed, Melody was standing near the window, Kia was sitting in a chair behind the door and Regeane was standing behind him. John was feeling uneasy about her standing behind him. The other day they had some words in the street; she wanted to fight him and had even pulled out a box cutter to cut him.

"John listen," Melody said. "And listen good you'll only be told once. Number one, you're not wanted here, two, I'm putting my life on the line for you. Please remember that I'm your only sister and I can't be replaced; three, if you cross me in anyway, shape, fashion or form I'll be forced to kill you. Do you understand?"

"Don't think I forgot about that ass," Regeane chimed in.

Melody opened her hand passing him the white rock powder.

"What's this?"

"That's what we want you to tell us," Ava said. John tasted it affirming that it was dope.

"How good is it?" Toni asked.

"It's hard to tell I have to sniff it first." They all looked at him waiting for him to sniff. Kia suggested he go into the bathroom. When john walked out the room they started talking about their shopping sprees. Kia looked over at Melody, "John been in there fifteen minutes check and see if he's okay."

Melody knocked on the door and he didn't respond. She started banging and he still didn't respond.

"Is everything okay?" Kia asked as she came to check on them.

"John isn't answering." They both pushed the door open. John lay on the floor with white foam coming from the sides of his mouth.

"Get all of the ice that you'll have," Melody told Kia. The rest of them ran inside the bathroom to help. Melody turned on the shower," help me put him in." It was not the first time she'd been in this situation with John. Regeane was able to pick him up placing him under the cold water. Kia ran inside with the bucket of ice. Melody was slapping him calling out his name.

"Keep slapping him," she said while she undid his pants and started dumping the ice inside his underwear. He regained consciousness.

"You asshole!" Melody yelled out. Ava looked over at her, "Are you sure about this?"

Melody wanted to cry instead she shook her head yes. She was so hurt to see her brother looking like that in front of her friends. Kia handed him a clean towel and told him once he was cleaned up to come in the room. She didn't care what Ava said John was cool with her. They sat patiently waiting for him.

"Listen motherfucker, this is the last time that I'm saving your ass after you've OD'd do you understand? Now tell us what we need to know?"

"Where did you get that shit from?"

"None of you business," Ava replied. "Tell us what we need to know John."

"Well I hope ya'll did not try and sell that yet otherwise you'll all be in jail before you can make a dollar. This is the best dope I've ever sniffed in my life, it almost killed me and that's what's going to happen to the other dope fiends that sniff or shoot it. It's too pure, it has to be cut maybe eight or nine times before you could even consider selling it."

"That's the reason you're here," Toni reminded him. John started nodding out right in front of them; Regeane yelled out his name, he lifted his head for a second then it dropped back down to his chest. Melody walked over to him and slapped him with all of her might. John looked up at her, "Why did you do that?"

"Stand your dope fiend ass up," she yelled. Ava sat there shaking her head.

"You got to find morphine connect to cut this stuff up with, and you'll need a lot of it." John knees started to bend and his eyes started to roll in the back of his head, Regeane slapped him so hard that he fell on the floor.

"Close your eyes again," Regeane threatened as she stood over him.

"So John where can we get morphine from?" Toni asked.

John nodded out again; he heard Regeane and his eyes popped back open. He pointed towards her.

"What the fuck you pointing at me for?"

"Your brother is the connection. He works in a hospital, right? He's been selling it to Masada, the guy on 118th street and Lennox Avenue."

"John what are you talking about?"

"Your brother, he's the morphine connect you'll need."

"So he be selling it to that motherfucker Masada? I'll see about that, it's not going down like that," Regeane said.

"Mike is apart of that crew," Melody said.

"I hate that pretty ass motherfucker, his ass disrespected me about a month ago I'll kill his ass myself," Regeane said.

They were so into their conversation that no one noticed that John had nodded completely out in the middle of the floor.

"So listen if I'm understanding what John said that means that we have eight or nine times more of this stuff," they all started adding it up in their heads.

Melody blurted out, "We're going to be millionaires in a years' time." They all smiled at one another.

John was still lost in his nod as Melody stood over him. "If it gets all the fiends high like this, we're going to be them Bitches in charge. Get up John." When he stood up on his feet she stared into his bloodshot eyes.

"Now listen you got two weeks to clean yourself up, and at anytime if it becomes a problem, I'll have no choice but to kill you. It will hurt my heart to do it, but I won't hesitate. As a member of the Roses that's my duty." Melody looked over at Ava; she just turned her head away. John looked at his little sister then around at her friends, it wasn't a game! He had to kick the habit and fast otherwise he knew he was a dead man.

The Plot, The Takeover

The phone rang, Ava answered it, and it was Wayne. She walked out of the room to talk with him privately.

"Are we on for tonight, it's my treat?" Ava asked.

"Sure, why not let's meet at One Fish Two Fish, at 96th street and Madison Avenue."

"That's not too far from me," Ava said.

"I'll be there at 9:30."

"Deal, it's a date."

Ava walked back into her room, the Roses were plotting on the blocks that they knew sold dope. The first block was 123rd street and 7th Avenue.

"Kenny is a goner," Ava joined in the discussion. "I want to do his ass my damn self!"

118th street and Lennox was the next block. "I want that job," Regeane volunteered. I want my face to be the last thing Masada sees before I empty that clip into his face."

The Eastside 122nd Street and 2nd Avenue, Kia and Toni agreed to handle that one. "We're also going out of town branching out to Baltimore, Philly, and Washington all up and down the East Coast, New Jersey too?" Kia said.

"Let's worry about Harlem first, then the Bronx. We got all the dope in the world." Melody said.

"I got family in Baltimore that sells dope down there," Regeane revealed. "So we shouldn't have a problem setting up shop out there.

"Everything seems like it's going to work itself out. I think it's safe for me to leave now ladies, I got a date tonight," Ava said.

"A date?" Kia asked with an eyebrow raised.

"Yeah, with our manpower and if he plays his cards right I might give him some pussy too."

They all started laughing. Toni stood up.

"I got a few phone calls to make to some people in Brooklyn."

"Fuck it, I'm going to holla at my man," Melody said. "John let's go."

Kia and Regeane just looked at each other. Toni was on the phone with her girlfriend Marilyn.

"It's been awhile since I've heard from you," Toni's girlfriend said.

"I've been busy lately."

"How is it living in Harlem?"

"Girl, you don't know what you're missing."

"Did you go to the Apollo yet?"

"Yeah, I went but it was closed. It's no problem though, I live around the corner from it so I can go anytime I want. I'm coming to Brooklyn tomorrow, it's a lot we need to discuss, and I want you to be apart of something big I'm into. Oh hey do you still have Kane's number?"

"It's in my room somewhere, why you want it?"

"No, look I want you to call him for me and tell him we're coming to see him."

"What time will you be here?"

"About 3 p.m."

"I'll be waiting for you."

After she hung up the phone she looked under her bed for the Timberland boot box where she'd hidden her money and the .9 mm Glock that her father had given her after she turned fourteen for protection that her mother was unaware of. She counted out ten thousand dollars afterwards she loaded the clip. *It's too early to put you to use, please let tomorrow be a good day.* She thought as she walked over to her window. Kenny and his crew were standing next to the store, she pointed the gun the only reason she didn't pull the trigger was because she knew that his days on 123rd street were already limited. Either roll with the Roses, or get planted like one, her mind was set she was going to get rich, or die trying. Not even the police would stand in her way.

Melody called Mike for the first time in three days.

"What's up Boo, you don't have time for me?"

"It's not like that, I just had a few things to take care of. I'm trying to make both of our lives better. I need to see you."

"When?"

"Now I'm in a mood to make love."

"Come downstairs in five minutes," Mike said.

"Look Mike don't hurt my feelings, or you'll pay big time. Do you understand?"

Mike was a little confused but he answered anyway, "Why would I wanna do that?"

"I'm just letting you know, you've been warned, that's all," Melody answered. "A lot of things will be changing around Harlem."

Mike laughed, he didn't know exactly how serious Melody was, "Like what?" he asked.

"Just put it this way; it's your choice to go with the change, or get caught up in something that you can't handle. It's bigger than Nino Brown baby," Melody said. "If you make the right choice you'll make a lot of money in the long run trust me."

Mike didn't know what the hell Melody was talking about. He wrote it off as nothing too serious, "I'm on my way," he revealed.

This was the first time Ava had seen Wayne wearing a suit. It was a two-piece baby blue Giorgio Armani with a mock neck sweater. His left arm sported a Q blue face Rolex. While Wayne bent to kiss Ava's cheek she smelled the Issey Miyake and was thoroughly impressed when she peeped his manicured nails. Oh yes if he plays his cards right I can lay down, she thought.

"Ava, you looking good in that Gucci jumpsuit with the matching boots."

Ava smiled, "How do you know it's Gucci?"

"Come on now, I know today's fashions." Ava smiled even harder.

"Thank you. You looking good in that Armani also." They smiled at each other.

Wayne started the conversation talking about himself and his three brothers along with the eight years he spent in jail. He wanted to be honest with her so she'd understand who she was dealing with.

"So what did you do?"

"Murder," he said casually.

"So tell me about your brothers, what are they into?"

He smirked, "Everything from murder, mutilation, to marbles."

Ava looked at him knowing that the conversation was going in the right direction. All she needed was a way to get Wayne and his brothers to play by her rules.

"So let me ask you something?   Are you saying that you're not into the streets anymore?"

Wayne shook his head no.

"But what if the money was right would you convert back to your old ways?"

Wayne looked at Ava, "It depends."

"On what?"

"With who and if enough money is in it for me."

"Hypothetically speaking," Ava started, "How much would you charge me if I wanted to hire you and your brothers to put some work in?"

"Hypothetically huh, well friends are friends and business is business, regardless of who, or the money that they have. I'd just want my money."

"The problem isn't the money it's the fact that you didn't answer my question, and for the record you or your brothers don't scare me at all. Now that it's been said I have a deal and it's up to you to accept or reject it."

"To do what?"

"Murder and mutilation," Ava laughed, "we're too old to play marbles. All my partners and I need to do is lock down the streets and protect our investment. Anything goes as long as we come out on top. So tell me your price."

Wayne sat back in his chair. "Is this the reason that you quit you job?"

"It plays a part, but that not the real reason."

"$20,000 cash a week regardless if our services are needed or not."

Ava sat back in her chair with Regeane's voice clear in her head, *life is like a game of chess one crucial move or words from their mouth can cost a person their life.* She knew that the next move was on her. Ava wanted to be precise and avoid any signs of weakness.

"I'd need to discuss this price before I could agree, however our rules are simple, we don't care about what your personal lives consist of, when we call and tell you what we want, its done!" She looked straight in Wayne's eyes.

Wayne liked how a woman like Ava handled business, including the fact that she wasn't afraid. After they agreed to take the terms to their partners Ava took the liberty of placing the orders for both of them wearing a huge smile.

"So can I go home with you tonight?"

"I don't see why not," Wayne said.

Ava paid the bill and left a $20.00 tip. Wayne helped her wit her coat. Once outside she was shocked to find that he was driving a 2001 Tahoe that was sitting up on 22" Giovanni chrome rims. It was apparent that he was into more than serving coffee. Ava had been surprised by his suit, watch, and now his truck. The inside was hooked up, Wayne wasted no time selecting R. Kelly's *The Greatest Sex* CD.

They'd been riding about a half of hour on the highway to Queens.

"Wayne what else you into, there is no way coffee is selling like this. This is a fifty thousand dollar truck I'm not going for it."

Wayne pulled over on the side of the highway, he faced Ava. "I didn't ask you how you could afford to pay me that type of money so let's not get into one another business. You said that you wanted us on point when you call and that's all that counts, right?"

Ava knew that she had to respect his wishes. He put the truck in drive and ten minutes later they were pulling into a nice apartment complex. The parking lot housed a row of expensive trucks and cars. Wayne's apartment was located on the ground floor. The living room was adorned in black, gold and white. Furniture was black leather, glass tables, 60" television with black carpet, it was a nice two bedroom, but what caught Ava's attention was his huge photo of Phyllis Hyman. She'd been hearing Toni talk about her and this was the first time she'd seen her. She looked like an ice princess set against a black and gold frame in a flowing white dress, with a fur hat, pearls around her neck holding a white poodle.

Ava sat down and he turned on the television.

"Would you like some wine?"

"Yes that would be nice."

"Any preference?"

"Red please."

Wayne returned from the kitchen carrying two wine glasses and a bottle of Louis Jadot Montrachet. Ava smiled she didn't remember the last man that had been able to make her smile so many times in a single night, not since Todd whom she'd met five years prior.

Wayne reached out for Ava's hand helping her off of the couch and led her to his bedroom.

Finally Ava thought, she was hornier than a cat in heat and wanted Wayne to fulfill all of her needs. The bedroom was also black, white and gold. He had an extensive cologne collection that was neatly arranged on his dresser. It'd been eight long months since Ava had been with a man. Wayne wrapped his arms around her and began kissing her neck. She faced him as she teased his ear with his tongue she spoke seductively, "My pussy is dripping and begging for you to taste it." She unzipped his pants and made her way down in front of him showing him that she didn't have a problem going all out. She slid his dick deep in her mouth and brought it out licking all around it like an ice cream cone real slow. Ava enjoyed sex the kinkier the better, she knew that she and Wayne didn't know one another that well but she would be flinging new ideas at him and real soon. A low moan escaped from Wayne although she'd been out the field she knew that she was still a master at the head game, something she took real pride in knowing.

Wayne's legs began to shake; Ava moved her right hand to massage his balls and with her left she played with his ass. Wayne's body was ready to explode and with a tremendous shake he knew that he was getting closer to cumming inside of Ava's mouth. Ava knew that the pressure was on and she rammed her middle finger inside his ass. Wayne's eyes almost popped out of the sockets. Surprisingly this felt so good to him that he didn't know if he should thank her for giving him the best nut he's ever had or kick this freaky bitch out for shoving her finger up his ass.

He pushed her back on her ass, "Bitch is you crazy?" Ava smiled up at him with cum dripping from her mouth. Just the sight of her turned him on.

"Nigga stop playing you know you liked it. Don't worry I won't tell big man," she teased with a smile.

"So that's it Ava, you want it rough?"

Those words were like music to her ears.

"Bitch take off your clothes!" Ava stepped out of her jumpsuit and Wayne noticed that she was completely naked underneath. He enjoyed looking over her beautiful chocolate body it actually glowed in the dark, she looked like a Nubian Queen her hair was hanging over the side of her face. He was really taken back with her and knew he had to find a way to possess her.

"Why are you standing there with your mouth wide open, you know what I want; now get down on your knees and eat this pussy," she opened her legs wide and Wayne happily obliged. All night long they fucked and sucked one another in every room including on top of his 60" television.

The next day Toni was on the train wearing her black Roland Mouret leather suit with the gold buttons, carrying a matching Hermes picotin shoulder bag containing the ten thousand and her .9 mm Glock. She looked like a businesswoman. Her mind was set that she wasn't leaving Brooklyn without the guns she'd planned to purchase. She got off of the train and everything was just as she'd remembered, all except she didn't feel the same. Marilyn was glad as hell to see her best friend in the whole entire world. Marilyn began screaming, "Come in, come in!"

Marilyn's ice gray eyes were cold enough to freeze Medusa. Marilyn was mixed with Chinese and Greek, she was a golden brown complexion, with sandy brown hair that she usually wore covering her face to hide her chinky eyes. At 5' 4" and 126 pounds she was easily any mans' dream woman. After they hugged Toni walked into the living room noticing that there had been a change in there.

"Who's here with you?"

"No one," Marilyn looked at Toni, "Damn girl you're looking good."

Toni sat on the couch. "Look I need to talk to you about something important." Toni patted the cushion next to her. "I have some new friends in Harlem, and we're forming something big and I really want you to be apart of it with us."

"What is it?"

"There's a lot of money involved."

"How much money?" Marilyn curiously asked.

"Just say this, way too much to count by hands."

Marilyn smiled as she stood to walk over to the window. "What would I have to do?"

"Before I say anything more I need to know if you're in then we can talk about it."

"Are you sure about this?" Marilyn asked as she faced Toni.

"If I wasn't I wouldn't be here telling you about it." Marilyn took her seat next to Toni. "You're my best friend and if you're in, then I'm in."

Toni smiled, she began explaining how they found a shit load of drugs and money and that the best thing about it was that they didn't even have to share it with anyone.

"What about the people that it belongs to?"

"We killed them." Toni opened her bag and peeled of ten hundred dollar bills and passed it to Marilyn.

"What's this for?"

"Just for being my friend."

"It's been lonely without you around."

"That's because I'm the only one who likes you Ice Eyes," Toni teased. "Did you call Kane for me?"

"Yeah, he's waiting for your call." Marilyn dialed his number, his brother Vito answered. Kane wasn't home, but before Marilyn could hang up Toni reached for the phone to speak with Vito.

"This is Peter's daughter."

"Yeah, I thought I recognized the voice. How are you?"

"I'm fine; can we talk its important?"

"When?" he asked looking at his watch.

"Now in person."

"Okay come by my house, I'll be outside waiting for you."

"Marilyn and I are on our way."

Toni looked at Marilyn, "So are you ready to go shopping?"

As they turned the corner of Vito's block he and his pit bull were standing outside. Vito kissed Toni's cheek as they spoke.

"Girl you're looking like you work up on Wall Street, beautiful!" he spoke with a thick Italian accent.

"That's why I'm here for business."

"What's so important that you have to talk to me?"

"Can we go inside?" Toni asked. As they walked in she looked back. "Who else is in here?"

"Just us," Vito assured her.

Toni went into details about her need for guns, bulletproof vests, and whatever else he could get his hands on.

Vito looked at her as he laughed, "Get the hell out of here!"

"I'm not kidding I'm looking to do business," Toni said while reaching inside of her bag pulling out the stack of hundreds.

Vito noticed the butt of the gun stuffed inside of there.

"Marilyn and I are here on business Vito, this is nine thousand dollars and if you can't help maybe I should go some place else."

Vito looked at Toni, Marilyn and then the money.

"So what's it going to be?" Marilyn asked staring intensely at him with her icy eyes.

"Where in the hell did you come into this type of money?"

"That's none of your concern, now are we doing this or what?" Marilyn asked.

Toni pulled out a piece of paper. "I want all automatics, with ten bulletproof vests with two extra clips, three boxes of bullets and silencers. Is there a problem?"

Vito shook his head in disbelief, "Shit can I get ya'll some Army tanks too? What are ya 'll into?"

"Again that's not your concern. Do you deliver?"

Vito took the paper from Toni's hand to look at the extensive list of guns. He took a deep breath, "$11,000 more to fill this order."

Toni nodded in agreement, "When can I expect my packages?"

"Friday afternoon."

"Okay so this $9,000 is the down payment."

"Don't have us looking for you, Vito." Marilyn said. "I still haven't forgiven you for breaking my arm." She said with a smirk on her face. Vito knew that she wasn't playing. Marilyn and Toni had chased him for two straight months with butcher knives, he only got it to cease after speaking with Toni's father.

Toni definitely had her father's blood, he thought. Hell and that wasn't a good thing; the daughter of a hit man with more heart than some of the guys in his own crew.

"Shit, looks like the murder rate is about to go up," he said aloud.

"I'll be back on Friday," Toni stated looking at Vito. Shortly after she and Marilyn walked out the door.

"Marilyn ask your mother if it'll be okay for you to stay with me."

"That's no problem I'm looking forward to meeting some new people." The friends hugged, Toni was praying that she wasn't luring Marilyn into a trap.

Summer Madness

Melody woke up about 3:30 p.m. after making love with Mike for the very first time. He was the first guy that she'd allowed to get this close. Melody was in love with Mike and willing to do anything for him. She opened her bedroom door and called out John's name, when he didn't answer she knew it was a wrap.

She walked into the washroom to piss and shower. As soon as she got out of the shower she called Mike's to see if he wanted to shop with her at Macy's.

Mike's mother answered the phone.

"Hi Ms. Green, is Mike there?"

Ms. Green sound like she was on the verge of tears, "Mike was arrested this morning with two loaded guns along with two other guys," she managed to get out.

"What time did this happen, Mike and I were together last night up until 10 this morning."

"I don't know the exact time, but one of Mike's friends who seen him get arrested called me and that's what they claiming happened."

"Please if he calls tell him to call me," Melody said.

"I will."

Tears escaped Melody's eyes as she thought about Mike. She rubbed her body down with oil then got dressed; she put on a pair of Gap jeans with her tan Timberlands, a matching tan shirt. She pulled her hair back in a ponytail then she slipped into her tan suede jacket. She didn't care what the bail would be she was going to get him out of that place.

Regeane was walking down 123rd street talking to some guy Melody hadn't seen before.

"Regeane?" She turned noticing Melody and walked away from the man she was talking to.

"When we gone do this thang, a bitch ready to eat!" Melody laughed at Big Rage.

"In a few days be patient."

"Fuck all that," Regeane spat, "it's getting hot in Harlem, and I want to show my ass!"

"Don't worry you'll have time to do that for the rest of your life."

Melody was telling Regeane about Mike's arrest and how she was waiting on his call in order to bail him out.

Regeane's mind was drifting off to another place, "Look at him he thinks he's all that!"

"Who are you talking about?"

Regeane pointed across the street at Kenny. "Why are you so worried about him? He's a nobody in our world," Melody said.

"In due time he'll be working for us or he won't be working around here trust me. When he slip we'll be there to catch his ass." Regeane started laughing. "We'll be controlling half of Harlem, next stop 118th street, 122nd Street and 2nd avenue, after that we'll go to 110th Street and Lexington Avenue."

"You got this all planned out, huh?"

"That's right it's the only way we're going to control shit as a team."

"I know, trust me I know," Melody cosigned. "Don't think I forgot about Baltimore, Washington, Philly and Delaware we're going down there too."

Regeane started to get hyped. "That's the shit I want to hear!" she yelled. "Point of no return, let's get rich!"

Toni walked up on them.

"What's up Muffin you looking nice, what you selling I want some."

Toni put her middle finger up at Regeane.

"Okay so listen," Toni said. "Friday Regeane, my girl Marilyn and I are going to bring the guns as far as 42nd street. Melody you, Kia and Ava will bring them home.

"So you spoke with Kia and Ava already?" Melody asked.

"Does it matter? We're all in this together there are no bosses when it comes to us."

"She's right Melody," Regeane said. "It sounds good to me."

Ava, Kia and their mother were sitting in the living room watching television.

"Mommy you need to give that hospital your notice because we got plans of moving you out of this rat hole." Ava said.

"We don't have that kind of money on hand."

"Just find you a nice house in Texas somewhere it's time for you to retire and enjoy your life and we're paying for it," Ava said. "And I mean in two weeks so you need to start looking for a house now."

"Oh really," before Jacqueline could say anything more Ava and Kia were both putting on their jackets and heading out the door.

Jacqueline didn't know what to think of this. She knew that her daughters were both grown women. Honestly she liked the idea of them forcing her to move out of Harlem after all these years. "Thank you God!"

When Ava and Kia got downstairs it was the first time in quite sometime that they had all been together. It was the five elements of life forming all at once, fire, water, wind, sun and moon making them the Unfallen Roses; red, yellow, white, pink and black. They greeted the sisters'.

"Let's take a walk to the park," Toni suggested.

Once seated in Morningside Park on the bench Toni informed them that she'd secured the guns.

"What kinds?" Regeane asked.

"All automatics."

"How much did they charge you?" Kia asked.

"$20,000 that's not a problem cause we need them more than anything right now. Ava and Kia I need you both to meet us on 42nd street to bring the guns home and timing is everything so don't be late. I'll call when I'm leaving Brooklyn."

Regeane told them that her brother could get the morphine, but only in the liquid form they needed to find a way to turn it into powder.

"Just bring it tonight to Toni's," Ava said.

"So Regeane do you know anything about shooting a gun?" Toni asked.

"My brother taught me everything; how to clean them, shoot them, take them apart, load them, hell I can even fix them. Oh and yes my brother won't be doing business with Masada anymore, the guy I told ya'll about who disrespected me on 118th street." Regeane nodded her head, "but now it's my turn motherfucker."

"Regeane we're not plotting on him only business matters," Kia said.

"Fuck that," Regeane yelled. "I want him. I promised his ass that we would meet again, fuck business this is personal!"

"Okay Regeane just let it rest for now."

Ava told them about Wayne. "It's four of them and they want 20,000 a week for whatever we want done, I told them I had to speak to my partners first."

"Fuck it pay 'em," Kia said.

"Is it anything else we need to discuss?" They all looked over one another. "Good let's go and get something to eat before I fall out," Ava said.

Melody walked into there apartment as the phone started ringing. "I got it," she yelled out. It was Mike.

"What happened?"

"I can't say, but one thing I know for sure I didn't have anything to do with it."

"How much is your bail?"

"$7,500 cash only."

"Are your friends going to get you out?"

"No, I got half at my house the other half is the problem."

"Where are you?"

"Central bookings."

"Well just hold on, I'll be there to bail you out myself."

"You got that kind of money?"

"Yeah, we got that kind of money."

"I love you boo!"

"I love you twice as much," Melody said. "But listen Mike from now on you can't mess with Masada and his crew do we have an understanding?"

"Fuck them, it's all about you mami, understand?"

Melody smiled, "Let me go I'll see you tonight." She walked over to her closet and pulled out her old coat where she'd hidden her money. She counted out the bail and an additional $1,000 for his pockets. Someone knocked on her bedroom door.

"Come in."

"I found someone that's selling two ounces of morphine for $500 dollars, so grab your coat you're hanging with me today," John smiled, hoping he'd made his sisters' day.

"Who is this person?"

"A friend of mine, he lives in the St. Nick Projects."

As Melody slipped her coat on, she looked over at John, "come on are you ready?"

Once outside Melody noticed Kenny, Mellow, and Mannie standing across the street talking to some girls. The weather had gotten warmer since she was outside an hour ago. They started walking towards the projects.

"He's lives on 127th Street, in building 317."

"What floor?"

"It's the second so we can walk up."

Melody was watching John, in her heart she knew her brother wouldn't hurt her but the fact that he was a dope fiend kept her on point. John knocked on door 3-H when the door opened a skinny dark skin man wearing the filthiest wife beater, in a pair of ripped jeans answered. He wasn't wearing any shoes standing at the door. He smiled and his mouth revealed rotten teeth obvious that drugs were getting the best of him. He opened the door allowing them access to his home and Melody was shocked at the immaculate order his apartment was in. At least he's a fiend with some class she thought. Melody sat in a chair close to the window.

"How you doing I'm Raymond," he said.

Melody smiled as she introduced herself.

"Can I get you something to drink?"

"No thank you." Melody felt comfortable he appeared to be a gentleman. "Let's get down to business," Melody said.

"So John tells me that you're his little sister and you're looking to buy some morphine."

"That's true."

"I'm not trying to be funny or anything but you look kind of young to be interested in something like this."

"Listen Raymond," Melody said as she made certain that there eyes met. "I'm here to do business not for you to discuss my age or anything else."

"John if you had the heart your little sister had you'd be alright. I'm sorry if I upset you in anyway I have two ounces that I'm selling for five hundred." Raymond placed it on the table. Melody looked at John.

"Come check this out," she said.

John stared at the gray powder then tasted it; he shook his head to confirm that it was indeed morphine. Melody counted out the money and placed it on the table. Raymond counted it behind her.

"You don't have to count it I'm all business and I'd like to keep it that way," she said.

"You know you have a lot of class," Raymond said. "In this game you're about to join you'll outlast a lot of your opponents."

"Thank you. Whenever you get your hands on some more I'm buying it, just let john know when you get it."

"You got that Boss Lady."

"Plus if things go as planned I may have a job for you."

"I could use the extra money." Raymond said. "In case this matters to you I haven't used in almost five years." Melody looked at Raymond.

"I can tell," she said with a smile on her face.

When they got outside John looked at her.

"Where did you get that kind of money?"

"If you play your cards right you'll be having this kind of money also plus some. Now shut the fuck up I'm trying to think," she said as she flagged down a cab.

"100 Center street please," Melody told the driver.

"Why in the hell are we going to the court building?"

"I'm bailing my boyfriend out of jail."

"When the hell did you start having boyfriends?"

"John please, not now!" Once they got out of the cab Melody saw two police officers standing against the wall.

"Excuse me officers, can you tell me where you pay bails at?"

The officer pointed towards white street through the glass doors.

A female officer was sitting behind a desk when Melody walked up to the glass window.

"Yes may I help you?"

"Yes I'd like to bail out Mike Green." The officer keyed in his name on the computer.

"Yes he's here, his bail is $7,500 and that's cash only."

Melody pulled her money out counted it with John standing next to her looking. Melody passed the money through the glass and watched as the officer recounted the

122

money. Melody hated when people recounted her money like she couldn't count.

"He won't be released until later this evening."

That sounded good to her as long as she knew he'd be home tonight. The officer passed her the receipt, "don't lose it." Melody and John headed back uptown.

Regeane and her brother were walking into their building together when Melody and John pulled up.

"John wait for me upstairs," Melody instructed. They all walked up the stairs together. Melody knocked on Kia's door.

Kia opened the door and directed them into her room Ava and Toni were already in there watching Pretty Woman on DVD.

"Have a seat Tyrone," Ava said. "Long time no see."

"You're right about that," he said.

Toni stopped the movie. "So let's get down to it," Toni suggested.

"Tyrone we hear you can get morphine?" Ava asked.

"Yeah it's the liquid kind."

"How can we turn it into powder?"

Tyrone looked at Ava. "You need quinine blocks."

Ava looked around at the others. "Where can we get that from?" Melody asked.

All you need is a syringe to shoot it inside the quinine blocks then it'll turn grayish, then you have to let it dry out."

Tyrone looked around at them and landed on Ava. "Look we been cool a long time but I already got a guy who buys from me."

"Tyrone we been cool since we were kids," Ava said. "So this is what we're going to do, from now on," she pointed to each of the women in the room. "We'll be purchasing that morphine from you."

Tyrone looked at Ava. "I'm sorry; I can't do Masada like that."

Ava took a deep breath, "Look Tyrone he won't be in business too much longer cause we're shutting him down in the next week or two, now if you want to join us we are willing to compensate you with 3% a day of our cut. That's way more than Masada is paying you."

Kia winked at Regeane.

"I told you that things were about to change around here, now the question is what are you going to do about it?" Regeane asked her brother.

"So what ya'll saying?" Tyrone asked.

Kia reached under the bed releasing a roll of plastic sheet as Toni pulled her .9 mm Glock from her waistband and handed it to Regeane.

Tyrone looked over at his little sister. Toni sighed, "Tyrone I hate to be the one who has to inform you of this, but you've heard a little too much," she said as she punched him in his adam's apple. At that moment the lights went out, Tyrone dropped to his knees gagging for air as Regeane stepped closer to her brother placing the gun on his temple.

"This is the last time we're offering," Kia said.

Tyrone shook his head up and down; he was still on his knees. "We have a deal?" Toni asked again.

"Yes," he said as he held his neck. When he stood he looked at Regeane, her eyes let him know that she was seriously going to kill him if he hadn't agreed.

"So I get that 3%?"

"Yeah and if Masada comes to you, just tell him that you can't get it anymore. If he becomes a problem just let anyone of us know about it."

He shook his head like a little kid.

"When can you get some morphine?" Kia asked.

"Tomorrow it'll be a half gallon, that's enough for four kilo's of dope," he offered.

The Roses had a sensational feeling going on inside of them knowing that everything was going as they'd planned. Ava passed Tyrone $2,000.00. "It's nothing personal just the business that we're in I do hope that you understand?" Tyrone looked at them, still holding his throat, trying to ease the pain somewhat, "Ya'll really on some shit!"

"Nah it's just our turn to control shit," Melody said.

Facing Regeane he asked, "We're you really going to kill me?"

"This ain't no game we're not accepting any no's for an answer."

Tyrone just stood there; stone faced.

The next day Melody, Toni Kia and Regeane were in school laughing about the night before.

"Regeane you put the fear of God in your brother's heart. Would you have killed him?" Melody asked.

Shaking her head Big Rage answered, "Kia and Ava would've had blood all over the place. I ain't ever been a punk bitch!"

Kia and Melody looked at her like she was crazy.

"Don't look at me like that, 'cause one day it's going to be one of you who'll have to pull that trigger, and scared money don't make money."

Melody saw Mike walking towards them wearing a brand new Sean John jean suit with a pair of black suede Timberland boots that he had unlaced, sporting a black baseball cap.

Melody smiled when he walked up on her and wrapped his arms around her neck she whispered in his ear, "I know that you're the man I'm going to marry."

Mike spoke to them as they left. He passed Melody a brown paper bag. She looked inside and it was filled with money.

"What's this for?"

"Bailing me out."

Melody passed the bag back to him. "I bailed you out because I love you I wasn't looking to get repaid. Look in the next couple of weeks I'll have something big for you, just don't you get into anymore shit. Pick me up after my computer class tonight and we'll talk some more." Melody stuck her tongue in Mike's mouth. I love the shit out of you!"

She tried to walk away but Mike grabbed her by her waist, "C'mere."

"What's up?" Melody asked.

Mike look real deep into Melody's eyes, "You know you my bitch, right?"

"Make sure that you know," Melody smiled as she walked away.

Toni and Regeane were on the train professionally dressed. They looked good as usual in their designer fits, DKNY, Cesare Paciotti. Inside of Toni's Fendi bag concealed $11,000. They were heading to Brooklyn with only one thing on their minds, the guns. Marilyn was at the train station awaiting their arrival. She was also dressed in business attire wearing a Channel dress with a long leather coat and leather boots. Toni made the introductions. Regeane and Marilyn exchanged friendly smiles.

"Have you heard from Vito?"

"He's been waiting for us since this morning," Marilyn said.

Marilyn opened her cell phone calling to let Vito know that they were ten minutes away. Vito was standing outside when they arrived.

"I've been waiting for your call all day."

"And we've been waiting all week for you, so I guess that makes us even." Marilyn said as she tossed him one of her infamous stares.

"Let's get this over with," Vito suggested as they followed him inside down into the basement. He looked back at Regeane, "who is she?"

"That's not important she's here with us," Marilyn said.

Vito pulled out three duffel bags filled to capacity with the guns, vests, and ammo. Regeane tossed the bags on the table and checked each one of them thoroughly investing the vests for any form of defects. A half hour later Regeane gave off a Rose signature wink signaling that everything was there. Toni passed Vito the remainder of the money.

"If you should ever need my help give me a call," Vito offered as he walked them back up the stairs. "Your father was a real good man and because of him I was granted a pass, I'm real sorry that he's gone. And if you need me call. I mean it Toni."

"I will," Toni said.

Each lady carried a duffel bag and headed out the door. Toni asked to use Marilyn's cell she call to let Ava know that they were on their way. When they got off the train on 42nd street Ava, Kia, and Melody were waiting. Toni made the introductions as they exchanged the bags. "Meet us at our place in an hour," Kia said.

"Listen up Roses," Melody said. "The games begin, we're about to become so very rich and powerful ladies. We got the guns, the morphine and we're working with the best dope in the city. All of this only took days to accomplish, our days of being broke bitches is over! This kind of an opportunity only comes once in a lifetime. We're going to have to protect our investments by any means." They all looked at Melody with knowing smiles on their faces.

"So Marilyn, Toni told you what we we're about to accomplish?"

Marilyn looked at Melody. She stood up, "Okay ya'll I was born and raised around criminals, murders, and drug dealers. After your first kill it gets easier especially if you maintain eye contact while you're pulling that trigger, knowing all of that power is in your hands is a wonderful feeling."

They all looked into Marilyn's cold gray eyes knowing that she was definitely the right candidate for them. After Marilyn finished talking Ava looked at Regeane.

"So you ready? It's finally your chance to get that revenge you're holding onto for Masada."

"Finally the moment I've been waiting on," Regeane smiled and kissed her gun.

"Regeane, could you just treat this like business instead of your vendetta? This way you won't make any mistakes which could be costly." Kia said.

"I got you Kia," Regeane assured. She placed her gun on her lap then pulled a .9 mm Glock out of one of the duffel bags along with the bullets and loaded the clip.

Kia looked over Marilyn, "You should be able to fit into Ava's old UPS uniform so you can serve as the backup just in case. As Marilyn tried on the uniform Toni loaded a .9 mm with a silencer for Marilyn's use.

"No mistakes, no witnesses and whatever you do make sure he's dead before leaving," Toni instructed.

"What about Kenny," Kia asked.

"That's all on you; he's always sweating you to go out on a date with him. Get him to drive you to East New York around the Flatlands, I'll be there waiting and he'll be dead before he can figure anything out." Ava said confidentially.

Marilyn walked into Masada's building wearing the UPS uniform with the hat pulled low over her face and a pair of ray bans to hide her eyes. The sun was out, plus it was about three guys standing in front of the building drinking beer not one even noticed Marilyn going inside. Moments later Regeane walked passed the same guys. Marilyn was waiting for the elevator when she knocked on the building's front door entrance. No one else walked to open the door so Marilyn let her inside. Once the elevator opened it was empty that was a good sign. Once moving they put on their leather black gloves, pulled out their .9 mm and cocked them. Cautiously they moved past the doors, it was both of their first time inside of the building. They found the apartment they were in search of, Regeane offered the Roses customary wink as Marilyn knocked on the door.

"Who is it?" Someone asked from behind the door.

"U.P.S."

Regeane could tell that it was Masada on the other side of the door by his voice. He looked out the peephole and then started unlocking the locks. Regeane was standing on the right side of the door with her gun in an upright position.

"Where do I sign?" Masada asked.

"On the red line." Regeane turned and extended her arm.

"Right here motherfucker," she said as she released the trigger. Masada's head exploded right in the doorway. He was dead before his body hit the floor. Regeane stood over his corpse and released the remainder of the clip inside of it. She looked at Marilyn, "Let's go mission accomplished," she said as they both walked down the stairs together. Marilyn's gun was in arm reach in case someone happened to see them.

Marilyn exited the building first and walked across the street to the waiting car that was being driven by Toni. Regeane walked in the opposite direction towards 119th with her gun securely tucked under her black jean jacket. Regeane reached her building and a smile was stretched across her face. It's just as exciting as a game of chess she thought to herself.

Toni pulled off in her mother's Honda Accord.

"That was fun, who's next?" Marilyn asked.

"Concentrate on getting out of those clothes," Toni said as she drove to the Hudson where they tossed the suit inside of a bag then into the river.

John was in front of there building pushing the very dope he'd almost overdosed on himself. Word had spread quickly and the buyers were passing Kenny and his crew up to get a taste of that *flash dance.*

"Damn it's slow out here," Kenny complained.

"Shit, John over by the building selling some shit called *flash dance*," Mellow said.

Kenny, Bobby and Mellow walked over to where John was positioned and without a word they started beating the shit out of him. Kenny struck first making John drop the bags on the pavement and the fiends scooped them up quickly without regards for John. They stomped his face, head and we're kicking him all over his body. Kia ran up on them in order to help, Kenny grabbed her by the jacket and slapped her to the ground, "Bitch play your position," he barked at her.

"You slapped the wrong bitch!" Kia told him with tears in her eyes. As she helped John up, she looked at Kenny, "Your days here on 123rd street are over motherfucker! Let's go John." She didn't bother trying to pick up her CD player that was still lying in the street.

Kia walked inside their apartment and Ava instantly knew that something was wrong. Melody noticed that there were tears in Kia's eyes also. She was yelling and talking so fast that no one was able to comprehend what she was saying. After taking a breath she slowed down and told them how she walked up on Kenny and his crew stomping John out in front of the building.

"...And Kenny's ass slapped me," Kia said as she wiped her face.

"WHAT?" Ava yelled out as Melody grabbed the phone to call Toni. Before she could tell her all of the details she and Marilyn were beating the door in. As Kia relayed the details to Toni and Marilyn Ava walked over to the window where she noticed Pam standing on the opposite side of the street looking around. Ava reached for the phone, "Ya'll be quiet," she said.

"Let's push his wig back, what we waiting for Roses," Melody wanted to know.

"Would ya'll please wait," Ava said as she walked back to the window watching as Pam retrieved her cell phone.

"I need you to take a walk," Ava spoke into the phone."

Pam looked around, "You got it," she said as she placed the phone back on her hip as she started up the street.

Toni was clearly upset as she recalled the numerous times when her father would hit her mother.

"This is the chance we've been waiting on to take over this block," Melody told them. Toni, Kia and Melody were all standing by the door with a loaded gun in there hands. "So let's do this right," Melody picked up a .9 mm for herself and cocked it. The five of them walked across the street where Kenny was standing.

"You like hitting girls?" Ava yelled as she swung a butcher knife at him. He blocked it but Toni came from the side and hit him in the head with the butt of the gun. Kenny dropped to his knees in excruciating pain. Ava and Toni continued there attack when Bobby and Mellow noticed and came to assist him. Still broad daylight Marilyn pulled out the Mac-11 and Kia upped the .9 she was carrying stopping the both in their tracks.

"If either one of ya'll think about taking another step I'm going to kill the both of you," Marilyn politely informed them.

She looked over at Kia, "You say the word and I'll kill them both anyway."

Kia made her way to where Kenny was laying on the ground with a bloody mouth. The fiends were enjoying the show as they stood around laughing at the humiliation that they dealers were faced with.

"Remember me?" Kia smiled, "I did tell you that I was the wrong bitch to slap," she cocked her gun the way Regeane had taught her and pulled the trigger twice shooting him in his legs. Kenny yelled out in pain.

"KIA, I'm sorry!" Melody began stomped his wounded legs as she got down on her knees to place the barrel of her gun on his head, "You ever fuck with John again I'm going to blow your motherfucking brains out."

"Melody I'm so sorry," he pleaded as Melody stood aimed and shot him a second time in his left leg. Kenny yelled out even louder. "AVA PLEASE!" he begged, "I'm sorry," he repeated over and over as Ava walked away with the others following behind her.

"So what can I kill them?" Marilyn yelled.

"Let's go," Toni said.

Marilyn smiled, "well guys I guess this is your lucky day." She said as she walked back across the street.

"Damn them bitches got some big ass guns, you think they were going to kill us?" Bobby asked.

"Hell yeah!" Mellow said.

More and more people seemed to gather around as Kenny was lying in the street riddled with bullets. By the time Pam and her partner arrived Kenny yelled out, "Bitch get me to a hospital." Pam didn't pay him any attention as she keyed her radio requesting a bus. Her partner was talking to potential witnesses when her cell rang.

"Fix that," Ava said.

"I'll handle it no problem," Pam said.

Pam walked over to Kenny, "So who shot you?"

"I don't know," Kenny lied. "Some bitch!"

Pam smiled, "You mean a big drug dealer like yourself let a woman shoot you?" She walked away as the ambulance workers made there way through the crowd. As they loaded Kenny on the stretcher, Pam waved at him.

"Money man I'll be at the hospital to get your report tomorrow."

After the commotion cleared Pam called Ava to give her a number of someone who would be beneficial to their organization as well.

"Who is this?"

"He's a lawyer and he has a lot of juice that may be a benefit to you. As a matter of fact he's waiting for your call." Pam read off the numbers.

Someone knocked on the door, Toni answered and Regeane walked in. "What the fuck happened?"

"Kia and Melody shot Kenny." Regeane looked at them.

"Why didn't one of you kill him?"

"Too many witnesses out there." Kia said.

"Well I was out there and the police are questioning them but no one has said anything."

"That's good," Marilyn said.

"I'll go to the hospital and visit Kenny. So I guess this is the right time to incorporate ourselves on the block seeing that his workers witnessed what happened to their boss. So it's either work for us or stay off of 123rd." Regeane said.

"Well we might as well keep applying pressure," Melody said. "Regeane you and Kia need to get to the Eastside 122nd Street and Second Avenue. Me, Toni, Marilyn, and Ava will move on 110th Street and Lexington Avenue."

"I know the guy that run that shit over there; he's a Puerto Rican with a beer bell older maybe in his 50's."

"And what does that mean?" Ava asked Melody.

"Not one damn thing to us," she said.

The word was out that Masada was killed in his apartment. People were saying that it had to be someone that he knew because he didn't just open his door for anyone. Toni, Marilyn and Ava looked at Melody.

"It's clear for now, but what about his workers?" Toni asked.

"No Masada, no dope to sell they're all on standstill so let's move before someone else tries to come over here. I'm giving this set to Mike and hell if he refuses I'll kill his ass my damn self. My money at this point is more important than even my heart."

"We're going to call this one *city food*, remember the old corner store?" Melody asked Ava.

"God bless Mr. Jay," Ava said as she laughed.

"So I'm thinking a 70/30 cut for Mike?" Melody asked. Toni, Ava and Marilyn nodded in agreement.

"So Regeane has the morphine and I got six boxes of the quinine upstairs," Melody said. "John and I can shoot the morphine in it tonight and let it sit over night so it can dry and tomorrow we can bag this stuff up all together. All of need to make sure we're wearing cotton and we need to find a place to mix this at."

"My place is fine," Toni offered. "My mom won't be coming home."

The next morning in Toni's kitchen they were all dressed in white. John had strainers, boxes of glassine bags, scotch tape, scales, spoons, and a pound of powder morphine. Kia reached into a brown plastic bag and pulled a kilo of dope out. John looked curiously at all of them.

"Is that real?"

"Don't you worry about it, show us what to do with it." Kia said.

"We need a blender otherwise we're going to be in here cutting this stuff for weeks."

"We want it strong we want all the fiends in Harlem spreading the word to Brooklyn, Queens, and the Bronx! We want all the fiends to know all about *flash dance* and *city food*."

"That's right John, you heard your sister." Ava said. "We want them to all fall out." She yelled.

Six hours later they counted up fourteen thousand bags; half stamped with *flash dance* the other with *city food*. The next morning John was out on 123rd Street selling *flash dance* with a line like he was giving away money.

Pam walked into Kenny's hospital room. He was sitting there watching Jerry Springer's morning show.

"Hello Ms. Police officer."

Pam didn't say a word until she was close enough that people walking by couldn't hear her. She sat on the side of the bed.

"So do you remember who shot you?" Kenny just looked at her. "Well I guess we both know that you don't cause you won't be pressing charges will you? You think you and your crew so slick, think that I don't know ya'll selling out on my post? I've been turning my head to what ya'll doing and this won't be any different, unless of course you don't plan on making another sale because I can assist with getting you ten years up in Clinton, Comstock or Sing-

Sing." Pam stood. "So we do understand one another, right?"

She laughed, "You have to respect the streets in order to get it," she said before leaving.

It'd been an hour since Kenny dozed off and awoke to Regeane sitting next to his bed holding a .9 with a silencer attached to it. "It's a good day, isn't it Kenny?" Regeane asked as she smiled at him. "I have to admit you look a little fucked up," she nodded. "But damn I had to come myself to let you know that I've taken over 123rd and the only way that you're coming back is if you're working for me." She leaned closer to him. "The only reason that your life was spared was because there were too many witnesses." She looked around, "we won't have that problem here so I'm going to finish the job." She stood up, "so Kenny are you working for me or not?" she asked as she aligned the gun with his dick.

"You wouldn't dare," Kenny said in a shaky voice.

She pulled the trigger and both bullets pierced the bed between his legs.

"Come on now Kenny this is a silencer the next time I won't miss!"

"OKAY!" he yelled. "You got it!"

"When you get out of here come and see me I got a job for you." Kenny just looked at her as she reached inside of the blue suede jacket she was wearing and revealed a knot of money and tossed it on the bed. "Kia and Melody said that this should cover the hospital bills." She walked out the room and came back "this is all about business," she said as she winked before leaving the room again.

After Melody counted up the proceeds from the day she called Ava to tell her that John finished the entire package and they'd need to do double or even triple next time. "I'm going to go and talk to Mike about his options today."

"Do you want me to go with you in case he act up?"

"That's a good idea meet me outside in a hour."

Melody had Mike meet her on 116th and Lennox, when he arrived Melody was already there and Ava was standing ten or so feet away drinking a grape soda with her gun in close reach. Melody kissed him, "Let's walk towards the Eastside."

As they walked Melody looked over at Mike, "Do you really love me?"

"Yes, I have since the first day I saw you, you know that boo."

Melody took a step backward. "I need you to really listen to what I'm about to say to you cause I don't plan to repeat myself."

Melody's demeanor was instantly cold. "Remember when I mentioned that things were going to change around Harlem? Well it's as simple as this either you're going to follow the path I have for you or you'll be joining Masada. With me you can be the man around here and I'm willing to give you a 70/30 cut, and in a couple of weeks 60/40, but shit starts tomorrow and the stamp you'll be pushing is *City Food*, it's the best dope in Harlem."

"Melody somebody on ya'll block already got the best dope its *flash dance*. It got all the fiends going crazy."

She looked in his eyes. "That's my dope too. "So what's it going to be Mike, or do I need to alert my friend to do her damn job." She pointed at Ava who had her hand in her pocket pointed in his direction. Mike couldn't believe what Melody had just said.

"So you killed Masada?"

"That wasn't mine, it was personal. You didn't wonder where the bail money came from; I know that you didn't think welfare paid like that. It's from these very streets you walk every day. So the change is here Mike now I need to know where you stand so I know what has to be done."

Before Melody could blink Mike drew his gun and had it pointed against her waist. Because the couple was so close Ava couldn't really see what was going on. The two looked more intimate than violent. Melody gasped from the feeling of cold metal pressed up against her skin.

"Mike what the fuck…"

"Shut up!" Mike demanded. "Now listen to me and listen to me good. All this threating me and having ya girls come for back up is wack!" he continued to speak through clenched teeth, "I told you I'm ya man, you my bitch and that's that! I love ya little tough ass and that ain't gon' change, now I'm gon' play for the team no doubt, but it's 'cause I want to not 'cause I have to, remember that shit! Now when I put this gun back on my hip I want you to kiss me real long and hard. I'm not gon' even make you apologize right now, you'll tell me how sorry you are in the essay you gon' write tonight."

"Essay?" Melody asked.

"Yeah, essay, an essay on respect, five hundred words.

Mike placed his gun back on his hip then leaned in to kiss Melody. She raised her hand to slap him, Mike caught it in mid-air. Faster than the speed of light Ava appeared with her gun cocked on ready! "Just gimmie the word," she looked in Melody's direction as she held her gun pointed at Mike's temple.

"Melody looked at Mike," Despite the gun pointed directly at his temple he remained stunningly calm. Melody reached inside his waist and grabbed his gat. She unloaded the clip then tossed everything in her bag. "Ava, put the gun down, I'm good." Ava put the gun on her side, but her eyes remained focused on Mike.

Melody got up in his face, "I thought I told you to stay out of trouble? I bail you out only for you to do the same shit that got you locked up in the first place; then you pull the gun on me? Have you lost your mind?"

Mike looked at Ava then at Melody, "Make that a six-hundred word essay yo! I gotta go," he kissed Melody then walked away, "Make sure you get that to me tonight," he spoke without turning to look back.

Damn, Melody thought to herself, *I love a man that can take control. I guess I better get home to work on that essay*, her pussy got moist just thinking about the way Mike took charge.

By Friday the Roses had full control of two of Harlem blocks. Melody reached out to Raymond using his apartment to bag, and he had ten workers to watch over.

Regeane and Kia were standing in front of Kia's building talking.

"Kia let's go to the Eastside and visit, we're not doing anything we can check the cash flow over there."

Kia looked at her watched, "That's cool with me."

As they got out of the cab Regeane tapped Kia on the arm.

"That's one of the bosses that run shit around here." Regeane was pointing to a light skin guy wearing a black Von Dutch jean suit with a white gold chain and a diamond encrusted pendant around his neck and a black gator band

Ice-Tek diamond watch. He was standing next to a Red "99 Ducati motorcycle.

"His name's Yo-Yo," Regeane told Kia.

"Come with me?" Kia said as she walked right up on Yo-Yo. "I need to talk to you," Kia said.

He looked at Kia from head to toe, "Do I even know you?"

"Nope we don't know one another but after we have this conversation you'll know me."

"What's up pretty eyes?"

"You know you out here playing yourself Yo-Yo," she smiled at him. "I want this block and every dollar that's being made on it."

Yo-Yo laughed in Kia's face. "Look whatever your name is you need to get the fuck outta here with all that big talk."

Regeane strolled over closer to them.

"Yo-Yo my partners and I don't understand the word no. Look we're willing to work with you here; we'll give you an ounce of pure dope just for you. Or the only other option is to buy your product from us or suffer the consequences. Looks as if there's a dilemma on your hand so we'll give you 48 hours to get in touch with us," Kia said as she passed him her number and Regeane handed him a brown paper bag. "I know that you won't disappoint us."

Yo-Yo looked at them both, "So what, you two chicken head bitches think that you can just walk over here and tell me that ya'll taking my shit over?"

Regeane looked at Kia, "I think we're doing a little too much   talking."
They winked at one another. Big Rage pulled out two .45's. Yo-Yo was standing between two parked cars away from his team and they had no idea what was transpiring.

141

"I'm starting to think maybe you don't hear so well either that or you're ready to die." Kia pushed his bike over and as he leaned to catch it she shoved her gun in his face. "In 48 hours this is going to become the Roses block."

"Can you hear her now?" Regeane taunted as she placed her gun in his ear.

"Yeah I hear her." He said.

"This is not a game," Kia repeated. "It's a lot of money for all of us so be smart."

Kia stopped a cab riding past and they got in. Yo-Yo knew if he mentioned this he'd get clowned. He was especially happy that they hadn't pulled the trigger. He looked inside of the bag and it was a ball of white powder. He passed out 8 of the samples and watched as six of the dope fiends overdosed in the middle of the block.

"Man," one of the fiends said, "that could stand to be cut some."

Yo-Yo smiled to himself as he thought about doing business with them.

Ava had two meetings that she absolutely had to attend. One was with Wayne and his brothers and the other; the high powered attorney.

Wayne and his brothers were standing in the park when Ava arrived, they were all 6 feet or taller weighing at least 250 pounds or better looking like linebackers. Wayne made the introductions Clad, Melvin and Parker who was the biggest of the four.

"So my partners are in agreement with the price," they all smiled.

"Any problems regardless the size we're just a phone call away."

Ava nodded. "That's what I'm paying to insure. Now I need ya'll to make guest appearances on 123rd and if you see anything out of the ordinary contact me."

Ava got out of the cab and instantly knew by the way he was impeccably dressed that he was the one and only Mr. Jay Roth Esquire. Although it was the middle of March his skin was tan. He extended his hand and introduced himself. They walked and talked about his retainers' fee and he spoke about some high profile cases in which he had the right influence with the right people. Ava was impressed enough that she assured him that she'd have her payment in his office by the morning.

The next day Kia got a call from Yo-Yo, he wanted to do business.

"If you want to talk meet me on 118th and Lennox on the downtown side of the street at 3:30 and come alone." Kia didn't wait for him to protest she hung up. She'd made it there before him and was leaning against a blue car when a white Mercedes Coupe pulled up in front of her. He blew the horn.

"Get out," she said.

"What if I told you that I wanted to buy it all?" Yo-Yo asked.

"You couldn't afford it," Kia said smugly.

"Well what can I get for a hundred thousand?"

"Let me just be honest with you; your money don't mean shit to me. So you can stop actin' like you holdin' like that 'cause you're not impressing me! Now your hundred thousand can get you ten ounces." Kia looked around. "Come on let's go inside Mama's and continue this." Kia made eye contact with Ava and Toni as she made her way inside. She headed to the back of the restaurant and when the waitress came over she ordered a slice of apple pie and a ice tea to go. "Can I get you anything?" Kia offered.

"Nah I'm good," Yo-Yo said as he noticed a female sitting across from them whose steel gray eyes were shooting through him.

"So I can work with the price when can I get it?" Yo-Yo asked.

"Call me when you ready," Kia said as the waitress returned with her order. As Kia stood so did Yo-Yo she looked back at him.

"How about you stay awhile and take in the atmosphere." She said as she walked out the door. One of the patrons from the table across where the female was tossing those evil stares followed her out the door. Yo-Yo sat down and the female smiled at him while tapping the table he looked at her and underneath he saw she was holding a .9mm pointed at him. She smiled even wider, "Be nice and act like you don't know my partners and I are watching you." She said as she got up from the table.

Yo-Yo made a few calls; one was to Chad, Wayne's brother he knew he would be down for this stick up. Yo-Yo's mind was set that if he killed Kia and hit Chad off with forty thousand dollars for himself he'll be on top of his game for real.

"What's up dawg?"

"Just chilling for now," Chad answered.

"Listen I got something hooked up for tonight," Chad knew off the top it was some foul shit, Yo-Yo was known for doing some underhanded shit. "Only if you interested it's an easy job."

"What is it?"

"There is this girl that got some good dope they want to sell me; ten ounces tonight."

"What's her name?"

"Kia is the one I'm doing business with. The buy is for 8 p.m."

"Does Corey know about this?" Chad asked.

"No and I want to keep it that way."

"Just call when you're ready."

As soon as Chad hung up with Yo-Yo he called Wayne to find out if any of Ava's partners name was Kia.

"That's Ava's sister, why?"

Chad explained the details of Yo-Yo's plan to stick her up tonight. Wayne informed Ava about Yo-Yo's plans to rob Kia and that he might even try to kill her. Don't worry she'll be safe Chad will be there."

"So will we," Ava said. "After we get his money I want his ass to vanish."

"You got it!" Wayne said. Ava told the Roses Yo-Yo's plan to get Kia.

"OH REALLY!" Kia yelled, "what he think something sweet here, okay," she said as she shook her hear up and down.

"I would love to see the look on his face when he finds out whose holding the ace in this game." Melody said.

"Melody I need you to go to 112th and make a call to 911 saying that shots have been fired, that way all the cops will rush down there." Kia said.

Yo-Yo called Kia to let her know that he had the money that they spoke about.

"So meet me in Mt. Morris Park by the stage oh and you can only bring one other person with you, if I see more I'm gone, you feel me?"

"Yeah, I got you boo."

Kia walked in the park wearing her bulletproof vest and a Mac 11 tied under her arm. Ava and Marilyn entered the park from 122nd side. Yo-Yo was already standing there with another dude and from the way dude looked and Ava's description Kia knew that it was Chad. Kia passed her bag to Yo-Yo first so he could test the dope, he then handed her a bag of money. As Kia looked inside Yo-Yo pulled out his gun, it was at this precise moment that Chad disarmed him and wrapped both of his arms around him.

"What the fuck are you doing?"

"I hate to have to tell you this, little sis here is part of my team and you've just fucked up!" Kia smiled as she pulled out her Mac-11 sub machine gun as Ava and Marilyn walked over to them.

"Why would you try this when I was still going to put money in your pockets?" Kia asked.

"Remember me?" Marilyn asked as she stepped in closer. "Remember this?" She said as she pointed her gun at him.

Chad pushed Yo-Yo down on the ground.

"Look I'm sorry, I swear I'm sorry and we can just work this shit out!"

Yo-Yo tried to get off of the ground to run and you could see a flash coming from Marilyn's gun as she pulled the trigger. This didn't stop Yo-Yo from trying to move.

"DAMN Marilyn!" Ava said "Kill that motherfucker already!"

Marilyn released her trigger 8 times with all of the shots landing in his face or what was left of it.

"DAMN! His ass don't have a face," Chad said. "That's going to have to be a closed casket service."

"LET'S GO!" Ava yelled.

"Thanks again and we'll be sending your half of this."

"Ya'll still got to get Corey if ya'll want that territory," Chad informed them.

"What he look like?" Marilyn asked.

"He's brown skin, about 5 foot 8, maybe 228 pounds or more. He drives a 430 cream white Lexus Jeep with brown tints."

"Thanks for the information," they said heading out of the park.

Toni was driving her mothers Honda Accord with Regeane and Melody in the back seat dressed from head to toe in all black with pullover ski masks. They were searching for the cream white 430 on the Eastside. It had been about an hour and they hadn't seen one and finally Regeane hollered, "Bingo!"

They pulled their masks down, cocked their Uzi's and waited for Toni to pull up on 122nd Street and Second Avenue.

"Are you ready?" Regeane asked.

"Let's do this!" Melody said as the jumped out the car blasting on the Lexus. Glass flew everywhere bullets riddled the exterior of the truck. They both released the clips; Regeane refilled hers and stepped closer to the Jeep she looked inside and noticed that the four people inside were dead. The streets were crazy as people ran for cover.

"LET'S GO!" Melody shouted. Regeane jumped her big ass in the back seat as Toni pressed the gas causing the car to jump into full speed down 2nd Avenue.

"COREY!?" Someone from the crowd yelled as onlookers now felt safe to come out of hiding. It was obvious from the sight of the Lexus that there were no survivors.

All the Roseswere all seated in the living room, "Tomorrow we're going to hit 110th Street and Lexington Avenue we can't stop applying the pressure. We're going to have to instill the fear of God in them so that they know. We'll give the Eastside a week and then we start pushing up on their workers and either they'll roll or we'll bury their asses!" Melody said.

Kia tallied the body count, "Five bodies in one night. I guess it doesn't end until we say so!" This is woman's work, we gone have all the men working for us." They all laughed as Kia and Ava exchanged winks.

The next day Marilyn was driving her brother's black Mini van in Spanish Harlem. Ava, Toni and Marilyn were on 110th Street watching as Melody approached Porky. Porky was yelling something in Spanish, Melody said something back to him and gave the signal for the Roses to kill Porky's fat ass and everyone on the block around him. They gave her five minutes before they would begin the killing spree. Ava and Toni cocked their guns.

"Are you ready?" Ava asked.

"Two more minutes," Toni said as she watched her watch.

Melody saw Kim, a friend from school walking with a baby in her arms heading towards 110th street, she knew in a matter of moments it would be a bloodbath. She immediately stepped in front of her.

"Melody, girl shit you scared the hell out of me! What you doing around here?"

"Just chilling, where you going?" Melody asked as she looked at the baby.

"One-Tenth to the chicken place."

"NO, I mean I need to talk to you, walk with me to 107th Street." Melody took the baby out of Kim's arms.

"NOW!" Toni yelled as Ava slid the door open. They jumped out of the mini van with MAC-11 submachine guns wearing costume masks. Ava ran straight towards Porky while Toni began firing at everyone standing around. As Ava reached Porky she yelled, "TRICK OR TREAT MOTHERFUCKER!" as she pulled the trigger. By the time Porky's body slammed down to the ground Ava's clip was unloaded. Toni had reloaded and aimed for the windows and let the bullets soar. Marilyn blew the horn and they ran towards her.

"Turn left on 110th and then a right on 3rd," Ava instructed.

"**B**oo we need to talk. It's important." Mike said into the phone.

Melody was still tired from the shooting with Porky and the the day before, but she if Mike said it was important than it was important. "I'm on my way." Melody replied.

Since Masada's murder Melody wore a bulletproof vest and carried two loaded .45 Desert Eagles.

"I need to ask you something." Mike said as he looked at Melody. "Did you have something to do with all this stuff going on in Harlem these last few days?"

"Mike what I do in the streets is my business and you're safe so fuck the rest!" She said callously. She really wanted to spaz out but since Mike put her in her place she learned to choose her words more carefully, "Because you're my man and I don't plan to ever lie to you, yeah I had some involvement with Masada, Yo-Yo, Corey and Porky and it's not going to stop until we're on top baby, this is not just for me; I'm doing what has to be done for us."

Mike placed his hands on top of his head as he spoke, "You got Harlem fucking scared to come hustle!"

"Good 'cause that's the way I want it. Either they selling my shit or nothing at all! Mike you don't have nothing to worry about as long as you making that money and I'm making money we good," she kissed his cheek.

Mike pulled her in his arms. He could feel the guns. "You need my help; you know you can ask me."

"It's cool I already got people who move on my account."

Mike started telling her about the dope fiends and how they loved *City Food* and made lines as long as the block just to get it. "We sold over fifty thousand yesterday."

"Just save your money baby, let everybody else run out and buy some sixty thousand dollar car or truck, we got bigger plans."

"Hell no I ain't gon' do no stupid shit like spending mony recklessly! We got better things to do with our money."

"How many workers you got over here, Mike?"

He laughed. "Shit I had to get a whole new crew ya'll scared the rest of them off."

"So you're telling me these so called Harlem money makers afraid of little ole me?"

"Hell not just you, that crazy ass white girl Toni, Regeane big ass, Kia with her ole evil ass sister, and who is this chick with the iced out eyes? Mellow on the blocking telling everybody how she was standing in the middle of the block with a machine gun on him and Bobby. Shit scared Bobby ass so bad he moved down south!" They started laughing.

"What ya'll trying to be on some mob style shit in Harlem?"

"Who are they?"

"Them guys in the 80's they was getting all the money."

"Well it's 2001 now, they all probably in dead, in jail or worse. The ones who still here are broke; their shit don't means nothing to me."

Kenny pulled up on the block in his white Yukon, he was with some light skin guy that Regeane hadn't seen prior and she didn't trust this.

"Get out the truck," she said.

"What's up?" Kenny asked as he looked up and down the street. "I see you really got the block on pumping. Is that offer still on the table?"

"Yeah," Kenny noticed that John was standing where he normally would stand.

"So I'm about to park, it's still 60/40, right?"

Regeane nodded as she smiled.

The guy sitting in the passenger seat with the ice grill didn't worry her a bit she was strapped with her .40 caliber.

"It's a hundred bundles behind the door in the hallway." Kenny and his friend went inside to get it.

"So you got me working for some bitch? When I was on lock down I was told that you had shit on smash around here what's the deal?"

Kenny looked in his friends eyes, "Shawn do you want to work or not?"

Kenny watched as Regeane walked into the Laundromat. Moments later Marilyn and Toni walked out of the building.

"Oh shit look," Marilyn said. Toni looked.

"Don't worry that's Kenny the one Kia and Melody shot last week."

"What the fuck he doing around here? Shit let's finish this!"

Kenny turned to tell Shawn to come on and noticed Marilyn and Toni standing behind him.

"You looking much better than the last time I saw you," Toni said.

"I thought all of that was behind us?" Kenny asked.

"I hope so 'cause finishing the job wouldn't be a problem."

"Look you need to talk to Regeane she said everything was cool. We can get this money together."

"Okay," Toni and Marilyn agreed as Shawn walked up.

"Damn dawg you even got white bitches on your dick?"

Marilyn and Toni's eyes traveled from Kenny to Shawn. Marilyn took off her Alain Mikli dark sunglasses, "Who in the fuck you calling a white bitch?" she asked.

"Yo Toni, Marilyn," Kenny called out to them. "Please he don't know anybody around here."

"Fuck all that Kenny are we fucking with them or what?" Shawn continued.

"Money what's your problem?" Marilyn asked.

"All of a sudden white people moving into Harlem thinking they black?"

"SHAWN!" Kenny yelled looking at his boy.

"Man why you out here acting like you scared of these bitches!"

"Say something else slick and I'm going to plant your ass right here," Marilyn threatened.

"Whatever!"

Tony looked at Kenny, "Your boy out here talking shit, but he's out here selling our shit!"

"Don't worry I'll handle him."

"You better or I will."

Regeane was standing in the Laundromat talking to Tyrone when she saw Toni and Marilyn returning with bags of food. Ava, Kia and John were out on the stoop talking.

"Tyrone I'll see you later," she said as she walked out. Marilyn was telling Regeane how disrespectful Kenny's friend was and the next time she was going to handle the situation herself.

"Let me talk to him first." Regeane walked over towards where Kenny and Shawn were standing. Kenny already knew that there was a problem from the scowl on her face.

"I need to talk to you," Regeane said as she got closer to the car they were standing by.

"What's on your mind?" Shawn asked.

Kenny didn't budge he didn't want anymore issues with the Roses he was now going to walk with a permanent limp thanks to them.

"Listen Playboy don't be disrespecting my friends because in my eyes you're not built like that, so be nice, okay!"

Shawn looked at Regeane up and down, "BITCH, if you don't get the fuck out of my face I'll slap the shit out of you and take your shit!"

Regeane was ready to pull her .40 Caliber from under her oversized J-Lo sweatshirt, then stick it in Shawn's mouth like a lollypop, but she just got up in his face real close instead, "You know what Playboy you could do that, but I know one thing for damn sure you won't live long enough to enjoy it." She walked away without another word.

They were standing in front of the Laundromat when Kia and Ava walked out carrying a handful of yellow number slips.

"What's up?" Ava asked as the ladies heading towards Ava and Kia's apartment.

"Make his ass vanish! He's disrespectful towards the Roses, hell women period. If Kenny ass acts up he can go too!" Regeane said.

"I'll handle it," Ava assured her. She called Wayne and told him that she was having problems with some loud disrespectful guy.

"I'll be there in ten minutes, don't worry about it. I'll call you right back," Wayne said.

Regeane started in about the Eastside and when they would move in over there asking who they could get to control it when Ava's cell rang.

She described what Kenny's friend looked like and was wearing.

"I see him," Wayne said.

"Just wait until I'm downstairs before you do anything," she said. They all headed back outside towards the door. Once outside they didn't see anyone.

"We're waiting," Toni said impatiently and a bit annoyed. Ava noticed Parker and Chad on the other side of the street near where Shawn was standing talking to two dark skin females.

Kenny looked up and saw all of them standing on the stoop and knew that something was about to happen. Chad walked up on Shawn who was leaning against the wall like he was running shit.

"Yo money let me get three bags of *flash dance*."

When he reached in his pocket Parker came from the side and punched Shawn so hard he was unconscious before he hit the ground. The two girls walked away from them not wanting to be involved. Chad snatched his body up off the pavement as Wayne pulled up in a red hooptie and Chad through his limp body inside the trunk like he was garbage. Kenny stood watching helplessly knowing that would be the very last time he saw his friend. He looked over at the stoop and they were laughing as they walked back inside of the building.

Petals and Thorns

Kia was in Apollo Express Department store on 125th Street looking at the latest pair of Jordan's. A brown skin guy wearing an Enyce sweat suit with a fresh pair of uptown sneakers approached her.

"May I help you?" When she turned and looked at the guy standing in front of her she smiled.

"Sure you can help me in many ways Cutie." Kia said flirtatiously.

"I'll do my best," they both smiled at each other.

"You can start by getting me a size six in the new Air Max."

"My name is Joe, and yours pretty eyes?"

Kia smiled wide, "Kia."

"It's nice to meet you Kia."

"Same here Joe."

"So let's start by getting you in the new sneakers you want." Joe reached for her hand Kia placed her small hand inside of his and he lead her to a seat. Kia got a funny feeling just from holding his hand.

"I'll be right back," Joe said. Kia spotter a pair of red suede Manolo Blahnik Timbs when Joe returned carrying two boxes, Kia leaned over to unlace her shoes.

"Kia let me that's what I get paid for."

Every time Joe said something Kia smiled, not only that but she felt moisture between her legs. Kia wondered if this was what love at first sight felt like. Even if it was lust it would be nice to get to know him.

"At least your feet don't smell that would've been a turn off."

"Never that," Kia said as she tried on both pairs of shoes.

"They look good on your feet."

Kia looked over at the Manolo Blahnik Timbs.

"Give me these and those," she pointed at the Manolo's.

"Those cost eight hundred dollars."

"I didn't ask you how much they cost!"

"You're the boss," Joe said as he carried her boxes to the counter.

Kia felt bad about the way she came out to him, he was nice the entire time.

"That'll be $1,100.32," the cashier said.

As Kia pulled out a stack of hundreds she realized not only didn't she have on her bulletproof vest, she wasn't carrying a gun either as she hurried and put her money back up and reached for the bags.

She walked over to Joe, "I apologize for coming out my mouth the way I did."

"You didn't do anything wrong."

"Can I ask you something? What's wrong and don't lie. You got a girlfriend?"

"No, I just moved to New York three months ago."

"Where are you from?"

"Utah."

Kia smiled and knew that she was open for the season with him. "Would you like to have dinner with me, my treat of course?"

"I sure would, are all of New York women this friendly?"

"Only in Harlem. What time you get off?"

"7:30."

"I'll be outside waiting for you."

125th Street had people coming and going. Summer was quickly approaching. Kia walked down 8th Avenue to H.M.V. record store where she picked up some CD's. The boxes and the blazing sun were wearing her down, she didn't want to go home but she needed to put this stuff away. As a blue Jeep rode past blasting Jadakiss' *knock yourself out*, Kia stopped and looked real hard. *I'm getting me one of those, because this summer I'm showing my ass* was the only thought that came to her mind.

As she walked back past 7th Avenue that same Jeep was parked on 124th Street and four girls were sitting in it with L'il Kim's', *Get Money* blazed through the speakers. Kia walked over to the driver side.

"Could you turn the music down for a second?"

"What you want?" the driver asked, looking at Kia like she was stupid.

"I want to buy your Jeep, how much?" Now the other three girls were looking at Kia like she was stupid and crazy.

"Look if you don't have twenty thousand dollars there is nothing to talk about."

"My name is Kia," she said as she pointed across the way. "I live over there, drive me to my building." Kia hopped in the backseat.

When the driver pulled up Marilyn was sitting on the stoop eating beef jerky. She walked over to the Jeep. "What's up?"

"Go upstairs and bring me $20,000 I'm about to buy this."

Marilyn laughed, "For this piece of shit?"

The driver yelled at Marilyn, "My Jeep ain't a piece of shit!"

"It's a piece of shit, now what the hell you gone do about it bitch? You trying to beat my girl, I'll take this shit and make your ass walk home."

"Marilyn just go and get the money," Kia said.

About five minutes later Marilyn and Melody came down carrying a plastic bag. Kia looked at the driver.

"That's my girl Marilyn, we call her Ice Eyes, and please don't say nothing to her, that bitch is crazy don't say anything to her," she warned again.

"What's going on Kia?" Melody asked.

"I'm buying this Jeep."

"Drive it around for about ten minutes to see how it rides." The driver and Kia switched seats as the other three passengers stood out on the street.

Kenny pulled up in his X5 pumping P. Diddy's *Le's Get It.*

"What's up Melody?" he passed her a gym bag. "It's a hundred thousand in there I'll be back tonight."

One of the drivers friends walked up on Melody and her and Marilyn reached for their guns. She stepped back with her hands in the air. "I'm sorry, I don't want any problems. I just wanted to speak to you. My name is Jill," she looked back at her friends. "We like how ya'll holding it down and was wondering if we could get a job?" Marilyn looked at Melody, "What makes you think we're giving out jobs where I know you from?"

"Like I said before we don't want any problems, we're just trying to get paid too. Why the men always have to run some shit is all I'm saying!?"

Melody looked and Marilyn had a smile on her face.

"I'm feeling that! What about your friends?" Marilyn nodded. Jill waved them over. "This is Seena and Missy."

"I'm Marilyn and this is Melody. I don't like ya'll friend; with that wack ass Jeep so don't bring her around understand?"
They all nodded.

"Where ya'll from?"

"Wagner projects on 122nd Street and Second Avenue," Jill said.

Marilyn and Melody shared a knowing smile.

"What's happening over there?" Melody asked.

Jill talked about the two main bosses being killed.

"What they sell over there?"

"Dope."

Do you think you can get 122nd without any problems?" Melody asked.

"Hell yeah!" Jill said. "My brother is strong over there and they don't want any parts of him or the wolf pack crew."

"I've heard stories about them," Melody said. Seena and Missy just stood by listening. Melody pulled out a pen to write down a number.

"Call me at 8 tonight, but let's get something understood now if anyone of you is thinking that you can play me or The Roses, I'm going as far as having your entire family killed, and anyone who resembles them. So all of you got that right?" The three of them nodded their heads at the same time. Kia and the driver pulled back up.

"Pay her," Kia said. Marilyn walked over to the driver and dropped the plastic bag on the ground. "The next time you get fly out your mouth you'll be on the ground with a bullet in your head."

"Fuck you bitch!" the driver responded.

"Damn why did she have to say that?" Kia asked.

Marilyn lifted her lime green silk pullover hoodie with her left hand and with her right hand she pointed her .45 in the girls face. She reached for the girls' hair, "Bitch get this money and get the fuck off of this block while you still can!"

"That's enough," Kia said, running to the girls rescue. Kia looked at the girl, "Didn't I tell you not to say anything to her!"

People walked past as if nothing was happening. Marilyn made it clear the day in the street when she was holding that Mac-11 that she wasn't to be fucked with. The girl grabbed the bag and opened it.

"No need to count it, it's all there now beat it bitch!" Kia handed Melody the bags, "Nice doing business with you," she said as she flagged down a cab and hopped in, she wanted to get as far away from Marilyn as possible.

Marilyn and Melody about faced to the other three girls who introduced themselves earlier as Jill, Seena and Missy.

"Now, listen up, this is what we gon' do first..." Marilyn spoke.

Kia drove to 140th Street and Lennox Avenue; that was one of her favorite blocks. There was a mural of the late rapper Big L, she looked over at the picture. "Gone but not forgotten, I love you Boo!" She proceeded towards the Polo Grounds on 155th Street just to see if the ruckus had started yet. All four corners were crowded Kia made certain her presence was known as she turned up her music as loud as she could playing *Shake your ass*, by Mystical. The crowd looked towards her and she was loving the attention she was getting from Uptown. Kia hit the FDR headed for Queens, her first stop was the 40 projects, from there she went to Baisley Projects and then 150th Street where she drove around the Southside of Queens before going to Jamaica Avenue. There was just something that she loved about being in Queens, she'd set her mind that she was going to buy her a house out there.

Melody told Ava about the Jeep that Kia purchased.

"What kind is it?" Ava asked.

"The one without the top."

"Is that bitch crazy?" Ava flipped out. "That makes her ass an easy target. She's going to have to get rid of that shit! Who gave her the money for it?"

"I did." Melody said.

"Why did you do that?"

"What could I do? She has an equal amount of control of the money like all of us, remember?" Ava nodded her head.

"Where's Rage?" Melody wanted to know.

"With her mother," Ava answered.

"We finally got a way to open up on 122nd Street."

"How?"

"The girl Kia got the Jeep from lives over there, and her friend's brother is the leader of the Wolf Pack."

"That's them crazy motherfuckers who's always shooting something up?" Ava asked. "Fuck it we might as well have them on our team for free."

"Everybody can play a part in the Rose's Garden," Melody said. "I hooked up a meeting with them tonight.

"Them who?"

"The girl Kia brought the Jeep from had three friends and they asked if they could get put on."

Ava looked at Melody. "You're as crazy as Kia. I'm not mad; I just don't want to meet anyone."

"Whatever Ava!"

Ava was furious as she tried reaching Kia through the walkie talkie of the Nextel phone. "She's out here doing dumb shit like she don't know what we've been out here doing in the streets."

Toni and Rage had managed to make their way to Ava's house, but still, no had heard from Kia.

Then just like clockwork Kia walked inside the living room smiling, "Ava, I bought me a Jeep."

Ava, Regeane and Toni were sitting there.

"We heard, listen Kia you have to get rid of it!"

"WHAT?"

"You heard me," Regeane said. "It's not safe you're too open for anything to happen to you."

"She's right," Toni added.

"That's fucked up; I buy me something that I want now all of you want to spoil it!"

"Fuck all of this," Ava said. "Get rid of it by the morning or I'm setting the shit on fire!"

"You touch my Jeep and I'll beat the holy shit out of you!"

"Well me and Toni helping Ava," Regeane said calmly.

"I got a date tonight afterwards I'll get rid of it, maybe ya'll right. But I'm buying me a bigger truck!"

Kia was parked in front of Apollo Express at 7:30 on the dot wearing a tight black Dolce and Gabbana leather suit with a pair of Armani Exchange 6" leather boots, and a Piaget gold watch with a diamond face, she was feeling like somebody important. Joe walked out and noticed that Kia was sitting there wearing a smile.

"Get in what you waiting for?" Joe got in. "So how do you want to start this night off?"

"Whatever," Joe said hunching his shoulders. "I'm just happy you really came through."

Kia smiled, "Okay let's go and getting something to eat, what you like?"

"I got a taste for seafood."

"Let's go to City Inland."

"What's that?"

Kia smiled as she rubbed the side of his face. "Put your seat belt on and relax Cutie Pie, you're in good hands."

That's a nice watch you're wearing," Joe said. "Did I mention that this Jeep was hot, but you being in it makes it hotter!"

"Thank you. My sister and friends want me to get rid of it. They say that it isn't safe."

"That's true people are always getting killed in these kinds of Jeeps." He smiled at her, "but you still look hot in it!"

Kia turned on 7th avenue zooming Uptown towards 155th Street Bridge to get on the Deacon expressway heading north to City inland. There were a line of seafood restaurants. Kia parked in front of Sammy's in Harlem, it was a well known place to eat. She ordered king crab legs with lobster tails for the both of them.

Joe talked about Utah and enrolling into John Jay College to study Law following in his father's footsteps. Kia told him about the Do's and Don'ts in New York City. She went so far as telling him about all of the con games and other shit that happens to out of towners. Kia was a virgin but her mind was already prepared Joe would be the first. It was already midnight, "How time flies," Kia said.

"You're a beautiful young woman."

Kia smiled, "Would you like to go to the hotel with me?"

"You were reading my mind," Joe licked his lips.

While driving to the Whitestone hotel in the Bronx Kia told Joe that she was a virgin. Once there he tried to pay for the room.

"My treat, remember?" Kia winked. Joe stepped back from the counter. Kia laughed as she noticed the key ring read 123, just like her block.

"What's so funny?"

"Don't pay me any mind."

When they walked into the room Kia put her arms around Joe and kissed him. At this point she was feeling good.

"Take off your clothes," Joe whispered in her ear.

He reached for her shirt and she unzipped his pants. "I want you to take it all off, remember it's my treat."

Joe Just nodded his head as he smiled standing in front of her butt ass naked.

"Don't move," She said as she ran her hands up and down his body, slid her tongue in and out of his ear as she blew on his neck. When Joe tried to touch her she stepped back.

"My treat!"

She slid her tongue up and down the middle of his back. She was enjoying the pleasure she was experiencing, she was moist between her legs and her nipples were rock hard. The leather that she was wearing was heating her body up.

"Stand here and just watch, this is a treat for you," she said as she winked. She took off all of her clothes in the middle of the room as Joe smiled appreciatively. She reached for his hand and led him to the bed.

"Please remember it's my treat, so be easy." Joe laid her back and started sucking on her toes, kissing her feet and kissed up her legs until he reached the black satin panties she was wearing. Joe could smell the sweet aroma that was throbbing behind as he slid her panties to the side with his tongue. They were soaked with pre cum. With the very first lick Kia's body began to shake she grabbed the back of his head and wrapped her legs around his neck. The more he sucked the more pressure she applied. It felt as if her heart was going to stop she was so overwhelmed with pleasure. "OH MY GOD," Kia yelled breathlessly. "You're good!"

"I'm not finished with you yet."

Kia smiled she knew at that very moment that she was in love with a guy name Joe from Utah. He flipped her over and slid his tongue inside her ass. Kia had no idea that sex could be so good, it was an even better feeling than she got from counting her money. They fucked from the bed, to the chair, the bathroom and on the floor until Joe came.

"Let's shower."

"Anything as long as it's with you," Kia said.

The water was lukewarm; Joe washed Kia and then slid his tongue back inside of her with the water cascading down her body. She felt so good that she lost her balance and they both fell out the shower on the floor.

"Get off of me I know what you're trying to do!"

"What are you talking about?" Joe asked confused.

Kia got off of the floor and kicked him in the ribs, "You're trying to turn me out!" But she knew that it was too late. She looked at her watch, she was already turned out. "Oh shit I got to get home."

Kia passed Joe the keys to her Jeep.

"Where to?"

"123rd Street and 7th Avenue." When he pulled in front of the building Joe asked where she wanted him to park it.

"It's yours, the papers are in the backseat, just remember that your tongue belongs to me and only me, understand?" She walked away from the Jeep feeling good. She'd had sex for the very first time, she paid a little over 20,000 for it, but it was well worth it.

Melody was downstairs waiting on Toni so they could go to the Eastside to meet with Jill, Seena and Missy when John walked over to her.

"Melody I need more help at the table," John said. Melody looked at him.

"We paying you $8,000 a week and Raymond $4,000 to handle that so why are you telling me this?" Her phone started ringing.

"You ready?" Toni asked.

"I'm downstairs already."

"I'm on my way down."

Melody and Toni made it to the Eastside meeting. Only two of the three girls were present.

"My brother says that his crew will be willing to work for you," Jill said excited.

"Where's the other girl?" Melody asked.

"Missy is putting things together with my brother," Jill replied.

"I'll be sending some of my people over here to help hold it down just in case," Toni informed them.

"You're not the girl from yesterday are you?" Seena asked as it was hard to see her face because it was concealed by a New York Mets baseball cap.

"No, why?"

"Nah, she scared the hell out of my friend."

Melody smirked then passed Seena four bundles of dope. "Use these as samples."

She handed her another bundle of twenty to sell. "Call me when you're ready for some more."

"No doubt." Toni and Melody turned and left.

On their way home Melody and Toni stopped at the fish restaurant on 125th Street and Madison Avenue. Melody's phone rang and it was Jill telling her that she needed more *Madman* and fast.

"Damn already? Send the money back by Seena; I'll be waiting for her in front of the building."

For some reason Melody wanted to know more about Seena and wondered why she was in the streets.

By the time they walked up Seena was standing there waiting for them. She handed them the money to Toni who then proceeded into the building.

"It's going to be a minute before she comes back down," Melody told her.

"That's not a problem."

"Come on let's take a walk," Melody suggested. "What made you hustle?"

"I'm an only child to a crack head for a mother and my father's dead. I don't have any money and I need to eat, plain and simple. I've never sold my body to any man. I finished high school and was taking classes at City College, but my mother kept stealing my clothes," she sighed. "So what could I do?" Seena had tears in her eyes. "This is why I'm so happy that you and your crew gave me this chance to prove that females can control shit too, I'm happy to be a part of the team. I don't need a man to give me anything; I can hold my own, always have and always will."

Melody was feeling her, but looking at gear totally contradicted half of the things she just said, "Look at you, you're dressed real nice," Melody complimented.

Jill stopped and looked at herself, "You really want the truth? All of this is Jill's, that's my home girl and her and her brother look out for me."

Just then Toni walked out the building carrying a brown paper bag with fifty bundles of *Madman*.

"This is for you," Melody looked at Toni then Seena. "Tell Jill and Missy that after tonight you won't be working with them. They'll control it; you're going to roll with me out of town where the real money is."

"Thank you!"

"It's not easy," Toni said.

"What do you mean by that?" Seena asked.

"Are you willing and ready to kill?"

Seena looked at Toni and Melody. "Killing won't ever be a problem for me. I know what comes with this street life and pulling a trigger won't ever be a problem.

"Yeah that shit sounds good now; we'll see when the time comes." Toni said.

"Call me tomorrow because we're going to Baltimore to open up shop for you."

Kia walked out as Seena was walking away.

"What's that all about?"

"I want Seena to go to Baltimore with Regeane," Melody told her.

Kia looked over at Toni, "What you think?"

"It sounds good to me," she said biteing on an apple.

Melody got on her Nextel pressing the speaker.

"What's up?" Regeane responded.

"It's time," Melody said.

"For what?"

"Baltimore."

"I can't talk right now I'm with my mother. I'll be there in ten minutes, but I'll make a few phone calls before I get to you."

"Why are you taking her with ya'll?" Kia asked.

"Its something about her I like. She's hungry like us."

"Well you're the boss," Kia said.

"No, The Roses are the bosses." They all started laughing.

Kia's cell rang it was Joe. "What's up Boo?" Toni and Melody looked at Kia as she covered the phone whispering, "It's a dick call!"

They all erupted in laughter again.

"It's good to hear from you, I had a nice time last night, can we do it again?"

"Let's do it tonight. It's my treat this time," Joe said.

"Uh-huh, what are you trying to do turn me out again?"

Joe laughed a devilish laugh, "I wouldn't do that," he said.

"Yeah right! I can't tonight, but I can freak off with you tomorrow."

"Okay I'll pick you up in front of your building tomorrow at 8."

"Nope I'll meet you at your job at 7:30."

"Deal I'll be waiting."

Kia was going to keep Joe away from her street business as long as she could. The last thing she wanted was for him to get hurt because of her.

Melody informed them that she had papers for all of the Roses to sign off on. "We are all officially stockowners in Nextel, Dell, Wendy's and Microsoft. We can't touch the money for ten years it's in case we go broke, but I wouldn't let that happen." Melody smiled. "*Flash dance* is making $70,000 just from Kenny a day and Mike is doing the same thing not to mention the Eastside is putting up big numbers."

Kia smiled. "Ya'll know what? We'll be millionaires before we're twenty."

"It's easy to make the money Kia, the question is will we live long enough to enjoy it?"

"Damn Toni you always got to fuck something up!"

Toni looked at Kia, "Look the Roses are going to have to pay the streets, the devil and God for all of our bad deeds. You've heard that saying for every action there's a reaction. All of us won't live to see this out, and that's how it is!"

Regeane got out of a cherry red Lexus 400 and joined her clique, "What's good? I spoke to my people in Baltimore and they are ready for us. I told him that we would be there in a week. Their bags go for twenty."

"Tell your people to make a bomb," Melody said. "Fuck making them nod, make them want to fall out and give they self some head. I want them to love and fear us."

"The way I see it if we give them six dollars off each bag and pay each one of them five dollars to carry for us we don't lose." Regeane looked at Melody, "What you think?"

"I got somebody to carry for us."

"Who?"

"One of the girls from the Eastside, Seena. I don't know for some reason I like her."

"The Baltimore thing sounds good, but Regeane that's all on you," Toni said. "It don't take all of us to handle that so you deal with that. We'll set up shop and let Seena run it; then we can move on to other cities."

"I agree with Toni," Kia said.

"So fuck it we'll leave Monday," Melody said.

Who's upstairs?" Regeane asked.

"Ava," Melody answered. "I think Marilyn might be up there with her too.

"What Ava doing upstairs? She ain't been outside in days." Regeane asked.

"Counting money, you know she worked at a bank so she can count faster than anyone of us could." Kia said.

Melody nodded. "That bitch sitting up there like she's Oprah with all that money around her."

"Let's go knock her ass off her high horse," Kia joked.

When they knocked Marilyn let them in. Money was all over the floor, table and chairs stacked neatly by denominations. Ava hadn't heard them knock and when they walked in she pulled her gun out.

"Bitch is you crazy?" Toni yelled.

"I didn't hear ya'll come in, I'm sorry. Next time at least warn me." Toni motioned to sit down. "Don't sit down grab a stack and start counting, Marilyn and I have been here counting the last three hours." Each of them picked up a stack. Melody was sitting at the table counting a stack of ten's.

"Ava you and Marilyn will need to keep a watch over Kenny and Mike. Toni, you watch Jill and Missy and Kia you keep track of the books; Regeane, Seena and I are going to Baltimore on Monday."

"Who is Seena," Ava asked as she looked around the room.

"That's one of the girls from the Eastside."

"Not the one I pulled my gun on is it?" asked Marilyn.

"No, not her."

"Ava I want you to stay on top of my brother and make sure that he's on top of Raymond. Marilyn check all the apartments every two hours. I'm going to buy a new stamp, we'll call it *No Name*."

B-More

Monday morning Regeane, Melody and Seena were on Amtrak headed for Baltimore carrying 100 bundles of *No Name* along with two Glock 21 shot pistols with three extra clips. It was June and the weather didn't feel the same as it did in New York City, they all got in a cab and headed towards Motel 6. They checked into different rooms as a precaution.

"I'll meet you in your room Melody; I'm going to call my cousin from the payphone."

Regeane dialed her cousin Rick, "What's up fam, will I see you next week?"

"No, you'll see me in an hour give me your address."

Seena was the first one out of the cab, followed by Melody then Regeane. Rick was standing in the front of his house drinking a beer.

"What's up Cuz?" they embraced. "It's been some years, look at you." He smiled as he looked at her. "Damn girl! The last time I saw you, you looked like a female linebacker with a chessboard tucked under your arm. Did you learn how to play yet?"

Rage laughed, "I happen to be a reigning teenage champion three years in a row."

"What!?"

"I got a new hobby though."

"Yeah what's that?"

"Making the public nod off this good shit I got." They all started laughing.

"Come on inside," Rick said. Regeane introduced Melody and Seena.

"Well let's talk business," Rick said.

"We got some samples for you to pass out. We want to see how the fiends react to this dope, if they like it, then we're willing to work it out." Melody looked at Regeane then at Rick. "Now I realize that you and Regeane are family, but you're not mine, so if you get the wrong idea about this thing here," she used her finger to point to them respectively. "Your fam here is going to kill you!"

"Shit, I will about this money," Seena said in a matter-o-fact tone.

"This is not a game!" Regeane assured her cousin.

Melody made eye contact then spoke loud and clear to Rick, "This is the only time you'll see me, unless I have to come back to put somebody down."

Regeane looked over at Rick, "So who is the competition around here?"

"Jo-Jo and his crew."

"Will they fuck with you?"

"Nah, it's these two brothers; Ronnie and Jazz that everyone is paying off."

"Rick I don't know how things work around here, but The Roses don't pay any man unless they fucking us," Melody told him. "Where can we find them brothers?"

"In the park we can meet up with them later." Rick told her.

Seena lifted up her gray Gap sweatshirt and pulled out two bundles. Rick noticed the .9 mm Glock in her waistband. He knew his cousin and the chicks she was with meant business!

175

Rick was passing out the samples and in one hour's time he had seven fiends over dose and passed out all fifty. Regeane and Melody went back to the hotel to get the rest. The next morning they were on the train headed back to New York and Seena had five thousand dollars more than she did the day before.

Back in New York a lot of shit happened. Four men concealing their identities with ski masks robbed Mike's dope spot while he was upstairs counting. Tey made all of the workers lay faced down with their pants down. They wanted to know which apartment was the stash. None of the workers knew there were five different stash apartments in that same building so the robbers only hit one. One of the assailants got pissed and killed Almo, who was one of the workers because he wouldn't tell which apartment Mike was in. They got off with five thousand dollars cash, and two thousand dollars in drugs. Almo chest had a bullet hole in it with blood pumping out of his mouth. Mike got a call from Eric, another worker telling him what happened.

"I recognize one of them by his voice," Eric said.

"Who was it?"

"It was Ice's brother; you know the one who was stealing money from us. His ass set this up."

"I'll deal with his ass later; don't worry about the money or drugs call me when the cops leave so I can get out of here."

"I got you," Eric said.

Mike called Kia to explain what happened at *City Food* spot and Almo's murder.

"Almo who graduated with us?" Kia asked.

"Yep."

Kia always liked Almo; he was a cutie pie just too wild for her.

"Where does Ice live?"

"112th Street and Lennox Avenue."

"I've never liked that black blunt smoking motherfucker anyway! We're going to handle it for you, don't even worry about it!"

Kia told Ava and Toni what happened over at *City Food*.

"Is Mike okay?" Toni asked.

"Yeah."

"Ya'll know Melody would flip out if something happened to him." They all agreed.

"What we gone do? You know someone has to feel it!" Kia said.

"Wait until we can talk with Mike and then we can get Wayne involved." Ava suggested.

"FUCK THAT!" Kia yelled. "Send that hit out now! I want his ass dead, they live at 112th Street and Lennox Avenue he's a black blunt smoking motherfucker you can't miss."

"Why don't you just wait!?" Ava snapped back.

"Wait for what Ava? We paying them $20,000 a week regardless if they kill or not, I'm not paying if I have to go kill that bastard myself."

"She's right Ava, we're paying them big money while they sitting on their asses." Toni said.

Ava picked up the phone and dialed Wayne.

Wayne picked up his phone and Ava shared all of the information that Kia had relayed to her.

"What do you want done?"

"First I want to know who his friends were, then I want you to torture his ass, cut his damn hands off and leave them taped to his mothers' door."

Jill and Missy were now moving more than 180 bundles of *Madman* a day, with the help of Jill's brother K-B and the Wolf Pack Crew. In days they'd taken control of 122nd Street and 2nd Avenue locking out the competition. 110th Street and Lexington Avenue was hurting since The Roses went down and mashed the whole block including Porky, the team on the opposite side of the street was loosing money, customers, and respect in the streets fast.

One of the competitors was mad and said, "Fuck the Madman Crew, the Bull Crew still runs the Eastside." A fiend said. Telling K-B how the Bull Crew was beefing about the Wolf Pack Crew. Since Jill let K-B control the streets, he put all of the Wolf Pack Crew down with him; if he eats, his crew eats, that's why they loved him, and he showed love in every situation. Wolf pack was known for kidnapping, sticking up drug dealers, and murder. He knew as long as he was around that his little sister was safe. "Things didn't change, I'll still put my gun in a motherfuckers' mouth for that money, then pull the trigger; don't get it twisted!"

"K-B, I'm just putting you on point," the fiend said.

"Thanks, it's nothing personal with you."

K-B walked to the corner to take a look at the competition. Of all the guys over there it was just one that he grew up with, but since drugs hit the Eastside they stopped talking since they were in conflicting fields. The only thing that worried him was that Jill and Missy were the bosses and they all knew it. He wondered if Boe would try them. They all came up together from kids, but the streets changed people for the worst. His street instincts kicked into overdrive, if she's the boss, why not? He would've. K-B pulled his partner Uni to the side, "Listen Homie, I think the Bull Crew might be plotting against us."

Uni looked at him, "What do you want me to do?"

"Let's mash the problem before it gets out of hand."

K-B looked back across the street then at Uni, "Let me speak to Jill and Missy first."

"K-B, look you know how this thing here works, if it's a problem just give me the word, I'll go over there and lay the entire Bull Crew face down, and rob they asses for recreation." Uni boasted. "I'd prefer doing that than standing around getting paid for doing nothing."

"Just hold on! I want to talk with them first Uni."

"You know what?" Uni asked. "Tell Jill I said just give me the word, I'll clear that whole side of the street! It'll sound like the 4th of July came early." They both laughed.

"I only got 10 bundles left."

"Get 50 more then call it a day." K-B told him.

Missy walked around the corner carrying a black plastic bag, "What's up guys?" they both smiled at Missy.

"You still sound white," K-B said.

"That didn't stop you from trying to get in my pants."

Uni laughed at her comment.

"We only got 10 left."

"I got 60 more bundles on me," she told them.

"Give them to me," K-B said.

"No, give me the money for the 100 Jill gave you earlier."

"Give me five minutes Missy, we'll be right back." Uni said.

"You better take this shit," she said as she forced the plastic bag into his hands. As she walked away Uni grabbed K-B, "Damn Missy is a bad bitch," shaking his head from side to side. "I'd make her wifey, I love that girl! Do you know the only reason I didn't push up on her because of you big homey."

"Hell she didn't give me no play, Jill ass was cock blocking." They both watched as Missy walked across the street.

"MISSY!" Uni yelled. "Are you going to the dro spot?"

She nodded her head yes.

"Pick me up two bottles."

"I want my money back," she yelled.

When she got on the other side of the street the Bull Crew was standing out in front of the building. Missy knew most of them from Wagner projects or school.

"What's up guys?"

"What's up Missy?"

"Just chilling," she said.

"We don't sell *Madman* over here."

Missy turned her head, it was Boe. She was shocked that he was coming at her like that. They both lived in the same building since they were kids.

"What's your problem Boe?"

"Like I said we don't sell *Madman* over here, so why are you on this side of the street?"

"Boe if you got something personal with me then bring it to me; don't stand behind your friends and talk shit."

All the guys started laughing. One of the guys standing on the stoop said, "You're going to let her dis you like that? You're soft!"

Boe walked up on Missy then punched her in her face knocking her off her feet. Two of the guys standing out there who knew Missy pushed Boe away from her. He was standing over her like he was preparing to stomp her.

"What the fuck is wrong with you, Boe?" Jake asked.

"Fuck that bitch! She's down with the Madman Crew, there's no love for her over here."

Jake helped Missy up. Missy was still dizzy.

"Are you alright?" Jake asked concerned.

K-B and Uni walked out the building together talking. A little girl walking pass told K-B that Boe had just punched Missy in her face.

"Where?" The little girl pointed towards the Bull Crew across the street.

"WOO-WOO," K-B yelled out and the whole Wolf pack and Madman Crew knew that code was when something was wrong. The crews ran across the street to help Missy. K-B and Uni were standing in front of Missy, Uni's gun was out.

Uni yelled out, "What the fuck you want a war in the streets?" Uni leaned over and whispered to Missy, "Give me the word I'll blow his brains out right here." Missy shook her head in disagreement.

"No, forget about it," Missy spoke calmly. "I'll handle it! Besides we're making too much money just to lose it all on him, he's not worth it," Missy told them as she laughed. "But, you can bet this on my yellow ass he'll never hit another woman again! Let's get money!" She yelled as she walked into the smoke spot. When she came out Missy stopped in front of Boe, "Damn Boe you're hating on us like that?" She shook here head. "Now listen I didn't tell so you won't tell, right?" she taunted as she blew him kisses. K-B passed her a bag of money and she handed Uni two bottles of dro without even asking for her money back.

Uni looked at K-B, "You know she's going to fix his ass, watch!"

This was Jill's first time meeting Ava. Toni introduced them. Jill was telling them about Boe hitting Missy.

"We got people to handle problems for us," Ava told her.

"She wants to handle this herself."

"Why didn't your brother or someone from his crew handle it?" Toni asked.

"She told them not to."

Toni looked at her, "So otherwise things are okay?"

"Things are good," Jill told her.

Toni walked back to retrieve a shopping bag, "It's 200 bundles in there; it should carry you until tomorrow."

Jill smiled while passing Ava the money, "You want to count it together?" she asked.

"If we have to count it then that means we don't trust you," Toni responded.

Missy just got out the shower when she looked in the mirror and wanted to cry. The entire right side of her face was bruised black and blue with a small cut above her eye. She was hurt more so that she and Boe knew one another. Missy moisturized her body with Cool Water body oil as she reached for the phone. She called the Harlem car service.

"I want car 515," she told the dispatcher. He drove a 2001 Lincoln Navigator with tinted windows.

"Where to?" the dispatcher asked.

"On hold for two hours."

"That's going to be $200 dollars."

"No problem," Missy told her.

"Where are you?"

"114th Street and 3rd Avenue."

"He'll be outside in 15 minutes."

Missy put on her brand new lady Enyce sweatshirt, with the hood and tied up her black matching Air Max sneakers. She reached under her bed to find her nickel plated .380 pistol. She hit the release to make sure that the clip was full and slipped the gun inside her left side pocket. On her way out the door she grabbed the unlit hi-dro blunt and the Diane Von Furstenberg shades sitting on the table.

When she got outside of her building the black Navigator she'd requested was waiting for her. Four guys were sitting in front of the building shooting dice.

"What's up Missy? Money's in it."

"Not now," she yelled behind her. Missy loved to shoot dice with the homeboys around the way. They think because she's a woman she doesn't understand the game. Precisely the reason after every game she's walking away with at least $5,000 at a time. Yeah they were her herbs." Missy climbed in the back.

"Where to Missy?" Driver 515 asked.

"122nd Street and 2nd Avenue." Missy only used 515 to take her places because not only was his truck nice, but he always had the newest CD's before they hit the streets.

"Turn that up," Missy told him; it was something new by the Lox's she hadn't heard before.

When the truck pulled up on 122nd Street the whole Bull Crew from earlier that day was still out, now they were drinking Courvoisier and Grand Marnier while smoking, with five girls standing around with them. Not one of them noticed the black Navigator parked across the street.

"Just relax," she told the driver while retrieving her blunt. She took a long pull from the blunt trying to relax and put her mind at ease. She glanced around again and noticed that Boe wasn't one of the ones standing out there, but she knew that it would only be a matter of time before he showed back up.

Ten minutes later a cab carrying Boe pulled up on the other side of the street. He joined in and picked him up a cup drinking with the rest of them. It took a lot of composure to keep Missy from jumping out the truck blasting, plus she remembered a few of them stood up for her. Her beef was definitely with Boe, not the rest of his crew. Missy watched every move Boe made. They were all laughing, talking, and hugging up on the girls. Missy looked closely as she noticed Boe make his move towards the projects still carrying one of the small cups in his hand; he turned into 45 Schoolyard as was headed toward his building.

"Drive slow," Missy told the driver, "I'll be right back."

As Missy got out she slipped her hand in her pocket and pulled out the gun preparing to fire, while pulling her hood over her head. Boe must've heard footsteps as he turned around facing the barrel of Missy's .380.

"OH SHIT!" Boe yelled out. "Missy I'm sorry for hitting you," Boe said noticing her attire was all black and her face was void a smile. "I was wrong for hitting you," he pleaded like a bitch.

Missy just stared at him, "Don't you remember our deal?" she asked mockingly. "I told you that I wouldn't tell, and now you won't be able to tell," she said as she let loose five shots. Boe's body hit the pavement hard. Missy stood directly over him and noticed that the bastard was still breathing with his eyes stretched wide open. Missy took off her glasses and placed her right foot on his chest while looking in his eyes as he gagged for air with blood heaving out of his chest, she closed her eyes and fired three more times. The bullets ripped Boe's face wide open. As Missy started walking away the cops appeared. She started walking faster through 45 Schoolyard and the undercover police car flipped its sirens. Missy began running in the direction of the waiting Navigator as the police car cut her off. One of the officers jumped out the car yelling, "FREEZE, or I'll shoot!"

Missy was still holding the gun.

"Drop the weapon!" The officer demanded.

Missy was uncertain what to do. She knew it was all over so she could just turn and start blasting. She dropped the gun disguising her face inside the hood.

The Bull Crew noticed that the cops caught someone in the middle of the street.

"Didn't Boe go that way?" Jake asked.

"Hell yeah," another guy answered, "I hope they ain't locking this nigga up." They all headed over to the schoolyard as the officer pulled off Missy's hood.

"It's a woman," the officer yelled to his partner.

"OH SHIT, it's Missy," Jake said.

The black officer pulled out his radio calling in a homicide that had taken place on 122nd Street and 2nd Avenue. Jay saw a motionless body stretched in the middle of the Schoolyard.

"DAMN!" Jake yelled out. "That's Boe," he said as he identified him due to the three carat diamond earrings he'd only purchased the week before. He could see the three bottle cap holes in his face.

"You yellow bitch!" Bobbi, the ring leader of the girls who were standing outside with the Bull Crew yelled. "If I ever see you again I'm going to fuck you up!" Bobbi spat as the rest of the girls chimed in, everyone of them was crying.

"Boe was wrong for punching her in her face like that," Jake said visibly hurt. "Now look this shit is all fucked up," he said as tears fell from his eyes. "We all grew up together and now one is headed to a grave and the other a cell." Jake walked off.

It was 2 a.m. when Jill got a call from Annie telling her that Missy killed Boe and the police caught her with the gun. Jill jumped out of the bed yelling, "Are you sure it was Missy?"

"Hell yes," Annie told her.

"Okay, thanks, I'll handle it!"

Jill hung up and called K-B to tell him what happened.

"Ain't nothing gone happen until she go to court just go back to sleep Jill, I should be home in about two hours."

"Where are you?"

"Jimmy's Café."

"Which one?"

"Up in Harlem."

K-B pulled Uni away from the Puerto Rican girl that he was dancing with.

"Jill just called, Man Missy killed Boe."

Uni looked at K-B, "Didn't I tell you that she was going to fix his ass? But hell I didn't see her killing him."

The next morning Kia, Ava and Marilyn were talking to Melody and what happened with the robbery, and Almo's murder. Her concern wasn't for the money, or the product; it was for Mike and Almo. She felt responsible for insisting that Almo be put in the second position. She cried; they'd been cool since they were little kids and she was taking this personal. Finding out that Ice was responsible really set her off.

"Wasn't he down with them?" Melody asked. Kia nodded.

"Fuck that have them niggas kill they whole family," Melody viciously said.

"Melody no," Ava said. "No children or women."

Melody nodded, "Okay deal, kill his ass and all of his brothers."

"I can agree to that," Ava said as she looked back at Marilyn and Kia. "What ya'll think?"

"It won't be my lost," Marilyn said. "I don't know him."

Ava's cell rang, it was Jill calling. "I got a big problem," Jill said.

"What is it?"

"Not over the phone," Jill said. "We have to talk in person. Plus I just finished that cake you asked me to make." That was code for the 200 bundles that Toni gave her the day before.

"Well come over now," Ava told her.

Ava was shaking her head as she hung up the phone.

"What's wrong?" Kia asked.

"It's Jill she's telling me that she has a big problem."

"Did she tell you what it was?"

"No, but she's on her way over here."

Jill got out of the cab carrying a brown gym bag. Four men were installing a big black metal door.

Marilyn let Jill in, Melody was working on the computer and Ava was standing in the middle of the living room wearing a black silk robe with a black rose on the right shoulder barefoot. On the table lay two Mac-11 machine guns with silencers attached, a Roit pump shot gun lay across from it. Ava walked over to her and hugged her, "What's wrong little sister?" she asked as she led her over to the couch.

"You want something to eat or drink?"

"I'm fine." She sighed, "Missy's in jail."

"WHAT!?" Kia yelled.

"That guy who hit her yesterday, she killed him." Ava looked back at Kia, Melody and Marilyn.

"Well Ava, what you waiting for?"Kia asked, "Get her out of there."

"We can't have our main people staying in jail," Marilyn added.

Melody got up from the chair and passed Ava the phone. "Call that expensive ass lawyer we got on retainer. Whatever her bail is we got it. Get her out of there!" Melody yelled.

Jill looked around the room and she liked how they cared about Missy, and neither of them really knew her; that's love she thought to herself.

"What's her name?" Ava asked.

"Mishell Sinclair."

"Don't worry, she'll be out no later than tomorrow. Do you want to chill for the day?" Kia asked.

"I can't, people depend on me; if I don't eat then they don't. It's money to be made," Jill said. "And Like P. Diddy says *'Let's get it.'*"

"I like you," Marilyn told her.

Ava called their lawyer, Jay Roth and described the situation surrounding Missy.

"Bail in the cases of murder are usually very high if the judge will even grant it," he said. "But I'll go check on her."

"No! Mr. Roth I don't think you understand, with the amount of money you're being paid I expect her to be out of there and soon."

Ava hung up the phone without waiting to hear another word from him.

"What's wrong?" Kia asked her.

"These overpriced lawyers think they are slick, that's all."

That afternoon in Downtown Manhattan Jay Roth Esquire was inside of the female bullpen, "Mishell Sinclair?"

She was asleep on a metal bench, hoodie over her head with her left sneaker off her foot.

"Mishell Sinclair?" He yelled again, "Excuse me," he pointed at a white woman who appeared to be drugged sitting on the bench. "Could you please tap the young lady there sleeping?" The woman tapped Missy as she raised her head she heard her name, "Mishell Sinclair?" She jumped up off of the bench sliding her shoe on.

"That's me!" she stepped towards the gate.

"I'm Jay Roth," he introduced himself as he passed her his business card. "I was sent here to represent you by Ava Wilson, your sister."

Obviously she was puzzled being that she was an only child, plus she didn't know anyone by that name. It must be one of the Roses she'd never met, she thought. She began to feel better knowing that they were willing to help her out.

"You're being charged with first degree murder."

When the other females in the bullpen heard that, you could hear some of them whispering, "She's fucked."

"We're going to court in about ten minutes, when we get in there I don't want you to say anything, okay?" Missy nodded her head. "I'm going to try and get you home today."

Missy was amazed, to say the least. She couldn't believe what her attorney was telling her. "I'll be in the courtroom waiting for you," he assured her.

Missy went back to the bench and took a seat next to some young girl dressed in all blue.

"Excuse me, Miss?"

Missy looked over at her. "Did you really kill somebody?"

"Why, are you the police?" Missy turned her back to the girl and pulled her hoodie back over her head. Five minutes passed and a white female court officer was walking towards the cell, "Mishell Sinclair court!" Missy removed her hood and pulled her hair into a ponytail.

"Put your hands behind your back." The officer secured the cuffs. "Follow me."

Missy was escorted into the courtroom. Her attorney was standing behind a long wooden table waiting for her. The District Attorney for the State of New York read the charges pending against her.

"How do you plea?" the judge asked.

"Not guilty."

After listening to the defense and the prosecutor the judge set the bail at $75,000.

Missy's head fell down; she knew in a million years she couldn't raise that type of money.

"Your honor, my client would like to post bail at this time." Missy's head flew up amazed at what she was hearing. Drug dealers she knew that had been in the game for a long time wouldn't be able to raise that amount of money.

"I'm going to pay your bail, I'll be back to talk to you."

As the court officer escorted her back to the bullpen she talked to Missy, "It would take me two and a half years to make that kind of money, someone must really love you." Missy just smiled. Not every comment deserved a reply. Missy took her regular seat awaiting her attorneys' reappearance.

"Damn looks like you're going to be in here a long time," the girl said trying to strike up another conversation. Missy began laughing aloud when she saw Mr. Roth approach the gate.

"Your bail has been paid, we'll have to be back in court as soon as two weeks, and it shouldn't be long before you're walking out of here." He reached inside of his wallet and handed her a crisp hundred dollar bill. "Don't forget I'll see you in two weeks," he said.

Missy couldn't resist the urge to annoy the girl., "Looks as if I'm leaving and you're the one who is staying."

"Mishell Sinclair?"

"Right here!" Missy turned around and looked at the girl, "If you're ever Uptown and you need a job, look me up!" She said while walking down the hall laughing.

Missy called Jill as soon as she walked inside of her apartment.

"What's up bitch?"

"Bitch, have you gone cuckoo for coco pops or what?"

191

"Nah, Jill listen I didn't really want to kill Boe seeing how we all came up together, but he punched me in the face. Shit I'm too light for that shit. I never did anything to him; I thought we was mad cool, we used to be all up in the projects smoking dro till 4 in the morning. If I could I'd change all of last nights events, but just between us; pulling that trigger felt good." She inhaled deeply. "And who is Ava Wilson?"

"She's Kia's older sister."

"How did she find out about me?"

"What do you think? I told them the entire story. Oh and to be on the safe side, they want you in Baltimore with Seena."

"That's cool."

"Well I'll be over there to see you later," Jill said.

K-B and Uni were standing on 122nd Street and 2nd Avenue when a hot red escalade with tinted windows blaring Black Robs' *'That's Crazy'* came rolling up. The music was so loud and clear that people on the other side of the street were bopping their heads to the beat. That side was crowded. There were people buying dope along with the dealers selling.

Missy sat in the passenger's seat watching as K-B and Uni talked. She stepped out of the truck like she was someone famous decked out in a sky blue Donna Karan linen two piece with matching open toed lace up leather Cesare Paciotti sandals and carrying a matching Coach bag.

"What the fuck is wrong with you?" Uni asked.

"What are you talking about?" K-B looked back thinking Uni was talking to him.

"Why did you kill Boe?"

Missy looked at both of them, "Why? Ya'll saw my face after he hit me?"

"We were there, remember?" K-B reminded her.

"Sounds to me like ya'll defending the dead," She said as she removed her Selima Optique sunglasses. "Look at my face, how can I explain this? K-B if it had been Jill what would you have done?"

"Missy we did offer to handle that situation for you."

"I have to be able to defend my damn self."

"Damn how you get out so fast anyway?" Uni asked.

"They gave me bail."

"Yeah, how much that run you?"

"$75,000."

"WHAT!" Uni yelled.

"It was paid as soon as the judge called it out," Missy bragged. "Don't worry the same people who bailed me out, would do the same for the two of you."

"They don't know us," K-B said.

"Trust me, they know of both of you and they would do the same thing." Missy said with a smile etched on her face.

"What's funny?" Uni asked.

"The person that paid my bail, I've never even met her."

"Missy," K-B looked at her, "You said it was a female who got you out?"

Missy curbed her excitement she knew all too well how K-B and Uni got down. "I'm going to get me some dro to hold me down for a few days, I'll catch ya'll later."

"Here we go again," Uni said.

"I'm going with you," K-B informed her.

When Missy walked up on the Bull Crew side of the street, Jake was standing out there next to the stoop by the weed spot with four other guys. K-B pulled his .9 mm out of his waist, cocked it and pushed it back inside his pants.

"That's fucked up Missy," Jake said. "You didn't have to kill Boe!"

"What the fuck are you talking about?" Missy screamed. "He didn't have to punch me in my face!"

"But come on Missy, killing him?" Jake shook his head in disgust. "A week ago it was all good."

"You're 100% right about that, but he chose to use his hands to hurt me, so I chose my gun; now I consider us even!"

Jake turned his head. Bobbi walked out. "Bitch I'm going to whip your high yellow ass!" Bobbi charged in Missy's direction, Jake stepped in front of her as Missy stepped back opening the flap of her coach bag.

"I whipped your ass out on this Avenue before, I ain't got the time for a repeat but if I have to reach in my bag shit is gone get ugly!" Missy angrily warned.

"Go get the smoke," K-B said so they could leave.

"Bitch this ain't over," Bobbi promised.

"SHUT THE FUCK UP PLEASE!" Jake yelled at Bobbi noticing that K-B's hand was on the butt of his gun with members of Wolf pack and Madman waiting across the street to get the word. When Missy returned Bobbi looked her up and down.

"The Madman Crew ain't gone always be around!"

"Bitch check this, when I pumped them eight bullets into ya man Boe the Madman Crew wasn't around, but you keep running your mouth I'm gone unleash this Madwoman on your ass." Missy smiled as they crossed the street. K-B knew all to well that could be a deadly sign in Bobbi's case. Once across the street Missy hugged K-B and Uni. "I'm headed to B-more to open shop with Seena."

"Stay safe," K-B told her. Missy got back inside the waiting red Escalade. Cam'Ron's *'Oh Boy'* was so loud the truck was literally shaking from side to side.

"Uni, I been asking around about these females Jill been getting this work from; they call themselves The Roses.

"Word?"

"Yeah, and you know that night Corey and his brothers got killed inside of his truck?"

"Yeah what about it?"

"I was across the street talking to Kimmi, it was girls' that jumped out the car with Uzi's and killed them."

"Are you sure?" Uni asked.

"It was the same night Yo-Yo was killed in Mt. Morris Park by the stage. A week before Masada was killed. Then think about it, before we could jack Porky some females wearing masks carrying machine guns got him and his crew right on 110th Street. It's because of this we're making so much money."

Uni was puzzled, "So what you saying is these females are cleaning up the streets so they can take 'em over?"

"I don't know what to think, I'm just stating the facts. It is what it is," said K-B holding his arms out.

"You need to school Jill and let her know what she's dealing with, and why Joanne ain't down with it?"

"Jill said one of them bought her truck for $20,000, another one of them felt like Joanne was beating her friend; words got exchanged between her and Joanne and she put her gun in her face, Jill said Joanne damn near pissed on herself and won't even go back on the Westside." They laughed.

"How many of them is it?"

"Jill doesn't know for sure, she hasn't met them all." They both looked around at the females holding up the block wondering if any of them were Roses.

"Shit," Uni said. "These bitches all look like gold diggers!"

Kia, Melody and Mike were shopping on 125th Street.

"Can we stop by Apollo Express? I need to see my Cutie Pie."

Kia walked up in Apollo Express store, Joe started walking towards her smiling.

"Give me a few minutes," he said.

Mike was explaining to Kia and Melody how Ice was Downtown bragging, about how he robbed him, and killed Almo, for trying to play hero. He and Melody laughed at the end; they both knew what had to be done, too bad Ice didn't. Kia hadn't heard any of Melody and Mike's discussion as she watched some light skin girl with curls in her hair getting overly friend with Joe. Kia strolled over to where they were and looked the girl up and down.

"Bitch, I paid $20,000 for this niggas tongue so if you can't match it, you need to buzz off!" Kia looked at Joe then back at the girl, "He's mine all mine!"

"Excuse me," The lady looked at Kia, "do you know me to speak to me in this manner?"

Joe grabbed Kia by the arm, "What are you doing? This is my job!"

Kia snatched away from Joe then focused on the chick, "Bitch bring your broke ass outside so my feet can do the rest of the talking up your ass!" Kia proceeded to the door with Melody and Mike looking around trying to figure out what happened.

Melody and Mike introduced themselves to Joe.

"Joe don't worry about Kia, I'll talk to her. Just call her tonight, as you can tell my girl really likes you." Joe smiled. As Mike and Melody made there way out the store Joe reached to shake Mike's hand, Mike pulled him forward, "Kia's holding dawg you better lock that down," he whispered. "Plus, I know she feeling you so treat her right, she a good girl.

As they walked out Melody looked at him, "What was that about?"

"It's a man thang, you wouldn't understand."

Kia was standing outside with her hands on her hips waiting.

"Girl, bring your ass on, we got bigger problems to deal with," Melody yelled.

Ava's phone rang it was Wayne. "Chad and Melvin got Ice tied up in the basement."

"Did he tell you the names of the other men who helped him?"

"Yeah, he did it was two of his brothers and the other guy he's not sure what his name is. So how do you want to handle this situation?"

Ava slid her hand over the phone and relayed the message to Regeane and Toni. "So what's the problem?" Toni asked. "You told him to cut his damn hands off and taped them to his mothers' door, right?"

Ava nodded. Toni reached for the phone. "Wayne, Ava told you how to handle Ice, so what I want you to do with the brothers is to remove their heads and place them on the Westside highway and their bodies on the FDR Drive, you understand?"

"I got it."

Toni went back to finish counting the last of the money on the table.

Regeane opened the door, Marilyn walked in carrying a duffel bag.

"What's up, what's in the bag?" Regeane asked.

"I went to see Vito, Toni." She sat the bag down. "He just got a new shipment in, so I got six of them metal things and he blessed me with three silencers."

"What kind?" Regeane asked.

"Three .44 Magnums, two .357 Magnum's, one .40 Caliber with Hollow points and shredded bullets." Marilyn said as she placed the guns and the silencers on the table.

Regeane knew the moment her eyes saw the .40 Caliber that it was for her. Ava walked over to the table; she picked up one of the .357's, "These are all too powerful for us. Just keep them anyway; you'll never know when they may come in handy."

"I'm going to Club Cheetah's tomorrow night," Toni said. "Anybody rolling with me?"

"Fuck it, let's all go together." Regeane said. "Matter of fact tell Jill and Seena and make sure the one that we spent all that bail money on comes along, hell least we could meet her ass!"

Ava walked in her room and back out, "I'm not going in any club I can't take a gun inside. These young motherfuckers' like to act up, and those hating hoes too!"

"We will all be carrying, just in case." Toni stated.

"Let Kenny know that we want to use his trucks tomorrow." Ava still didn't really like Kenny, but she knew that he was apart of the Roses bottom line so she backed off of him.

Regeane dialed Kenny's cell phone. Toni called Jill to see if they wanted to party with them. Ava updated them about their finances. So far they each had $90,000 that she had packaged and separated.

Kenny parked his Yukon Denali and his X5 BMW in front of the building. The Roses walked out wearing all the latest fashions. Ava's Link Pave diamond choker was the most stunning of all the items the Roses were sporting. Each Rose was adorned with a custom made Gucci gun holster. Kia was in the drivers' seat of the Denali with Regeane and Marilyn. Melody was driving the BMW with Ava riding shot gun. They headed towards the Eastside with the booming sounds of Ja Rule '*Put it on me.*'

Kia pulled up on 122nd Street. Missy, Jill and Seena were standing on the corner talking to Uni and K-B and the Madman Crew who were secretly watching over Missy. After Kia hit the horn three times Seena noticed Melody sitting in the drivers' seat of the X5. "That's us," she said as the three of them kissed K-B and Uni. K-B was trying to get a look inside of the trucks, but the tint was too dark until Seena opened the door and he got a glimpse of the Diamond choker and then the matching bracelet when the arm came out the window. Ava made eye contact with K-B and liked what she saw; she smiled and he winked at her as Melody pulled off into traffic before anything more could develop. Ava turned around and looked at the three women in the back seat. "Which one of you did the Roses bail out?"

Missy smiled softly, "That was me. Thank you."

"No problem," Melody said as she looked at her through the rearview mirror. "This one was on us; the next one is on you."

Kia pulled up at Club Cheetah followed by Melody.

"Park, I'll be right back," Toni said as she jumped out of the Denali and walked up on the bouncer, and pulled on the back of his shirt. He turned around, "Damn!" Toni said as she took him all in, he was about 6 foot 8 and weighed 329 pounds, he looked down at Toni.

"Yes, little lady what can I help you with?"

Toni said a few words he began smiling and she passed his four hundred dollars. Toni's father taught her that money could talk for a mute, blind or crazy person. In the words of the WU; cash rules everything around, and I got plenty so I guess I rule. Toni thought as she waved them to come on.

Melody and Kia paid the valets as the nine of them strutted towards the front of the club. The bouncers' attention started at Regeane's platinum rose that contained 72 blue cut diamonds. Then he focused on the .45 tucked in her waist.

"The tea in China just went up three hundred more dollars," the bouncer alerted Toni.

"You trying to play me?" Toni yelled.

"Listen, its insurance," he told her. "You won't get searched 'cause I can see them guns," he said as he pointed to Regeane, Ava and Kia. "Hell for all I know all of you could be carrying!"

Regeane dug into her pants pockets and handed him the money.

"Don't shoot up my club!"

The Roses laughed as Melody smirked, "I'll buy this shit!"

"You couldn't afford it!"

"Try me."

When they got inside Ava and Melody walked to the bar as Kia and Toni went to grab two tables.

"Eight bottles of Cristal with nine glasses," Ava said to the bartender.

She looked at Ava, "That's going to be four thousand dollars."

"I didn't ask you for a price quote, I placed an order, so get it!"

The bartender returned carrying four buckets filled with ice containing two bottles of champagne in each. Ava peeled four thousand of a roll of hundred dollar bills. She waved her hand so the Roses could come help them carry the buckets. Before walking away Toni passed the bartender a hundred.

"No hard feelings, just keep them coming."

Missy walked up to grab a bucket.

"What's up Missy?"

She looked up and smiled. "Evelyn, I forgot you worked here." Ava and Toni walked away.

"So what's this I'm hearing that you killed Boe?"

Missy nodded nonchalantly. She knew that some things were best unsaid. "So I see you with some real ballers, is that Jill and Seena at the table too?"

"No doubt! The Madman Crew making a lot of money on the Eastside."

"Look if you ever need some help put me on!"

"I'll talk to Jill for you."

"Missy I got to get back to work, just keep me in mind."

"No doubt, I got you Evelyn." Missy said as she walked away carrying a bucket through the crowd while bopping her head to Shine. The music was loud and she was totally engrossed in it. Ava passed her a glass.

"Our first toast tonight ladies is to Missy,"Ava announced. "She committed her very first murder, that baby ain't no virgin. Our second toast is to Kia, my baby sister's birthday is next Sunday." Missy danced around the table and passed Seena an unlit Dutch master blunt filled with hydro. Kia, Melody and Ava looked at them, "What's that?" Ava asked.

"Dro," Missy answered, "is it a problem; us smoking around you?"

"No, just as long as you're on point."

Ava looked over at the DJ's booth; the sign read *HOT 97 Ladies night.* A female DJ' was also spinning the music; to her left she noticed a table of four females sitting three tables away enjoying Cristal as well. Ava smiled as she lifted her champagne glass in a toast to them; they all returned the smile and toast. The fashionable clothes they were wearing and the glistening diamonds they had on told Ava that they were into something big. Kia was pulling hard on the Dutch master before passing it to Regeane.

"What the hell you two doing?"

Kia and Regeane just looked at Ava; Regeane took another pull before passing it to Toni. Toni was never into drugs, she shook her head no, Ava waved it away from her, and Marilyn took two puffs and passed it back. Melody refilled all their glasses back up. Kia and Marilyn were drinking like it was water.

"Slow down girls," Melody said.

"Fuck that get me four more bottles, I'm enjoying myself," Kia yelled over the loud music. At that moment Biggie Smalls *One more chance* started booming out the speakers. Missy was dancing at the table, "I'm going to dance."

"Hold up," Kia said. "I'm going too." Missy, Kia, Seena, Toni and Marilyn were all on the dance floor. Seena and Missy were dancing with some white guy that favored Ben Afleck. Missy's hands were under the guy's shirt from behind, as Seena was grinding her ass into him. Seena turned around and looked in Missy's eyes "Let's freak him." The disco lights were blinking off and on and the constant thumping beat of the music had them feeling good. Seena moved even closer and slid her hands inside his pants massaging his balls. Missy moved closer and they were both rubbing his chest, back and head. The dance floor was so crowded no one really cared hell they may have been high off something themselves. The guy started touching Missy when he reached her waist and felt the gun she was carrying she looked at him, "Be easy, Pretty boy."

"What's wrong?" Seena asked.

"Nothing," Missy said as she continued to sway to the music.

Kia was so into the music enjoying herself; she didn't notice that her gun had fallen out of her holster. Toni and Marilyn were watching her, knowing she was tipsy from all the champagne she'd consumed. Marilyn pointed to her gun lying on the dance floor. Toni pushed the two guys dancing on her aside as Marilyn grabbed Kia by the arm. "You're slipping," she whispered in her ear. Toni reached down and picked up the gun with the two guys both watching her.

"What the fuck ya'll looking at?" Toni yelled as she unbuttoned her jacket to reveal her gun as well.

"Oh shit!" Kia yelled, "Marilyn I dropped my gun."

"Kia you fucking up, don't worry Toni got it."

Marilyn walked Kia back to the table where Ava, Jill and Regeane were sitting sipping champagne and talking. There were four unopened bottles of Cristal sitting in front of Regeane.

"What's wrong?" Jill asked as she looked up.

"Kia dropped her gun on the dance floor not paying attention."

Kia looked at Marilyn yelling in her face, "I don't need you to watch over me!"

Marilyn waved Kia away, "If we don't watch over one another, then who will? Take this," she handed Kia a piece of big red gum. Melody laughed, Kia pushed her so she could sit down.

"Kia slow down," Ava warned. Melody draped her arm around Kia's neck and whispered in her ear, "We're getting cash! We've spent ten thousand dollars tonight on champagne, and we didn't miss it. We've got four garbage bags of cash that's uncounted. Kia it's time for me to start Hi-Surf, next week I'm going to try and find me a store front and set up shop."

Kia looked into Melody eyes before whispering, "I'm here for you, and if you need any type of help don't you ever hesitate to ask, understand?"

Melody and Kia smiled at one another. Toni took a seat next to Kia, "Here take your gun, and next time pay attention." Regeane and Melody both looked at Kia.

Ava looked at the four women sitting three tables away, "Jill take them a bucket of champagne; make sure you tell them it's complimentary of The Roses."

Jill approached that table, "Excuse me ladies, this bottle is complimentary of The Harlem Roses," Jill pointed so they could see where it came from. All four ladies looked at them and smiled as Ava, Regeane and Toni raised their glasses.

"Gracias a todos (thank you all)," the darkest of the four said in Spanish. Jill wondered if they were Cuban, Dominican or Columbian.

Jill sat next to Ava telling her about the exquisite diamonds that each of them were wearing. Ava made eye contact with the group once again. Kia looked at her, "Why are you sweating them bitches? Hell if anything let them sweat the Roses!"

"That's right," Marilyn agreed. Marilyn raised her glass to Kia, "FUCK THEM!" They toasted.

Ava didn't like what Kia said. Everyone else was laughing.

The DJ played Jadakiss *Put your hands up*. "I'm going to dance," Toni said as Marilyn followed behind her. Toni's eyes connected with a dark skin guy standing by the bar wearing a two-piece grey suit with a white t-shirt underneath it.

"DAMN! Marilyn look at that black guy over by the bar."

Marilyn turned around to see who she was scoping out, "Toni you know if you touch that you might not come back."

Toni looked at her, "I don't believe you're saying some shit like that! What the fuck is wrong with you? You don't like black men?"

"Toni don't put words in my mouth, it's not like that at all!"

Marilyn pushed past Toni as she walked back to their tables with an attitude. Toni walked up to the guy that she was eyeing. She tapped him on the shoulder and when he turned around she smiled, "Can I buy you a drink?"

"No, but may I buy you a drink?"

Toni laughed, "I asked first."

"Okay," he said as he stuck out his hand, "My name's Terrell."

"I'm Toni," she said as she shook his hand. "So T & T," Toni said as they both laughed.

"What are you having?"Toni asked as the bartender from earlier walked over.

"Whatever you're drinking will be fine for me."

"So the same girlfriend?" The bartender asked. Toni nodded affirmatively.

"So what you order us?" Terrell asked.

"The best, and if it's not good enough then I'll order the whole bar until I get it right."

"You're funny," Terrell said as he smiled at her.

"No, I'm dead serious!"

The bartender placed a bucket with a bottle of Cristal and two tall champagne glasses on the bar in front of them.

"Big Dog Style, huh!?" Terrell joked.

"What this isn't good enough for you?"Toni waved the bartender back over. "What you want some Don-P, Thug passion, Moët whatever it is that you want baby, you name it and it's yours!" Toni said earnestly. "Hell I'll buy the bar out for a week until you can make up your mind."

Terrell looked at the bartender. "You want her to buy out the bar or what; I'm trying to go home?"

"The Cristal is good enough," Terrell said.

"Are you sure?"

Terrell laughed as Toni poured him a glass of champagne and handed it to him, then poured herself one.

"Drink up, there's plenty more. Can you dance?"

"No, not really."

"Guess what? Tonight is your lucky night; I'm going to teach you how, plus a whole lot of other things if you act right." Toni said seductively.

Jaheim's *Just in case* was playing as they made their way to the dance floor. Toni and Terrell were playing one another close like they came to the club together rubbing up all on one another. Terrell hand glided across Toni's .380 she looked at him as she put her arms around his neck, "That's not for you Boo!" They danced about a half an hour before Toni suggested they get another drink. While waiting for the bottle of champagne Toni began to rub up against him.

"Don't start something you can't finish," Terrell whispered in her ear.

"Anything I start I finish one way or the other," she said as she bounced her ass back into him. "What's that sticking me?" she asked as she boldly reached her hands inside his pants. "DAMN! You a Mandingo down there, I want to see that before tonight is over."

"Toni it's on you we can make this party short so our night can be longer."

"I like that," Toni said as she grabbed his hand. "Follow me big mouth."

"Where we going?"

"Shush," she placed her fingers across his lips. "Don't get scared now, I got your back not to mention I got my gun." She teased. As Toni pulled Terrell through the crowd of partygoers she couldn't focus on anyone else's good time, not even the Roses, it was her night and she was going to enjoy herself without regard to what anyone thought or said. She pulled him inside the women's bathroom. The crowd of women inside of the bathroom looked at them like they were crazy.

"You're in the wrong baffroom!" Some girl drawled.

"Bitch shut the fuck up, he's with me!" Toni pulled Terrell with her into the last stall and locked the door as she plopped down on the toilet placing her gun on her lap. She slid his zipper down slowly while looking up into his eyes as he smiled wide. Toni extended her tongue and met the tip of his dick and drew him in as much as she could. As she slid her tongue over the pulsating head she smiled as she looked up. "How was that for a start?"

He bit down on his bottom lip, "I want you to go home with me."

Toni zipped his pants back up.

"You don't know me; I could be a professional killer." She picked her .380 up.

"You don't scare me. At least if I die I'll have a smile on my face."

"Let me tell my friends that I'm leaving with you, meet me at the door at 3," she said after looking at her watch.

"I'll be there."

Regeane started getting a funny taste in her mouth, ever since she was a kid when something bad was about to happen she got this funny taste and she had it. She put her champagne down and pulled out her .45 and laid it on the table covering it with the table cloth.

"Is everything alright?" Kia asked.

She shook her head. "I'on know what it is. Maybe the effects of the champagne, the weed, the loud music and this crowd got something to do with it."

Seena was rolling another cherry Dutch master with purple haze, and Marilyn was rushing her. Melody poured herself, Ava and Jill more champagne with Kia holding an empty glass. "You're driving, Kia, remember?"

"Fuck it I'll buy my own."

Toni walked over to the table, "I'm leaving call me if something happens."

Marilyn had the Dutch master in her hand when Uni and another guy approached their table. "What's up Jill, hello ladies."

"Oh shit what's up?"

Uni looked at Jill, "The Bull Crew is here, along with Drop Out."

Kia looked, "Who is Drop Out?"

"That guy Missy killed, it's his older brother."

Uni was staring in Marilyn's face hard. He knew from the description Jill had given to K-B that she was the female that had given it to Joanne.

"Why in the fuck are you looking at so hard?" A cloud of smoked was enveloped around Marilyn her usual icy grey tight eyes were blood shot red. She held a blunt in her left hand and her right hand was on her gun.

"Marilyn's that's my people," Jill said.

"We know Uni is your brother's partner. I want to know why he is staring so hard?" Marilyn asked as she pointed at the guy standing next to Uni. Uni looked at the table where the .45 lay.

"Ladies, he doesn't want any problems with either of you."

"I hope not!" Marilyn said.

Uni looked around the table to find that Ava, Kia, or Melody weren't smiling. Ava opened her jacket allowing her .9 mm to do her talking. Uni looked all of them in the face. "I assure you that the Wolf pack is with you, not against you."

"I hope so," Marilyn said, "'Cause all ya'll living good off of us."

Uni was certain now that he'd just met The Roses; he took one last look at all of their faces before walking away from the tables.

Ava searched the tables and noticed that Missy wasn't sitting at either of them.

"Jill you and Seena go and find Missy."

Jill got up from her chair with Seena following closely behind her towards the dance floor. After almost ten minutes of searching they spotted her by the bar talking to some guy. Missy was in the process of exchanging numbers when they walked up. The guys hand was still extended with Missy's number.

"Excuse me handsome, is that her number?" Jill asked through a strained smile.

"Yeah."

"Can I see it?" Missy looked at Jill like she was crazy as the guy passed her the napkin. Jill looked at it nodded and shoved it inside her pocket. "She's gay!"

"WHAT!?" Missy yelled as Seena pulled her closer to her.

"Drop Out and the Bull Crew are hanging out here come back to the table now!"

Missy pulled her .32 from her waist and cocked it; she lowered it so it wouldn't be noticed.

The club was packed to capacity, the DJ put on *Anty Up* by MOP and the crowd was going wild as the music boomed out of the speakers. One of the Bull workers pulled Drop out to the side pointing out Missy, Jill and Seena creeping through the crowd.

"WHAT!?" Drop Out yelled over the loud music.

"Look asshole, there go Missy with Jill and Seena. It was hard at first for his eyes to adjust with the blinking lights. Missy, Jill and Seena sat down and that funny taste in Regeane's mouth got stronger. "Melody you and Kia go and get the trucks it's time to roll out of here," she said as she looked around.

Kia and Melody headed out the club and gave the valets $50.00 to bring the trucks around.

Ava pulled her .9 out and cocked it, Regeane lifted her .45 off the table and Marilyn had hers in her pocket. Jill, Missy and Seena followed their lead, as they were about to get up four guys approached the table.

"What's up Missy?"

"Not a thing, you tell me Drop Out?"

"Missy you think you can get away with killing my brother?"

"Drop Out listen it's not the right time for you, PLEASE, don't make me kill again, because I will!"

"Motherfucker back your ass away from the damn table now!" Billy Bad Ass Marilyn demanded. "I'm gone give your ass three fucking seconds to back away."

Ava said, "One."

"Two," before three could get out of her mouth they all stood and Regeane discharged her weapon first. *That's so crazy* was playing inside the loud club and it began looking a lot like a Fourth of July firework show.

Jill started shooting into the crowd without care who she hit. At that moment she knew she was fighting for her life. All four men who'd approached the table bodies fell to the floor. The crowd started pushing and shoving towards the front door. Marilyn was behind Ava shoving her through the crowd pulling her trigger. Regeane was blocked in by a crowd of people all trying to get out, she raised her right hand and released two shots into the air trying to clear a path, in all of the chaos someone snatched her seventeen thousand dollar diamond rose from around her neck.

"FUCK!" She yelled as she looked at people running in every direction. Someone was now shooting from the other direction of the club. Wasn't shit she could do, she knew she'd been got and the retrieval of her diamond rose was unlikely to happen tonight.

Marilyn went down. Seena and Jill helped her to her feet.

"My back, MY BACK!" Marilyn yelled. They held her up by the waist. While helping Marilyn out the club they all were gripping their guns.

Kia noticed the commotion and the first person she saw was Jill standing in the door with her gun pointed inside of the club. Ava ran pass her, followed by Regeane, then Seena and Missy who were holding Marilyn by the waist backing out of the club shooting in it. Kia shifted the Denali into reverse backing up sideways blowing her horn, Melody did the same thing. Both trucks blocked the door so no one else could get out, Seena, Missy and Marilyn got in with Kia. Regeane, Ava and Jill got in with Melody. Both trucks peeled out into the night in different directions.

"I think Marilyn got shot," Melody said. "Did ya'll see how Seena and Missy was holding her?"

"If my girl dies, I'm going to invest every dollar to see to it that that entire bitch ass crew does." Ava said.

"Somebody snatched my fucking diamond rose!"

Melody looked at Regeane through the rearview mirror while shaking her head. "Don't worry about that material shit, you're still alive and that's all that counts."

"DAMN! I just paid seventeen thousand dollars for that."

"Buy another one, DAMN!" Ava yelled.

"No, I want that one back! And I'm going to get it to, watch. It's the only one like it."

Melody turned on the FDR Drive heading north. Kia pulled into St. Luke's Hospital parking lot. Marilyn didn't have tears in her eyes all she kept saying was that it burned.

"Can you walk?" she gave Kia an icy glare.

"No!"

"Seena help her out."

"I'm going to stay with her," Seena said. "We'll think of something to say." Seena was holding Marilyn by the waist.

"Whatever you do, don't mention anything about being at the club."

"I know that Kia!"

Toni and Terrell were having fun at his place. He started out licking her ears, trailed down to her neck then her nipples and finally his tongue landed on her pussy. Terrell parted her pussy lips with his two fingers and blew on her clit. It didn't take long for Toni to have an orgasm, she tried to push him off but it was feeling so good. Plus the way that they were positioned it was hard to do anything but enjoy it. Toni was screaming and moaning, "Daddy please don't stop!" while holding the back of Terrell's head.

Terrell looked up and made contact with Toni's eyes. "Do you think I can handle you now?"

"Yes," she said seductively. "It's time for me to prove myself. And so you know when I start something I like to finish it." She leisurely licked the head of his dick as she kneaded his balls, then she ran his dick across her face as she blew on it. "I want to make love to your dick," she began trying to deep throat him, Terrell was moaning and ready to cum. Toni looked at him, "I'm going to swallow every drop of you." His legs started to give out, as she sucked him harder bobbing her head from side to side up and down and Terrell bust a large nut straight in her mouth with her swallowing every droplet.

"I hope that it's not over?" Toni smiled seductively with cum still on the sides of her mouth.

"Not at all," Terrell rubbed her pussy as reached inside the nightstand and pulled out a condom.

"Let me put that on for you," she put the condom in her mouth as she slid between his legs and slid it up like a pro.

"Turn around and get on your hands and knees."

As Toni obliged he parted her legs and began his thrust. Toni looked back at him, "Be careful, you're too big for me." Her pussy was tight it took some time for him to glide his fingers in and out to loosen up the entry. As he entered her he wrapped his hands in her hair and pushed himself inside of her as he pulled her back into him.

"You black motherfucker, you know how to treat a woman like a hoe," she said through deep loud moans. She looked back at him. "Who told you to stop?"

He slid his fingers inside her ass. "That feels good, what you want to put your dick in there?"

Terrell smiled wide at her, "I'll take my time with you."

"You sound like a pro at this. I'll try to handle that big ass dick you got, but when I say stop you better or I'm going to kill your ass."

He rubbed her clit and made her cum again before he slid himself inside her ass. She was visibly uncomfortable.

"Relax, trust me," he slowly starting pumping while rubbing her clit.

"It feels good."

It wasn't long before he was cumming inside of her followed by another release from her. Toni smiled as she looked at him. "You're going to be my boy toy." They both laughed as they lay wrapped up in one another.

When Kia walked into the apartment Melody, Ava and Regeane were watching televisions. It was a Newsflash about what happened at the club.

What appears to have been a shoot out occurred about one hour ago. After speaking with several witnesses; allegedly four men approached a table of women where words were exchanged and shortly after shots erupted. We have a total of ten casualties four inside the club and six outside. The club owner says that nothing like this has ever happened in or around this establishment before.

"What's up with Marilyn?" They all asked, praying their girl was good.

"She got shot in the back. She's in St. Luke's hospital Seena stayed with her."

"What did you do with Kenny's truck?" Ava asked.

"Jill and Missy got it; I told them to take it."

Regeane reached for her phone trying to contact Toni. After the fourth attempt Toni finally answered then yelled, "What the fuck do you want?"

"Muffin the party's over, Marilyn got sick."

"I'm on my way."

"Listen things are getting crazy now," Kia said. "We got to make some changes.

"Like what?" Ava asked.

"For one Missy need to get the hell out of New York, then we need to get the rest of the Bull Crew or Jill will have to deal with them."

"I really don't care," Regeane acknowledged. "I mean I agree to both, but I want my damn rose back!"

"Girl you need to let it go, 'cause it don't look like you're getting that one back." Melody said. Ava just sucked her teeth.

"I promise you if I see anyone wearing it they asses will be meeting God that day!" Melody and Kia laughed.

Ava shook her head in disbelief, "You know that rose will be at the pawn shop."

"You think it's funny? Watch and see. Matter of fact, I'm going home, bye!"

Jill walked into her apartment, K-B was sitting in a chair closest to the window holding two M-1 machine guns. Uni just called me telling me that them crazy bitches from the Westside killed Drop Out, Kerry, DJ and Hasty, and was trying to finish the rest of them, but they got away. It's a fuckin' massacre down there!" He shook his head. "Jill, listen I think you might be in over your head, don't you? You know it was them who killed Corey and Yo-Yo in the same damn night, right?"

"K-B fuck them frontin' assholes, they got what they deserved."

"These bitches are cold heart killers and they are willing to kill anyone or thing that gets in the way."

"I was the one who approached them. My mind was already made to rock this city, and get rich in a years time, two at the most. I'm not planning on going to jail or the graveyard because you're going to do what mommy told you to do; protect me!" she yelled.

K-B looked in his little sister eyes, "I'll kill anyone that tries to bring harm your way!"

Jill hugged her brother, "I'll do the same for you."

"Listen you need to lay low for a few days just until I can find out what's going on. It might be a war and you, Missy and Seena are involved."

"Who is the real boss of the Bull Crew?"

"Everybody thinks its Jake, but he only the front man for a guy name Dino."

"Who that?" Jill asked with her eyebrows raised.

"Only a few people know him. You might've seen his car, it's a 2000 red bug eyed 430 Mercedes Benz four door."

"Just the other day I did see it parked on the Bull side of the street. He's a dark skin guy, about six feet, with waves in his hair?"

K-B nodded, "He fuck with some girl in Johnson or Taft projects, his car is always parked on 115th Park Avenue. If you cut the head off then the body will fall." K-B looked at his sister.

"That means he needs to die also." Jill's mind began racing, Missy lived in Johnson projects and Joanne in Taft, the thing was she hadn't talked to her in months. Now she was thinking about Jake, they were all cool, but now she wondered would she have to put a hit out on him.

"What are you thinking about?"

"Nothing," she lied.

"So what are you going to do J?"

"I need to talk to my people first, but you'll be the first to know."

"Do you have protection?"

Jill pulled out her empty .32.

"Did you use it?"

"Hell yeah! If I had two more those would be empty too, shit my life was in danger."

"Give that to me, it might have a body on it now." She passed her brother the gun. K-B walked into his room and came back out carrying two boxes, one contained a brand new nickel plated .380 and the other a A.P. .9 mm. He placed both boxes on the table, "Which one do you want?" She looked at them both carefully and picked up the M-1. "This one will do me just fine."

Jill picked up her phone then called Joanne, but that call was to no avail. Joanne didn't know who the hell Dino was on top of that she seemed very distant. Jill hung up the phone then made a mental note never to call Joanne again.

At 6:45 a.m. Toni was knocking on Ava and Kia's door. Kia had just gotten out the shower. Ava ran to open the door.

"What's up with Marilyn?"

"Have a seat."

"While you were getting your freak on, Marilyn got shot. Shit got so heavy we had to shoot our damn way up out of there."

"What the fuck happened? Where is she? She's not dead is she?"

"No!" Kia and Ava answered in unison. Kia had a towel wrapped around her wet body. Ava sighed, "The guy Missy killed, his brother and his crew approached us."

"So Marilyn was shot over Missy?"

"I hate to say it, but yeah." Kia nodded.

"The Bull Crew is on the Eastside so I'm going to send some of my friends from Brooklyn over there to gather all of the information we need." That's when Toni thought about Vito, she knew he'd handle that for her as a favor to her father.

Seena and Missy were on Amtrak headed to Baltimore with two hundred bundles, and two brand new .45 automatics. When the cab pulled up in front of Rick's, he was sitting out on the steps eating pizza. He was smiling, "You don't know how happy I am to see you! The fiends been bugging me since you left last week."

The next day Rick was outside making a sale as two guys approached him with guns out. Seena was looking out the window.

"What the fuck ya'll doing?"

"Bitch do you know who we are?"

"NO! And I don't care either!" That's when one of the assailants went inside of Rick's pocket and removed a knot of cash.

Seena walked out the house. "Seena go back inside, I'll handle it!" Rick yelled. Ignoring him she approached the two men. "What are your names?"

"Jazz and Fat Ronnie, you better ask around about us." The fatter one said. Seena smiled wickedly, "It's cool Rick give them the money. Now be prepared because if you take it now, I'm coming back to collect later, with intrest," Seena said as the smile disappeared from her face.

"You need to mind your business!" Jazz said.

"You are so right," she said sarcastically.

Jazz and Fat Ronnie walked away smiling, brushing Seena off as an angry girlfriend.

Seena called Melody and told her exactl what happened.

"WHAT!?" Melody yelled. "Don't worry about it, we're on our way. Shut it down for now."

"We finished anyway," Seena revealed.

Melody was sitting in the living room of Ava and Kia's apartment along with Kia, Ava and Toni. "Listen up we're taking a road trip. Somebody call Regeane and tell her she's coming too."

"What's going on?" Ava asked.

"There are two guys in Baltimore that like to rob spots, they got us."

Melody looked at Ava. "Tell your people we need two of their guys to come with us. We leave in the morning."

Melody told John that he'd be running things for a few days. The next morning they were all on the train headed to Baltimore with three hundred bundles this time. They also had a bag filled with guns; catching a body or two wasn't a problem, 'cause at this point they all had at least one under their belt. Ava had everyone checked into separate rooms and rented three Cherokees in different colors for the entire week. Regeane was driving the blue one, Kia the black and Chad was in the white one with his brother Melvin. All of the Jeeps stopped at the same address and the doors opened concurrently with onlookers wondering who they all were, and what they were doing there.

As Regeane banged on the door Seena let them in. Rick was on the phone. "Hang up," Regeane demanded.

"It's my girl."

Melvin snatched the phone from his ear and hung it up for him. Rick didn't notice the other big guy standing in the corner of his living room. Melody walked over to Rick.

"Didn't I tell you if you ever saw me again that meant death?" Rick looked at Melody with a distraught face.

"I didn't come all this way to talk,"Toni said. She looked at Rick too, "Who are these motherfuckers that are giving us problems? Point them out!"

"It's Jazz and Fat Ronnie," Rick said.

"Why we sitting here, let's move on these assholes?"Ava suggested.

Jill put the bag of guns on the table, and they all chose their weapon of choice and headed for the Jeeps towards the park.

"There they are!" Seena said as she pointed at two guys standing next to a brown 740i BMW. Seena was riding with Ava, Regeane and Jill.

"Let me talk to them, if they act up kill them both!" Regeane said. She got out the Jeep and waited for the rest of them to set up around Jazz and Fat Ronnie.

"Hello fellas."

They both looked at Regeane, "Do we know you?"

"I don't think so," she said as she shook her head. "But I'm about to introduce myself. I'm here to resolve some shit, one way or another. We both have problems, but yours is much worse than mine. So let me tell you mine." Rage was sure to make eye contact. "You two assholes robbed my cousin yesterday for two thousand dollars."

Fat Ronnie laughed. Regeane did the same.

"So what!" Jazz spat.

Shaking her head Regeane cut her laugh short, "You don't even realize that your life is in my hands as we speak. Look over there to your right." Regeane pointed. "Do you see them two young ladies against the wall?"

Jazz and Ronnie looked at Ava and Melody as they pulled out two .45's with silencers, then looked back at Regeane. "Now look to your left," she said as a smile crept across her face. Kia and Jill were standing there with .9 mm Glock's out. "I'm not finished yet, you see those ladies over there with the shopping bags?"

Ronnie and Jazz noticed Seena, Missy and Toni revealing the top of their .9 mm Uzi's. Chad and Melvin pulled up in front of them and you could hear the sound of shot guns being cocked. "So see that's all your problems." She allowed them to take another look around. "Now we can easily resolve the issues; you two can either work for me, or go to the Rose garden. Oh and in case you're wondering what that is; it's dying here in the streets." Rage paused then continued, "As an employee I'm paying three thousand a week to look after my cousin." Ronnie looked at Jazz.

"Your time is running out," Regeane warned.

"You got it baby girl. What's your name?" Jazz asked.

"Put it like this; I just saved your life. Oh and my partner still wants her intrest." Regeane pointed to Seena who had the Uzi completely out of the bag. Regeane nodded her head and Ava walked over and passed both of them envelopes then walked away without a word.

"Now don't try anything we wouldn't want to put your sweet family in the Roses garden; the ones who live on Main Street in that blue house."

They both looked at her shocked! "Starting tomorrow you two will be keeping the wolves away from my sheep. Do we have an agreement?"

They nodded, "Yes."

They all walked off as Sheena made her way over to them, "You two act up and I'm coming for my intrest," she said with a smile fixed on her face.

Jazz looked over at his brother. "Did you see that shit? They could've killed us."

"What do you want to do about it?"

"What are we going to do?" Jazz asked animated. "SHIT! We gon' get this money for watching over that bitch ass nigga Rick! Ronnie tore into his envelope to find thirty crisp hundred dollar bills. "Those bitches ain't playing." Jazz opened his envelope noticing the same.

MY BROTHER'S KEEPER

Back in New York John was fucking up, getting high, not taking care of business and not getting Mike or Kenny their packages on time. He was too busy acting like he was the man, talking slick to Kenny and his workers, Had the customers getting all mad. He gave away about ten bundles with Kenny looking at him like he was crazy.

Kenny hopped in his Denali and headed to Rucker's. Mellow was standing in the parking lot talking to two light skin females with curls in their hair. Kenny blew his horn; Mellow looked up and told him to wait as he exchanged numbers with the shortest one.

"What's up? Why your ass ain't holding the block down?" he asked as he jumped in the truck.

"John high off that shit, he don't wanna give us the work; that nigga giving it away." Mellow started laughing, "Fuck it let Melody deal with it."

K-B and Uni were standing on 122nd Street and 2nd Avenue when a black 325i BMW with tinted windows came flying around the corner. Two guys jumped out dressed in masks carrying AK 47 machine guns blasting at them. Uni pulled out his .44 bulldog pistol, and then started blasting back. The sound from the .44 bulldog made people run for cover as far as two blocks away. The car pulled off with only one of the attackers, the other lay dead in the middle of the street. Uni turned to find K-B to see why he wasn't blasting back. He noticed K-B laying on 2nd Avenue bleeding from two holes in his neck. Uni bent down to place his fingers over the holes and realized that his best friend was dead and his eyes were wide opened. Uni kissed his man on his bloody cheek and ran toward Wagner projects with his gun still out.

When the Roses got home Melody called Mike, he told her the shit that John was doing since they'd been gone, and mentioned that the police had found Ice's body on the FDR and his hands taped to his mother's door. One of his brother's bodies was found on the Westside headless and the other brother was nailed to a tree in Central Park West.

"Now the police asking people questions about me, and the City Food Crew."

"Don't worry about it, I got the best lawyer money can buy. Just keep your head up, we'll talk tonight."

"John cost us over two hundred thousand dollars, now he's getting high again?" Toni looked at Melody. "Fix that problem before it gets out of hand."

"Don't talk to me like that!"

"So handle it!" Ava yelled.

Melody looked over at Regeane and Kia who were also nodding their heads in agreement.

"Melody we don't have any room for mistakes," Kia said. "Go have a talk with him. The next time we'll have to handle it the right way."

Melody looked around the room no one had an inkling of a smile, "Ok, I'll handle it!"

Toni looked over at her, "He gets a pass on you, the next time he'll stop moving for good."

Melody didn't like what she was hearing, but at the same time she knew what they meant.

Ava's phone rang.

"No names," the voice instructed." Right away Ava knew who was speaking. "Listen there's been a lot of talk being kicked around here about the all of the shootings, and murders in the last two months. My captain said it's coming from a crew who call themselves, City Food, with some guy name Mike Brown as the leader. The drugs ain't so much the issue; it's these bodies popping up all over with missing limbs that has my captain, the commissioner and the mayor going bizerk! This is getting out of hand."

Ava listened. "I don't know anything about it, but I'll keep my ears open thanks for the information."

"What's wrong now?" Melody asked.

"The police may be looking for Mike."

"I already know."

"So what are we going to do?" Kia asked.

"Shit shut it down," Toni said. "We don't need that heat, fuck it let's Debo another block some place else."

Kia laughed, "Shit where this time Brooklyn, the Bronx? I hear in South Jamaica Queens they getting a lot of money out there. We still got six kilos of pure dope left. What's that about four million a piece, coming to us?" Melody started thinking about Mike, she knew she had to get him out of Harlem and as soon as possible. As his soon to be wife she knew her duty was to protect him by any means!

Jill got home and the first thing she noticed was that K-B wasn't home. He's at some gold digging bitch house, she thought. She removed the clip from the AP .9 mm and took a shower and made herself some microwave popcorn. As she lifted the remote the phone rang.

"Hello," it was Uni.

"K-B's not home," Jill said.

"Jill I know," he said seriously. "I got some bad news."

Jill sensed his glum tone, "Uni NO! Tell me that my brother is okay!"

"Jill he's not, the Bull Crew brought us a move yesterday." Jill began crying.

A tear fell from Uni eye as well, "I'm on my way to get you, don't leave your apartment for any reason until you hear from me!"

Jill dropped the phone and screamed out crying. K-B always protected her from any and everything regardless if she was wrong or right. Now she was all alone in this cold ass world, no mother, and an unknown father. She packed a bag grabbing all of the photos she and K-B were in together. She ripped open the black leather couch, it was their secret safe. She counted and there was three hundred and eighty hundred thousand dollars. K-B's room safe contained ninety thousand, he was known to trick off with bitches. Underneath his bed she found two, M-1 machine guns, she checked the clips before walking back into the living room. She loaded her two Coach duffel bags with the money, pictures and clothes. She held the M-1 in her hand mentally preparing for anyone that looked at her strange.

In less than an hour Uni called and told her to come downstairs. First she opened up all the Vodka, a total of two cases and poured it all over their beds, the rugs, and couches and walked in the kitchen and turned the stove up high. She placed her bags in the hall as she lit a book of matches and tossed it on the rug. The fire shot across the room as she locked the door.

When Jill got to the lobby Uni was standing there with his gun out; Jerry, Burt, and Paul were standing with him. "I got a car waiting for us." Jill passed K-B's money over to Jerry and Paul. "This is ninety thousand dollars for you two, kill Jake and his family, it's from K-B." Jill passed the money to Jerry. He refused. "I'm doing this for free, don't you worry about it 'cause he would've done it for us."

"OH SHIT! Look someone's apartment is on fire." Jerry yelled. They all looked up. "Uni let's go," Jill said.

Once in the car Uni spoke, "We're going to the Bronx for a few days then we're going to head to Philly."

"WHAT?" Jill shook her head, "I'm not going anywhere until Dino's dead, I know where his girl lives and that's good enough."

"Where?" Uni asked.

"Johnson or Taft projects." The cab pulled up in front of Uni's apartment in the Bronx on Valentine Avenue. Once inside Jill noticed that his apartment was hooked up.

"Uni as soon as I kill Dino then I'll go to Philly with you."

"You don't have to do that."

Jill grabbed his arm, "I'm not going to be satisfied until I pump those bullets into his head."

"Don't you think you taking a bad chance doing that?"

"That's the chance I got to take."

Uni exhaled noisily, "We'll go out later on my motorcycle and see if we can find him."

Jill walked into the kitchen to call Ava to tell her about K-B. "When I get back from Philly, I'll pay ya'll the money back."

"Don't worry about it," Ava assured.

"If you want you can put some new workers out there."

"We'll pass for now, we got some other problems, but I'll be in touch," Jill said.

"Remember if you need anything you know we're just call away, you know you're family."

"Thank you Ava."

Later that night Jill was on the back of Uni's 1110 Yamaha Motorcycle carrying K-B's M-1 underneath her Baby Phat windbreaker. They rode around Johnson and Taft projects up 115th Street, down 112th Street. Uni even rode up in the projects. They were riding on 3rd Avenue and Madison Avenue when Jill noticed a 430 Mercedes with buggie eyes. Jill pulled on the back of Uni's shirt.

"That's it right there," she pointed. Uni nodded and followed behind the car slowly. Uni could tell that it was a woman sitting in the front seat; he was still unable to see the face. The Mercedes pulled into a parking space and Uni stopped two cars away. Jill unhooked her Machine gun and cocked it at the driver side door. Dino stepped out Uni rode up slowly Jill jumped off with the M-1 pointed at him as she pulled the trigger and hit Dino seventeen times! He fell back into the driver's seat. Jill walked closer up on him side of the car and then pointed inside the car and continued shooting, cutting his body in half. She aimed her weapon at the screaming female. She paused as she raised her helmet and allowed her eyes to meet the girl's. That's when she noticed it was Joanne who was screaming and looking scared! "So you 'ont know Dino, huh Joanne?" Tears escaped Joanne's eyes as Jill backed up. "Consider this your lucky day and consider me your guardian angel. This one is on me Joanne,"

Jill said as she jumped on the waiting motorcycle. Uni rode up 115th Street towards the Westside.

Joanne looked at her boyfriend's body that was cut in half. She cried for him then said a silent prayer, thanking God for sparing her life.

Kia and Toni went to St. Lukes to pick up Marilyn; it was the first time that Kia had seen Marilyn since that night of the shootout at the club. Toni was pushing her out in a wheelchair.

"DAMN! Girl you look like you've been smoking crack."

"Toni that's all you have to say to me? What happened to I missed you Marilyn or as long as you're alive that's all that counts?"

"Until you're better, you're staying with me at my new place," Kia said.

"You got three hundred fifty thousand put up so far," Toni revealed.

"Shit I get paid for being in the hospital? Take me back upstairs!" They all laughed. Kia pressed the alarm, and Toni opened the back door. "Who truck?"

"Mines," Kia sang."

"OH SHIT," Marilyn screeched. "The rims are still spinning."

"What you know about that shit? I had to order them, there Sprewells' 22 inch Chrome Rims."

"What kind of truck is this?"

"A Ford Excursion, it's the biggest truck on the streets."

"Kia your ass always got to outdo the rest! I'm not mad at you, do your thing. Hell, you only live once." Marilyn said with a wide smile on her face, "I'm buying me a white

Range Rover 4.6 HSE with gold tints, those same rims and a 25 disc CD changer."

"Slow down you can't even stand yet," Toni replied.

"I can't get inside," Marilyn said looking around.

"Don't sweat it," Kia said as she pulled out a stool so Marilyn could step up.

When Kia pulled up in front boxes still lay in her driveway.

"DAMN!" Marilyn said as she looked out the window, "This house is nice!"

Kia smiled, "Thanks, I just got it. And I got a maid, so just lay up until you get yourself together. We can even have for some male strippers to come by and keep you entertained."

"Nah, I'll pass on the strippers, but I can use a hard dick up in me right about now."

"You got to get that yourself."

Ava and Regeane were in the living room when her cell vibrated; at first she didn't even look at it as she listen to Regeane explain how it was time for them to expand their operation to other cities. "We should start moving south, our best spots are getting shut down."

"I agree, but we need to find a more peaceful approach," Ava said as her cell vibrated again. She held up one finger, "Hold on let me get this. Hello?"

"Hey Boo, one of my coworkers picked up a guy that I recognize from your block."

"What's his name?"

"John Cruz."

"What about him?"

"He was caught pissing in the streets."

"So," Ava laughed.

"The problem is that he was carrying three ounces of uncut dope."

Shit wasn't funny anymore, "WHAT!?"Ava's voice caused Regeane to look over at her. "Are you sure about this?"

"I don't play games, the DEA talked to him and he's willing to talk for no jail time."

"Now he's talking, I got to go!" Ava slammed the phone down!

"What's wrong Ava?" she stood and walked towards the window. "Ava what's wrong?"

"John!" Ava snapped!

"What about him?"

"He got picked up today for pissing on the streets."

Rage waived her hand, "Girl that's nothing!"

Ava turned and faced her, "He was carrying three ounces of uncut dope on him. Now the DEA has him and he's willing to talk for no jail time."

Regeane's eyes nearly popped out of her head, "What do you want to do? We could kill him ourselves without Melody finding out."

"No this is how we'll handle it, we'll all have a meeting and if Melody refuses to handle it." Ava turned from the window facing Regeane, "We'll kill both of them."

"You know Kia ain't going for that!"

"And I'm not going to jail for some dope fiend motherfucker either!"

Regeane nodded. "What I want to know is what in the hell was he doing with three ounces in the first place?"

Ava hated to have to call Melody at work with this information. Melody had made it crystal that street business was not to be conducted on her business line; no exceptions!

Melody had been working long hours and attending seminars every other night determined to get her website off the ground. She was also battling other small companies looking for assistance from the bigger companies. She seemed to be picking up business day by day.

Melody's secretary connected Ava to her and Melody knew that this was important.

"We need to have a meeting ASAP!"

"I'll be there after work."

Melody rented a store front in the Bronx. She had a total of ten workers; five of them were students with her from her evening computer classes. They all wanted control, but she was the only one with money and the ideas. HI-SURF specialized in mail orders, restaurants, club locations and online ordering for whatever anyone could possibly need. Her personal adage became 'if she didn't have it, she'd personally get it.' HI-SURF also helped create website for other companies at better rates than what the competition offered. Melody sat back in her chair and looked around. Before her eyes her dreams were flourishing and the last thing she wanted was to see them end. She didn't need any more problems from the streets. Melody buzzed her secretary to inform her that she'd be leaving early. She picked up her light suede jacket that matched her shoes perfectly then checked for her car keys and headed for the door.

When Melody knocked on Ava's door, Kia let her in.

"What's up girl?" Melody smiled at her, she noticed she didn't smile back. She took a seat next to Regeane none of them said a word and it was obvious that there was tension between them. "What's going on?" Everyone was staring at Melody.

Ava started, "John was picked up today."

"For what?"

"It was told to me that he was pissing in the streets."

"That's nothing."

"I said the same thing until I found out he was carrying three ounces of uncut dope on him, and we all want to know where he got it, and what were his intentions, but that's not all. The DEA has him in custody and he's agreed to talk to for no jail time."

"WHAT!?" Melody yelled as she looked at Kia, Regeane and then Toni. Melody put her head in her hands and started to cry. She knew that this was the final step with John. Her eyes met Ava's, "Where did you get this information from?"

"The police on our payroll."

Melody stood up and looked at her best friend. "It's your call; if one goes down we all go down as one. So we got to keep it tight."

Melody's mind was racing; she knew what was on their minds. Besides it was the only way to keep the Roses happy or from flipping on her. This wouldn't have been a problem if it had been a stranger, anyone but her brother. *DAMN, John!* She thought. "I need some air!" She yelled out, "I'm going to the roof for awhile."

"None of us approved of him in the first place, he's weak for that shit," Toni said.

"I'll deal with it!" Melody said as she opened the door. She turned to look at the Roses. "Please don't say a word to him." She knew that if she didn't deal with him Regeane and the rest of the Roses would.

The next day Melody called a meeting with her Lawyers, Stock Advisors, and Accountants. She wanted to look over all the dealings since day one of starting HI-SURF. Melody didn't trust any of them, she assumed that they thought because she was young and from the ghetto that she was dumb and easy to manipulate. She didn't allow them to play her when it came to her money in the streets and she wasn't allowing it here. That was the reason she had lawyers watching lawyers to insure she wouldn't go broke; it's a dog-eat-dog world. Melody had a will drawn up; if anything were to happen her mother and Mike would get equal halfs of everything she owned. Melody signed all of the forms; afterwards she sat in her black leather chair with thoughts of John. The fact that she knew she'd have to kill her only brother disturbed her. She flipped open her cell phone and dialed Kia and asked for her help.

"I really don't want you to do this, just send his ass to Puerto Rico with your mother, I'll help you cover," Kia assured.

"No! Kia he might be a problem for us somewhere down the line. Believe me, I hate the fact that it has to be done, but it's the only way that I'm going to be able to sleep at night."

Melody called Mike and told him that she'd be home late. Since the police have been looking for him Melody bought a house in New Jersey and they were living out there as a couple. Mike kept a low profile and was staying in the house. His days now consisted of playing video games, making sure the help was doing the jobs he and Melody paid them for, fucking the shit out of Melody whenever she came home and he'd even taken a new interest in learning more about computers and the business Melody was in.

Melody took a very deep breath before she dialed John's number.

"What's up Melody?"

"I have to talk to you about something, meet me on the stoop at 8 tonight."

She made two other phone calls, one to a car rental place. She reserved two cars under an alias, both cars had tinted windows; the other call was to her mother to tell her she loved her. In a bizarre way she felt as if the Roses might snake her, and try killing her also, but she was prepared for either one of them if they tried her.

Kia, John and Regeane were standing on the stoop talking when Melody pulled up driving a brown Civic. Melody called out John's name.

"I got to go," he said as he headed towards the car.

Melody gave Kia their customary wink, Regeane noticed it.

"What's that about?"

Kia just looked at her without saying a word.

John was feeling uneasy wondering had Melody knew anything about him being arrested with the three ounces of dope. She turned on the highway heading towards Red Lobster in Queens.

"Where are we going?"

"To get something to eat," she knew that she had to change the conversation quickly. They began talking about their mother. For it to be a Friday night Red Lobster was empty. She had John order for the both of them while she checked some notes. They dined on king crab legs, with clams on the side and talked for about an hour about this and that. Her cell vibrated, before she answered it she looked at John.

"Is everything alright?" Melody asked her brother. Her plan was simple; if he told her the truth she'd give him the one way plane ticket she had in her purse so he could go to Puerto Rico, for good.

"Everything is fine, why?" Melody's heart sank as she looked in her brother's eyes. *This ungrateful motherfucker*, she thought. This time when her cell vibrated she answered it said a few words and hung up.

"Is everything alright?" John asked feeling that he'd upset her.

"No, it's not John!"

"What is it?"

"Nothing it's late, I'll deal with it." John paid for their food. Melody was walking in front of him she turned to face him. "You know what, our lives changed a lot since the money started coming in. I think you should go and live with Mommy for good."

"Hell No!" he yelled out.

Melody nodded her head then continued into the dark parking lot, "Okay," she spoke softly as a tear escaped her eye.

When they got in the car, Melody asked John to pass her the Maxwell CD inside of the car door. When he turned his back to reach for the CD she moved the .25 automatic equipped with a silencer from the drivers seat. She pulled the trigger twice both bullets entered the back of his head causing an explosion all over the passenger side window. She looked at his body; he was still moving, she shoved the barrel into his rib cage and released four more rapid shots. It only took a few moments for the realization to hit Melody, she reached over the seat and grabbed the towel she'd placed inside of it earlier wiping the inside out. She took a final look at her brother slumped Kennedy style with his brains oozing on the front seat. She reached out to grab his cell phone off of his pants. Then like a ton of bricks it hit her; she'd just killed her only brother!

When Melody got out of the car Kia pulled up next to her.

Melody's face was cupped in her hands, "Kia, that wasn't easy for me." She confessed, "He was my brother, my only brother! I know that he was a fuck up, but damn, what the hell am I going to tell my mother? *Mommy, I just killed John because my friends said that he was going to tell them*?" Melody just shook her head as she continued crying.

"Why didn't you just give him the ticket?"

"Kia he lied to me!" She yelled. "I tried to give him a chance to come straight with me, but he didn't." They drove the rest of the way in silence. For the remainder of the night Melody was hurt by the choices she'd made hours ago. The streets made her a rich young lady, but at the same time they'd turned her into a cold hearted killer.

Regeane and Ava were trying to locate Melody for the last four days. She hadn't returned anyone's phone calls. Whenever one of them would call she'd instructed her secretary to take messages.

Melody was upset with the Roses, and felt they hadn't given her any option on her brothers life, and all because Ava claimed he was about to talk. Her mind was running rampant, and she wanted revenge for John's death. Killing a cop would surely be going too far, but Ava, she would suffice. Melody wondered if Regeane would've killed her brother that night, or if Kia would kill Ava if she ever fucked up, or what about Toni and Marilyn. How could she possibly explain any of this to her mother?

"Miss Cruz," her secretary buzzed her.

"I don't want to be disturbed at all!"

"Yes Miss Cruz."

Melody picked up the phone and started dialing her mother's number to relay the bad news. When Melody used Spanish to speak, her mother knew that something was terribly wrong.

"¿Cuál es incorrecto?" (What's wrong?)

Melody took a deep breath then told her mother the bad news. Mrs. Cruz and Melody both started yelling, screaming and crying. Mrs. Cruz crying 'cause her son was dead, Melody crying because she was the one who did it. She hated when her mother was upset.

"¿Quién lo hizo?" (Who did it?)

Wasn't no way in hell she could ever tell her mother the truth, she hated lying, but there was no choice. God, please forgive me for my sins, she prayed.

"I don't know. I'm trying to find out." If only Mrs. Cruz had known her son's killer and her daughter were one in the same..., they talked for about an hour.

I'd give all of this back, just to have John, Melody thought. The longer she thought the more she realized that someone would have to pay for this. She opened her desk drawer and started scrolling through John's phone numbers. One name stood out, Kevin; he was a childhood friend of John's. He'd killed a man for slapping him, and the courts had given him ten years. She pressed the key to dial his number. A man with a deep voice answered after two rings.

"Hello?"

"Kevin? It's me Melody, John's little sister."

Kevin smiled, "Oh shit, what's up Boo?"

"Just chilling."

"What's up with John?"

"John's dead."

"WHAT!?"

"He got himself into something that he couldn't handle. On top of that he lied to the only people who could've saved his life. Listen I called because I need to talk to you."

"About what?"

About you, me and life. It's worth it, trust me."

"When do you want to talk?"

"Tonight 8 p.m. on 4th Street and Avenue D."

"Alright, I'll be there."

Melody looked at the clock on the wall it was 5:35, which gave her the time she needed. Melody had decided she was going to pay big money to have Ava and her police officer friend Pam killed. She opened her wall safe and counted one hundred thousand dollars, her next stop was to see Raymond about two ounces of dope that she would give to Kevin in order to insure to push Ava and the police officers shit back the way she did her brothers. "An eye for an eye," she said aloud as she opened her cell and dialed Ava's.

"Where have you been?"

"Oh, I guess you forgot I have a business to run, and a man who is running from the law."

"Even still you have an obligation to the Roses, or are you getting too big for yourself?"

"I don't work for you!" Melody snapped. "Since when do I have to report to your ass?"

"Melody please don't get it twisted! You're still apart of this thing, so what you says counts, that's the only reason I was checkin' for you at all!" Ava snapped back.

Bitch you're going to get yours real soon, Melody thought.

"We're having a meeting tonight, and you must be there."

Melody hung up the phone without saying anything else. She called Raymond to let him know what she was coming after work.

"You got it boss lady, I got something to show you too," Raymond announced excidetly.

"Fuck all that, just have the shit ready for me!" Melody yelled. She got up from the desk, checked for her keys, placed the money inside of her Fendi bag, and picked up her .45 and cocked it before sliding it inside of her pocket. As Melody walked to her 2000 blue Nissan 350, she knew that she no longer needed the Roses; she had over 5 million dollars in cash, her computer business serviced over half a million people now, and was starting to be gain respect with the large companies looking to do business with her. *Let me walk away a winner while I can, before some shit happens* she silently prayed. She wasn't that same little girl in the piss smelling hallways; she had a big house in New Jersey! DAMN, at only 19 years old she still had a whole life ahead of her. That made her smile.

Melody's first stop was Raymond's house, he answered the door and the first thing she noticed were ten women butt ass naked sitting around a large pile of powder, and clear bags. Raymond directed her towards the room.

"This is for you," he said as he passed her a small pile of white powder inside of a brown bag. "I haven't seen John, what's up with him?"

"He's dead." She rudely replied.

"What happened?" he asked compassionately.

"He fucked himself that's all you need to know, understand?"

Raymond shook his head affirmatively. Melody reshuffled the gun in front of the dope she placed in her pocket.

As she got back in her car she turned left at 124th Street heading towards the FDR Drive driving south towards the lower Eastside. On 4th Street and Avenue D she turned left and Kevin was standing on the corner with two other guys talking. She blew the horn three times when he looked up she was waving at him.

"Melody," he looked around the car, "That's you? Get out so we can talk."

"No, get it, it's important."

He looked in her face; she didn't look like the same little girl he remembered. He got in and Melody sped off about five blocks and then pulled over.

"John told me if anything ever happened to him I could come and talk to you."

"About what?"

"John got himself in some shit I couldn't help him with because he lied." She sighed "It's a long story." She looked at him, "Let's get to my reason for being here tonight. Do you want to make a hundred thousand dollars and two ounces of pure dope?"

Kevin folded his arms then sat back looking at her amazed, "How do you want the Mayor of New York killed?"

"No, not the mayor, but it is a police officer is on the bill. It's two people, both are women."

Kevin looked at her harder, "Is this business or personal?"

A smiled lined her face, "Both."

"They both police?"

"Just the white one."

He took a deep breath, "When do you want this done?"

"I'll let you know when they'll be together. Tomorrow I'll bring you pictures of both of them. I'm paying you now, but if you try and fuck me I'll kill you, your family and your crew." She reached inside her Coach bag and placed the money and dope on his lap. "Now you listen to me, keep your phone on at all times because you'll never know when I'll call."

Kevin smiled, "I'm only a phone call away."

While heading Uptown to her meeting with the Roses Melody thought about Kia, and how if it were ever discovered that she ordered a hit that they would probably end up killing one another.

She knocked and Regeane answered the door. Toni, Kia and Ava were watching *The streets is watching*, on DVD.

"What's up girl, how are things going at HI-SURF?"

"Just working hard to get this company off the ground."

Toni pressed the still button on the remote. "Let me fill you in since you haven't been around in sometime. Jill's brother was killed on the Eastside, she's in Philly cooling out. The Eastside is shut down for now. Kenny got some people in Washington D.C. that he wants to pump *Flash Dance* with him. With two of our spots down it's time to make moves into other cities on the East Coast, fuck New York for now!"

"I'm with you on that," Regeane said.

"What about *Flash Dance* up here, who's going to run it while Kenny's in Washington?" Melody inquired.

"We can let Mellow run things. He's been down since day one." On the low Regeane liked Mellow and took every opportunity she could to say his name.

"So that's a done deal," Toni concluded as she pressed the button so the movie could continue.

"We all need to count two shopping bags of money," Regeane added.

The entire time Melody didn't say a word to Ava. She knew that she needed to get a picture of her and that Kia had one in her room of all of them in Club Cheater's, that was the picture she wanted and knew that Kia would gladly give her a copy.

Five hours and 1.9 million dollars later, and all of their hands were covered in grime. They divided the money equally into six.

"I'm collecting Marilyn's share," Toni reminded them.

"How is she coming along?" Melody asked.

"She's driving me up the wall," Kia laughed. "But, nah she's good company and she's getting better."

Melody sat in a daze, thoughts of her business, brother, and the 1.9 she'd just counted flooded her mind. She was feeling uneasy being around and thinking about how Ava hadn't said anything to her even though she had no intentions on speaking to her either. Melody made eye contact with Ava, *bitch you won't be on this earth too much longer*, she thought.

"Melody let me holla at you," Kia said as she started towards her old bedroom. She put her arm around Melody's neck. "I'm sorry about what happened to John, he was like my big brother too." She sighed, "I know you hurt 'cause I'm hurt too."

"If you had to kill Ava would you?"

"I would have to, I was the one that wanted her to be apart of this thing. If she fucked up, yes I'd kill her. She wouldn't just be hurting me, she'd hurt you, Toni and Regeane. Melody you know what we're here for, to get your company off the ground and bounce that's it. I've listen to your dreams of owning your own company since we were little girls sitting in these very same hallways. I would kill anyone who tried to interfere with you living out your dreams."

"I called my mother this morning and told her about John, she cried the whole time on the phone. I'm shipping his body to Puerto Rico tomorrow. I'm not happy and it's time for me to fall back for awhile, I got too much to lose and nothing to gain fucking with this street shit, it's over for me Kia."

"Listen, do what you want as long as I'm around you'll still get your piece of the pie."

"Really Kia, I don't want it. When my mother asked me why he was killed and who killed him, I couldn't even think straight. I've never lied to my mother before about nothing until this drug shit came into our lives. It was one lie now it's about a hundred and one of them. How can I tell my mother that her only daughter, killed her only son because a police officer told Ava that he was about to tell on me? How could I Kia?" Melody paused. Kia remained silent. She felt her friend's pain. "She don't even know what I'm into and if she found out its drugs she'd drop dead on the spot. Me and Mike are flying out tomorrow. When I come back its over; I can't do this shit nomore Kia!" Melody cried and Kia hugged her bestfriend. Ava, Regeane and Toni were in the livingroom laughing at a repeat of *Martin*.

The next morning Mike and Melody were on the plane to Puerto Rico along with John's body. Melody didn't want to look her mother in the eyes and be forced to lie in her face so she'd arranged to only stay there a few days. She had the Roses under the impression that she'd be gone two weeks. That was enough time to plot; she wanted Ava out of the picture as soon as humanly possible!

Mike wanted to ask Melody questions surrounding John's death. Deep down in his heart, he knew she was apart of it, even worse he feared that she had actually done it. He could also tell that she was in enough pain; he didn't want to add insult to injury by asking her about it. He let his thoughts rest as he kissed her forehead and sat back enjoying the flight.

Melody's only thoughts on the flight were of Ava and her friend, Pam. She wondered when would they meet and where would it be so Kevin could hurry up and kill both of them at one time. Her only concern was that they both die for killing John. Although she clearly pulled the trigger; she totally blamed Pam and Ava for John's death.

Melody arranged a small wake in memory of John. The only people in attendance were her, Mike, and her mom. The entire time Mrs. Cruz cried out, "Mi hijo, Mi hijo!" (My son, My son).

Melody knew she had to go she couldn't stand to answer any questions her mother may have.

"I need you to stay with ma until I call for you, there are a few things I need to take care of," Melody told Mike.

He pulled her to the side, "When will this all be over?"

"What are you talking about?"

Mike shook his head as he walked over and hugged Mrs. Cruz. Mike drove Melody to the airport without uttering a word. Melody sensed that he knew she was behind John's demise.

The next day Melody went to see Kevin and gave him Ava's picture.

"Is this the police?"

"No, but they will both be together. I'll tell you when and where."

"That dope you gave me is the bomb, can you get some more?"

"No," she shook her head. "That's it." Rain started to pour out of the sky. The lower Eastside was a dope haven and she knew that he could make a ton of money, but she was there for one reason and one reason only. Melody gave Kevin strict orders, not to pull the trigger until she gave the final word. Because she was keeping a low profile she only spent a half day at the office, the entire time she kept envisioning her mother yelling out "Mi hijo, Mi hijo!"

The New Year was approaching and Melody couldn't find out any of Ava's movements. She was getting impatient, but she had to play it cool. Other than wanting her plans to work out perfect she knew she had a host of other reason why she needed to remain cool. One thing that kept Melody alert and on point at all times were the Roses; she knew she couldn't go up against all of them at one time and win. She seemed to be especially bothered by Regeane; Big Rage didn't seem to mind killing these days. Then Toni; she was sneaky, with connections to killers. And what about

Kia, her best friend in the whole world; if she were to ever find out, it would break her heart to have to go up against her. Melody couldn't forget Ice Eyes, a stone cold killer that happened to be Ava's road dawg.

Melody sat back in her plush leather chair while rotating the marbels in her hands. She closed her eyes and took a deep long breath. Shit was getting crazy! She needed to make a move, fast!

It was December 31, 2001 11:47 p.m. Ava, Kia, Regeane, Toni and Melody had money all over the living room floor. *Flash Dance* sold over three hundred thousand dollars worth of dope in the past three days. Missy drove in from Baltimore twice that week, with two hundred thousand or better each trip. Regeane pulled out five bottles of Moët for them to bring in the New Year. Melody thought about her unopened mail inside of her Coach bag. It was an invitation from Dell Computers for a dinner party, for a thousand dollar a person, on January 8th. Melody jumped up from her seat yelling out, "That's right HI-SURF, is making noise in the computer world."

Toni stopped what she was doing and looked at Melody, "Melody, what the hell are you talking about? Over there going crazy!"

Melody passed the invitations, Toni looked it over, "It's for five people; can I go?"

"We're all going!" Melody sang, still very enthused. She started feeling good, she'd never been invited to something so important in her life.

"I can't go!" Ava announced, "That's the night I have to pay the lawyer, the police and our manpower."

BINGO! And there it was; the night that Ava would be heading towards the pearly gates, Melody mused.

"When you finish you can meet up with us," Regeane offered.

"Where is it?"

"The Lincoln Center," Melody said precisely as Kia jumped up yelling out "HAPPY NEW YEARS!" They all toasted and hugged one another.

Regeane stood up, "We did it! We got all the money we need, plus plenty more money to make. 2002 is going to be a good year for all of us." She looked over at Melody. "I wish you the best of luck on your dreams, and if you need our help, we're here for you babygirl!"

"Thank you," Melody said as she looked at them. "As long as I'm on this earth none of you ever have to worry about anything."

Kia had a smile on her face,"We feel the same way towards you, Boo."

Seena and Missy were making tons of money now. The competition didn't understand how they had Ronnie and Jazz holding them down. For the last four months Baltimore was hit, and they had made a killing. The lines to cop their dope were sometimes two blocks long. At times it looked as if they were handing out rent vouchers.

It was January 2nd, check day the snow was coming down, but it didn't interfere with the dope fiends coming to cure that morning sickness. Jo-Jo was standing on the opposite side of the street watching how Rick and his two workers served the customers.

"The only reason, I won't send the crew over there," Jo-Jo stopped talking to take a look at his crew, "Is on the strength of Ronnie and Jazz. Rick just don't know how my cuz is saving his life."

Jo-Jo's worker Lowe spoke up, "Why don't you have one of them New York bitches killed, I guarantee ya do that and the other one would run!"

Jo-Jo pulled Lowe by his shirt, "There are rules in Baltimore, no women and no children, you understand? If anyone gotta get it its gon' be Ronnie or Jazz, I don't care if they are my cousins, but I won't allow ya'll to touch no woman or kid, understand?"

Lowe shook his head affirmatively, but he had other plans, if Jo-Jo wouldn't do it then he would. *They making too much money over there* Lowe thought to himself, *they have to be getting about two hundred thousand in a weeks time.* He mentally added it up; that was more than three times what they were making! Nah, he couldn't just let this go.

Missy was driving to New York every four days with two hundred thousand dollars at a time in the trunk of her 2000 brand new black Infinity Q45. Since she and Seena relocated to Baltimore they were subleasing a mini mansion with four bedrooms, two and half bathrooms and it was on the outside of Baltimore. Not even Rick, Ronnie or Jazz knew about the place. Seena brought herself a 1999 blue Saab 9000 S, things were looking real good for them.

Once Missy got to New York, her first stop was to see Ava. Ava informed her about Jill relocating to Philly with Uni. Missy wasn't worried; she knew that Uni would take care of her.

"Let me get back to Baltimore before the fiends get sick," she and Ava laughed. Missy packed the bundles in her Coach backpack. She turned down 124th Street driving towards the Eastside, her old stumping grounds. She pulled up on 122nd Street and 2nd Avenue; it looked like a different block, no dope fiends, no dope sellers, just kids playing in the streets that she once controlled. "DAMN! That was just months ago," she turned up her Alicia Keys CD and headed to Baltimore.

Once back in Baltimore Missy filled Seena in about Jill's move to Philly waiting for the heat to cool down on her. It was only right since Uni was K-B's partner that he looked after Jill.

"Why didn't she come down here with us?" Seena asked.

Missy hunched her shoulders, "I don't know. But I'm tired as fuck. I'm 'bout to go home."

"Okay, I'll handle everything."

Seena and Jazz walked Missy to her car. Jazz noticed Lowe sitting in the driver seat of a black BMW 740i with three other guys looking towards them.

"We got haters plotting on us," Seena said out loud. Missy and Jazz looked across the street towards the parked BMW. Jazz opened his coat flashing his .44 bulldog pistol. Seena and Missy had their .380 automatics cocked and ready to fire.

Lowe rolled down his window, Jazz gripped his gun.

"We cool," Lowe yelled. "There is no beef with you over here!"

"I hope so," Jazz yelled back. Missy got in her car, Jazz instructed her to drive around the block first before heading home and to keep her gun in reach. Missy zoomed by blasting *Can I live*, by Jay Z and Jazz just stood there in the cold watching Lowe and his boys.

THE BIG HIT

Melody told Kia to hurry up; they also had to wait for Regeane since she moved to Strivers Road. It was one of the quietest blocks in Harlem, where only the upper middle class and rich could afford to live. Toni had moved in the Valley, it's the middle class section of the Bronx. Melody sat on the couch watching as Ava wrapped rubber bands around large stacks of money.

"Ava, what time do you think you'll be finished?"

"To tell you the truth, I really don't know."

"Well we'll still be waiting for you."

Ava grabbed a long white cashmere coat. Melody knew that distinctive coat wouldn't be hard to miss, she got up from the couch and walked in the kitchen to call Kevin to tell him what she was wearing and to catch her on 123rd Street and 7th Avenue.

"Don't pull that trigger until I give you the ok," she reminded him.

"I got you!" They hung up.

Toni and Regeane walked in together, Kia came out of the bathroom with the house phone attached to her ear.

"Can we please go?" Melody asked.

It was 6:35 when a black Lexus limousine pulled up in front of them.

"DAMN, girl we going in class!" Regeane said.

A white female chauffeur stepped out of the car to rush over and open the door for the Roses. Mellow and the Flash Dance Crew stood across the street watching as they got in. When they pulled up in front of The Lincoln Center, lights were everywhere. The valet opened the door for them; Melody exited the car first followed by Kia, Regeane and then Toni.

There were a series of personal stretch limousines; Mercedes, Rolls Royce's and Lincolns'. Important men were wearing three and four thousand dollar suits, women were wearing the most expensive gowns and dresses in season.

Kia pulled Melody by the arm, "I am so impressed, I feel like a movie star!"

Melody smiled as they all walked towards the front door looking like young high power investors instead of the enterprising street dealers they were. Melody passed her invitation to the doorman.

"Please follow me, Ladies."

Toni glanced around noticing celebrities, The Mayor of New York and other big wigs all looking to steal new ideas. The waiter helped each of them with their chairs.

"What are you Ladies having?"

"Champagne, please," Melody said.

Over two thousand people were in attendance at the Lincoln Center. Melody recognized some from magazines. A man with gray hair walked on the stage. Melody knew precisely who he was, Mr. Royal, HI-SURF's lawyer. They all settled down to listen as he began to speak. Kia, Regeane and Toni didn't understand what the hell they were talking about, every few moments Melody courteously explained. None of it mattered to Kia, she was just happy to be there with Melody and she knew that all of the Roses felt the same way. Melody's phone started to ring, she picked up without looking at the caller id.

"Melody, it's me, I'm at the Mickey Mantle Restaurant in Midtown. The two ladies are together right in front of me, is it a go?"

Melody looked over at Kia whose attention was focused on the stage. She looked at Regeane who was sipping her champagne and then she noticed Toni, who was listening to her.

"Melody, Melody!?" Kevin yelled.

"Hold on!" she told him.

Toni exhaled, "I'll be glad when Ava gets here." Regeane nodded. At that moment Melody knew she possessed the power to take Ava's life, but could she live knowing that she'd been responsible.

"MELODY!?" Kevin yelled into the phone again, "What's up!?"

Melody closed her eyes then shook her head.

"Are you okay?" Kia asked as she opened her eyes.

"No!" she said. "Forget it, back the hell away!" she yelled."

"I can't hear you; your phone's breaking up." She looked up at the stage; a computer robot was knocking out her frequency. Melody continued yelling out, "BACK AWAY!" She was scared ass hell. Kia, Regeane and Toni looked at her quizzically. "What's wrong?" Regeane asked.

"Can you heat me?" Melody kept repeating. All she got was a buzzing sound. She got up from the table walking fast towards the hall. "Hello, can you hear me now?"

"What's up with your phone?" Kevin asked slightly agitated.

"Don't do it, forget about it!"

"Are you sure, because my people are lined up?"

"Forget it, keep the money." Melody hung up the phone. She prayed to God that Kevin didn't take matters in his own hands. If he did she would have to kill him herself, after all he was the only link to her.

Melody turned and ran right into Toni.

"What are you up too?"

"Nothing," Melody assured her, sweat covering her brow.

Toni locked eyes with Melody, "Melody don't underestimate me, I'm not some dumb white bitch. From your reactions you're up to no good. I've been around a lot of things, and that phone call sounds a lot like a hit that you have planned to me." Toni looked around, "And besides Marilyn the only other person that's not here is Ava."

"What the fuck are you talking about?" Melody asked defensively.

"You're still upset about John, but you pulled the trigger, we didn't." Toni stepped closer to Melody, "Now Ava better show up tonight, and if she doesn't then you'll be joining her." Toni took a deep breath, "If I've said something wrong I'll apologize now, but remember my bloodline, I come from a long line of killers."

"Are you threatening me, Toni?" Melody asked in a defending way.

Toni shook her head. "No, I'm not. But if I thought someone was plotting something against you, I'd be giving them this same speech, and I hope that you'd do the same for me."

"Toni you got me wrong, I wouldn't hurt any of the Roses."

"I hope not. We'll keep this conversation between us, but you better pray to God that Ava shows up here tonight; safe and sound, she better not even have a scratch."

They both walked to their table. "Where did you two go?" Kia asked.

"There were some important people standing outside I wanted to meet," Toni told them. About a half an hour later Ava waltzed inside behind the doorman. He helped Ava with her coat, pulling the empty seat away from the table.

"DAMN, I finally made it! I done rode all around New York giving people my money, Melody fill me in so I can make some investments." Toni looked at Melody. Melody looked away then started filling Ava in on what she had missed. The remainder of the night went well. The Roses all invested money in different computer companies. Kia wrapped her arms around Melody's neck, "My girls' getting all the money she need from me, fuck the rest of those other companies."

Seena and Missy counted up the money to pay the Roses.

"I hate driving to New York," Missy said.

"You got court this week, right?"

"Yeah," she answered Seena. "The weather is fucked up, it's snowing, plus the highway is gon' be a mess, and I gotta drive in this shit!" Missy shook her head.

Seena pointed at her, "I told you to buy some snow tires for your car. But look at it this way; at leaset you killing two birds with one stone. You going to see Ava and you going to court. Imagine if you had to do all that shit on different days."

Missy sighed, "Come on let's get this shit over with. Are you ready to go?"

"Yeah, come on."

On the way to Rick's house, Seena was telling Missy how things around Baltimore are different from New York. Missy pulled up in front of Rick's house, Ronnie was walking out.

"What's up Ladies? I'm going to Wendy's, ya'll want something?" Fat Ronnie asked while rubbing his belly.

"No," they said in unison.

When they walked inside Jazz and Rick were talking about the football game this weekend, Jets vs. Ravens. Missy joined in conversation. She bet Jazz three hundred dollars that the Jets win by three points. After about an hour of bullshiting Seena looked at her watch, "Missy I think you should be hitting on the road now. You know they said the snow s'pose to get heavier later."

Missy looked at the clock on the wall, "You're right about that. I'll call you when I touch down." She looked at Jazz, "Make sure you have my money when I get back too!"

Jazz laughed, "You the one that's gon' be paying, you want me to thank you now or later for them three bills?"

"Whatever," Missy waived her hand.

Seena walked her to the car. "If it wasn't for court, I wouldn't even be going to New York right about now. I'll be happier than a kid in candyland when this shit is over with! Fo'real!"

"I know girl. Right now you just gotta do what you gotta do. Don't even trip."

Seena kissed Missy on the cheek and watched her drive off. Missy checked her CD rack and pulled out DMX's *The Greatest Depressions*, she liked hard core rap music. She was the outlaw when it came to her Seena and Jill. Missy turned towards the highway and didn't notice the blue van following her since she left Rick's. She was about to turn on to the highway when the car in front of her immediately slammed on the brakes causing the car and van to box her in. The first thing that entered her mind was a stick up! She tried pressing the gas, but the car in front of her was too heavy to move, on top of that all the snow on the ground only allowed her tires to spin instead of move. Missy reached for her gun and remembered that she didn't drive with it while transporting drugs and money. She checked her rearview mirror; three guys wearing black masks covering their faces jumped out with machine guns in hand. By the time she realized what was going on it was too late! She opened the door to run and bullets ripped through her flesh.

"I'm sending you back to New York in a body bag bitch, and your sisters' next!"

Lowe wasn't content with twenty-one shots that had already ripped through her body. He ran up closer then stepped on her stomach and chest. He pressed his shot gun directly on Missy's face and pulled the trigger then watched as her head exploded!

Seena was making herself a cup of coffee the next morning and turned on the television. Her daily ritual, she usually made Missy watch with her, telling her that because they weren't from Baltimore didn't mean that they shouldn't know what's going on. The top story; *An unknown Black woman was shot and killed on Baltimore's highway last night.* Seena looked up and saw the car in the background was just like Missy's car. She walked closer to the television. *A total of* *two hundred thousand dollars was recovered in the car, at this time there are no witnesses, and the police are uncertain if this is a drug deal gone bad.*

Seena ran out the house and down to the corner store to grab a Baltimore Chronicle. Missy's story was located on the second page. Seena started to cry she knew that it was Missy. She paid for the paper with tears in her eyes.

"Are you okay?" the man behind the counter asked.

"NO!" she yelled out. Seena didn't care what the people in the store thought about her; the only thing going through her mind was her dear friend.

Once back inside she sat on the couch wondering who would want Missy dead. She knew that it wasn't Jazz or Ronnie; they were both with her all night. Then she thought about Jo-Jo and his crew. Since they've been in Baltimore, Jo-Jo had been hurting and money wasn't coming in like it use to. They had a few words, but nothing to kill her for. She heard stories about people being killed for smaller things than that though. Her mind drifted to the Fun City Crew, everyone knew that they were killers for hire, but they had always shown them love. They had even inquired about cleaning work, and they told them to holla at them. Then what about the Roses and their money Missy was transporting? Seena's mind had run wild. "DAMN!" she yelled out loud. If the Roses money had to be recovered she could do that but it would set her back. She dialed the Roses. Regeane answered. Seena explained as much as she could to her.

"Don't even worry about the money; that can be replaced unlike a friend's life. Make the arrangements so we can get her body back to New York."

"Thank you Regeane."

"Don't worry about it."

Seena drove to Rick's. When she walked in Jazz and Rick were in the kitchen counting money.

"I'm glad to see you," Rick said. "I was about to call you when we finished. Seena obviously wasn't paying him any attention.

"What's wrong?" Jazz asked.

Tears slowly fell from her eyes," Missy was killed last night on the freeway."

"WHAT!?"

"Rick looked at her, "Where did you get that from?"

"The morning news."

Jazz got up from the table, he put his .357 Magnum inside his pants," I'll be right back!"

Jazz walked across the street to where Jo-Jo was standing with his baby mama Tanya.

"Let me holla at you Cuz."

"What's up Jazz?"

"In private," Jo-Jo walked out to him, leaving his babymother stading all alone.

"What do you know about the girl that was killed last night?"

"What the fuck you talking about?"

"One of my people was killed last night!"

"So you think I had something to do with it?"

"You tell me?"

"You know the rules in Baltimore," they looked at one another and repeated them together, "No women, and no children."

"Cuz, before I have a woman killed I would've killed Rick, and the only reason his ass ain't dead is cause of you and Ronnie."

"Jo-Jo, you wouldn't lie to me would you?" Jo-Jo looked at Jazz, and repeated, "No women, no children." They were both staring one another in the eyes, like a Mexican standoff.

"Jo-Jo we family, me and Ronnie never crossed any lines with you. So don't do it to us."

Lowe walked up, "What's up Jazz?"

"You really think I had something to do with it?" Jo-Jo asked still stunned.

"I hope not!" Jazz said as he walked back across the street.

Lowe looked at him, "What was that about?"

"One of those New York chicken head bitches was killed last night." Lowe started laughing.

"What's so fucking funny?" Jo-Jo asked through clenched teeth.

Lowe shook his head, "Why the fuck do you care, you don't know her."

"You right about that, but Jazz think I had something to do with it."

Lowe knew if Jo-Jo found out that it was him who'd set that up that his life was in danger, he didn't worry because the people that helped him were from Delaware.

Jazz walked into Rick's house, Seena was on the phone.

"Let me call you back," she sobbed as she noticed Jazz walk through the door. Jazz told them that Jo-Jo didn't know about Missy being killed until he told him.

"Do you believe him?" Rick asked.

"I don't know, but the streets are always watching and listening, trust me it will come out.

Over the last three weeks Uni had been trying to convince Jill to open up shop in Philly, finally she agreed with him. Jill made a call to Ava telling her about her plans, hoping she would agree with her.

"It's good money down here. The dope their selling is weak, they couldn't win against us. I think all it would take is a month before I'm controlling this city of course with the help of the Black Star Crew."

"Who's that?"

"They technically run the city of Philly."

"I will never tell you how to get some money, but you're from out of town, so be smart and keep your eyes and ears open. When can I expect you in New York, and how much you want?"

"I'll be there tomorrow at 4 p.m. for three hundred bundles, just to try out."

Ava told her about Missy's murder on the freeway, and gave her the information about the funeral.

"Thank you Ava for looking out for us." Jill managed to get out between sobs.

"Don't worry about that, we'll see you tomorrow."

Jill was sitting by the window crying when Uni walked out the bathroom.

"Why you crying?"

"Missy was killed on a freeway in Baltimore."

"Damn, that's a fucked up way to die! Do they know who did it?"

"They didn't say."

Uni sat next to her. "Listen Jill, in this business anything can happen and bullets don't have names on 'em. People get killed everyday, it could be you, me, anybody Jill you have to understand that when you dealing with the streets, you never know if you gon' make it home. Always be prepared to kill or be killed, that's why I keep my gun on ready just in case I get company.

"Uni how do I know your homeboys won't flip on us when the money start rolling in?"

"They won't trust me, I grew up with them."

"I hope so, because I won't hesitate one second to kill anyone that's in my way, including you!" Jill stared Uni right in the eyes as she wrapped her arms around his neck, "Don't cross me, we're all we got."

YOU'RE BEING WATCHED; FED TIME

Toni and Regeane pulled up on the Avenue with their new BMW's. They parked behind Marilyn's spankin' new Range which was directly behind Kia's Excursion. When the ladies exited their rides Mellow waved to them from across the street.

"Yo, Mannie look, they are really getting money fo' real! Those Beamers are straight off the showcase floor."

"Hell yeah!" Mannie agreed.

On the other side of the street a black van was parked with three Federal Agents taking pictures of the Flash Dance Crew. The agents had been taking pictures almost a week now; they had Mannie and Mellow's real names, addresses and cell numbers. Primarily they were there to target the Flash Dance Crew, Operation Snatch Them, Mellow was their lead man in the investigation, they had inside information about him being the allege boss over the crew. They had watched Mellow go into 2010 West 123rd Street at least three times a day, with bags of money returning with drugs. The building he went inside was equipped with a metal door and they weren't clear on which apartment he was entering, nor did they know who the supplier was. It was imperative that they found out, they had calculated the spot on a daily was bringing in $80-90 thousand in a single day.

Pam called Ava, "Just listen and don't use any names, the FBI are investigating someone in the neighborhood, so watch yourselves."

"Do you think it's us?"

"We both know how they work, so you'll never know until the handcuffs are on."

"Well keep me posted. Let's do dinner your next off day then we can talk some more."

"I'll call you," Pam assured then hung up.

When Ava hung up the phone she rubbed her legs. Kia could tell something was wrong by her movements, she knew her sister. Ava went in her bedroom to see how much dope was left, she counted four uncut kilos. It's time to move this shit fast, she thought. Once back in the living room Kia questioned her, "What's wrong?" She stood in the middle of the room looking around, and kept checking for her gun.

"Bitch, what the fuck is wrong with you?"

"The FBI is in the neighborhood investigating somebody."

"Who told you that shit?" Marilyn asked.

"I just got off the phone with my friend."

"The cop?" Kia asked.

"Yeah."

Regeane and Toni knocked on the door as Ava finished talking.

"We just bought us two brand new BMW's!" They both yelled.

"Ya'll done what?" Ava rushed to the window to see the pair of vehicles with the bill of sale papers still in the windows. She laughed while shaking her head in disbelief, "Tell me that ya'll didn't pay cash?" she asked as she made her way over to the couch next to Marilyn.

"Yeah why?"

"Have ya'll lost your fucking minds? The IRS will be investigating your asses about that damn money!"

"The car dealer said that he would take care of all the paperwork. We paid him an extra fifteen thousand for that." Regeane said.

Ava still just shook her head disapproving of the choices they all made when spending money. After being in the banking industry, she knew how ugly things could get. She stood back up and looked at them. "From now on don't park any of your cars in front of this building," she said before walking to the window pointing out. "There is more than $200,000 worth of cars sitting in front of this piece of shit building, and not one you have a job." She looked back at them. "I'm not going to jail because all of you want to ride around in these high priced vehicles. Move your trucks from around here!"

They all looked at her like she was crazy.

"Who the fuck do you think you're giving orders to?" Kia asked.

"The four of you, "she pointed.

"The only person to pass out orders is the boss," Kia snapped. Ava looked at Kia with evil eyes and then towards the rest of them.

"Ya'll think this shit is a game, when the judge starts passing out 20-30 years because of the money that we're getting, all the money in the world won't save our asses. So please don't park the cars around here anymore!"

"Okay Ava, we understand." Marilyn said.

"Let's go," Toni said.

The FEDS were still watching Mellow and his crew filling up rolls of film. Marilyn, Kia, Toni and Regeane simultaneously walked out of the building together, laughing at Ava and her paranoia. Mellow walked across the street holding a conversation with them. The female agent alerted the other agents.

"What do we have here?"

"It looks like we may have found some bigger fish in the pond, get some pictures of all of them together," Agent Brooks said.

Agent Brooks was in charge of the field team.

"Stop taking pictures for a minute; let's see if those cars belong to them, there's what about a quarter of a million dollars sitting over there? We need to find an entryway; we need to get surveillance from the inside."

"I have an idea," the female agent said. "Why not have the phone companies interrupt the phone lines for a day or two?"

"Good idea," the other agents said.

"That way we'll find out what apartment we're looking for."

After Mellow was finished talking with them, he walked back across the street and all of the ladies got into their trucks and pulled off.

"Jackpot people! Now we know that it's an all female crew that is running the show," Agent Brooks said. Mellow walked back to the building with a bag in his hand, he pressed an unknown button and some unknown person buzzed him up. Ten minutes later he returned carrying a smaller bag. Agent Brooks called the phone company and had them shut off the phone lines at 2010 West 123rd Street.

Ava was on the phone with Seena telling her about the FEDS when suddenly the phone went dead. "What the fuck?" She threw the phone down and picked up her Nextel. She dialed the phone company to inquire about her phone.

"We're sorry for the inconvenience Ms. Wilson; we can have a technician out as early as tomorrow."

"So that's the earliest?"

"Yes, again I apologize for the delay."

Ava sighed, "Thank you," she hung up.

Dominican Power

Harlem was beginning to resemble a dead zone. On Broadway bodies were popping up everywhere. The word on the streets was theirs a million dollar reward for any kind of information about the three Dominican's robbed and killed on Convent Avenue.

Over the last six months, more than one hundred and ten homicides had been reported. The 33rd precinct didn't have any views on what the hell was going on, or what was the reason behind so many deaths in the streets. Twenty million dollars in dope was missing with a street value of sixty million, now everybody wanted it. Every block between 135th to 225th Street on Broadway became so hot with police that the cocaine business was hurting bad. No one dared to go on Broadway to purchase anything, unless they were looking to be robbed, jailed or worse murdered.

On the other side of the world in the Dominican Republic, the owner of the missing shipment of dope didn't care how many people lost their lives; all he wanted was his dope back.

"Mr. Ruiz you have a phone call from the states," his maid told him.

It was Keke, Mr. Ruiz's top cocaine dealer in New York. Keke had been employed by Mr. Ruiz since he was 16 years old. His control included 139th Street all the way to 170th Street, with the help of his people; AWDC, short for A Wild Dominican Crew that sell cocaine and contract killers.

"Good day, Mr. Ruiz."

"Same to you."

"Your product isn't on Broadway or anywhere around here. I personally shook all the dope connections up here."

"I don't care keep looking!"

"I think I may know where it's being sold at."

"Where?"

"The black side of Harlem, that's why it's taking so long to locate."

Everybody knew Dominican's didn't go past St. Nicholas Avenue in Harlem.

"So Keke, you're telling me that some niggers robbed me for twenty million dollars!?"

"I'm not sure yet."

"When the hell are you going to give me some information?"

"They've been selling dope down there for the last 50 years; it may take some time to locate."

"I don't care about who, what, or why just get my fucking dope! Keke I'm sending a tester to the states tomorrow on my private jet, there will also be something for you."

Mr. Ruiz turned to his under boss, Orlando. "Pack some bags you're going to New York to help locate my dope!"

Is this the end? Check for

UNFALLEN ROSES II: *Get 'em Girlz*

The follow up to Unfallen Roses: Petals and Thorns

ALSO AVAILABLE BY EBANDTE INC. PUBLISHING:

THE HOOD
A story by Danté "Te-Shoota" Clarke
Written by Ebony Stroman

THE GAME CHOSE ME
by Ebony Stroman

COMING SOON...

STREET GLOREE
by Lataica L. Thompson

CREATION OF A GANGSTER
by Danté "Te-Shoota" Clarke

UNFALLEN ROSES II: Get 'em Girlz
by Anthony Walker

KARMA
by Saheed Apanda

THE HOOD II: THE END OF THE STORY
by Danté "Te-Shoota" Clarke & Ebony Stroman

THE GAME CHOSE ME: REMIX
by Ebony Stroman

"A BOOK BY EBANDTE GOTTA BE GOOD!"

A SNEAK PREVIEW OF

STREET GLOREE

A NOVEL BY LATAICA L. THOMPSON
COMING SOON... VERY SOON!!!

"Where the fuck is this nigga in my car!?" wondered Kyla as she paced the floor of her three bedroom house getting angry. The phones' ringing offered Kyla what she thought was an answer to her question. She would find out where Tye was and how long it would be before he made it home so she could get her car. Kyla hoped it was Tye, her man for the past six months. Instead it was Evony, the two were cousins who had grown up together and were very close, just like their mothers' who were sisters.

"Where you at hoe, its 4 o'clock and we gon' be rushing tryna find something to wear tonight! Whatchu doin', what's up?" asked Evony.

"I don't know whe...," Kyla stopped mid-sentence and cracked a smile, as the sound of Tye's key in the door brought with it the reality that her car was home.

Good! She thought rushing Evony off of the phone and heading out the door without saying a word to Tye.

Kyla was well informed of Tye's reputation. He was known to spoil a woman rotten and then dump them. So she decided to milk this cow for everything she could. She knew all too well what it was like to have a man leave you with nothing. It wasn't a mystery to her that Tye could and would at any time lose interest and put another hoe in her place. Shit, she had taken someone's place. So while she was there she would play the role; the devoted and loving girlfriend. She would be known as more than just somebody who Tye fucked for a few months and then thrown into the pile with all of the others. She shopped until she dropped at his expense. She had a big ass house she only lived in because of him and his money, a car that was in his name only and more money than she could ever spend in his safe. She was set for life or so she thought.

Kyla used everything she had to get into Tye's heart; head, pussy everything! She was determined to make him love her enough to make her his wife. Tye had a heart of steel one no-one had ever been able to get into and she knew it would be hell to try and soften it, but she was devoted to trying. She knew the hood was laughing behind her back, but fucks what the 'hood said; she wasn't going anywhere! She was his woman and unlike the others she was here to stay. But inside she was feeling just like the 'hood; that her days were almost over and she was next to get kicked to the curb so she decided to enjoy it while she could, no matter how short lived she felt she deserved to live like a princess.

It was on Jamaica Avenue after getting her nails done that Kyla stepped out onto the pavement and her life was changed forever. Just as she emerged from the salon so did Tye and his little brother Nate from the barbershop, The Hut. Kyla stood talking on her cell, but she and Tye couldn't take their eyes off of each other. Every time he looked at her she smiled, every time she looked back he smiled just as hard as she did. Tye couldn't do anything less than be amazed at how beautiful Kyla was. She was 5'4" with legs that rivaled Tina Turner's, had the smoothest chocolate skin, long luxurious hair that hung so perfect you'd never know it was a weave. She had dark brown slanted eyes and lips so full you'd swear she was a female version of L.L. Cool J. And Miss Thang had a body that would make Beyoncé look like she was on

274

crack. Without a doubt, Kyla had grown into a lovely woman, especially growing up in an era where dark skinned women were considered to be unattractive.

At the time Kyla met Tye she was with Gregory, another local dealer. He hustled down on Sutphin Boulevard and 121st Ave. He wasn't *The Man* or anything 'cause he clearly didn't run shit but he made moves for the niggas who did. He was the nigga in the 'hood who did whatever, whenever, wherever. He cooked the drugs, bagged 'em and he even went hand to hand if he felt he couldn't trust a little nigga to do it. He never trusted anyone to do anything. He felt if something was gonna get fucked up and he was gon' get blamed for it then he might as well make the mistake himself.

Living life with two drug addicts, Kyla saw the worst of Forty. She saw her aunt and her mother go through so much bullshit behind crack. The offspring of two hot and horny teenagers, Kyla never stood a chance. She was destined to suffer. Growing up broke as hell on welfare struggling she vowed to one day leave this hellhole. Kyla hated everything about Forty Projects and planned daily on ways to get out and stay out.

It was at Farm Fried Chicken on Baisley Boulevard one October evening that she saw her way out. Gregory was at least 6'2", weighed 140lbs, and had cinnamon colored skin, perfect white teeth and oval grey eyes. He was gorgeous with three G's. He and Kyla made eye contact the moment he stepped in the chicken place. Kyla was with Evony, Quana and Nette. Gregory was in the chicken joint alone at first but was quickly joined by a local troublemaker the 'hood only referred to as LQ. He quickly caught Evony's eye who was in Queens visiting Kyla. Even though Evony had Mel at home she felt it didn't hurt to look as long as she never touched.

Kyla had Gregory's nose wide open and so turned out with her pussy that after only two months he moved her from Forty and in with him. Kyla was content with that. She went from starving to surviving. She had love for Gregory because he offered her a chance at a life she never thought she'd know. Greg kept Kyla in the finest of things. She wore all the best clothes, the best shoes and ate at all of the best restaurants she'd ever seen. Gregory showed Kyla life out of Forty and she loved every bit of it. No more did she worry about what she'd eat, where she'd sleep. Or anything like that. So even with all of his lies and cheating ways she bit her tongue and said nothing. She refused to go back to Forty just because of a little unfaithfulness on Greg's part. Kyla lived by one motto and one motto only; *I don't care about those other girls, just be good to me.* And good Greg was.

Besides that, Kyla didn't want to go back to living with two crackheads. It wasn't that she didn't love her mother but they never really had a real relationship. On top of that, Kyla couldn't understand *why the fuck she just wouldn't stop using that shit!* Evony felt the same way about her aunt and her mother. It was safe to say both girls had shaky relationships with their mothers. And Lord knows how embarrassed they were by these two crackheads! This explains why they distanced themselves. Things only changed for the worse when their grandmother, Cassandra moved to Charlotte, North Carolina. The only reason Cassandra left the apartment to her two crackhead daughters, Lynn and E'vett was to assure that Kyla and Evony would always have a place to stay. In that apartment is where their drug habit destroyed them and 'caused their daughters many years of grief. With no one else to rely on Kyla and Evony learned to turn to the men in their lives for basic needs such as food, clothing and eventually shelter.

Kyla knew Tye disposed of his women quickly, but feeling confident she would have him walked away from Gregory for a more comfortable life.

In her car on the way to Forty Kyla relived the day that her life changed six months ago. This was a record for a woman in Tye's life. No other woman was ever in his life for this long. Usually after a month or two he got another one. Tye changed women like he changed his drawers.

After scooping Evony, she and Kyla finally arrived at their destination. Kyla stepped out of the car and onto the pavement in her Fendi minidress. Dressed simply in Dior Capri's and a tank top, Evony looked amazing. Her 5'3" frame was only complimented by her very dark skin, full lips and lovely long legs which was a family trait inherited from their grandmother, micro braided shoulder length hair and a very ample ass. Stepping out of Kyla's LS-450, she threw shades over her almond shaped eyes, pulled her Dior handbag onto her shoulder and joined Kyla at the front of the whip.

Kyla and Evony were known to wear only the best. They were known to dazzle crowds with what they wore. Tonight would be no different, they would spend an even two hours trying to find a Prada minidress for Kyla and a close fitted Fendi mini for

Evony. Matching shoes and bags were a must for these divas. Never having much of anything growing up they decided when they grew up they'd never lack the fashions of the 'hood that they'd missed for so many years. Growing up outcasts had made them fashion conscious! Never again were they left out of the fashion trends, in fact they began to set them.

Mel was in no uncertain terms running his entire 'hood. He was *Dat Nigga* for real! He had all the cars, jewels, houses everything! Evony met Mel at the bar on Linden and Sutphin Boulevard. After three months of dating Evony got pregnant, she moved with him to Brooklyn and felt the baby guaranteed her a roof over her head.

Growing up the way they did each girl decided to never have children of their own. They didn't feel as if they had anything to offer a child, but Evony felt with Mel at her side she could do this!

On August 21st, 2001 Evony met the love of her life. E'monni Jadae Collins was born. She weighed 7lbs, 8ozs and was 18 inches long. She was destined to look just like her daddy, which made Evony very happy. Evony loved being a mother to E'monni and wouldn't trade it for the world.

Evony, Mel and E'monni lived the life. They both ran the streets but in two very different ways. He hustled she shopped, she shopped hard he made niggas hustle even harder.

Early one evening Evony's life would change forever. Leaving the house one night headed for the club Evony noticed a blue car sitting on the corner of Lorraine Avenue. Too busy worrying about reaching Nia, Mel's sister on the phone she didn't see the car following her. As she turned her car onto the expressway it became clear she was being followed. Fearing a robbery, Evony turned the car around and headed for home.

"Move nigga!" Evony heard the voice yell as she stepped into the home she and Mel shared.

"Open this shit up!" Evony knew exactly what was going on and headed for the phone. Just as she pressed the nine on her phone it was snatched from her hand.

"Nah bitch! Ain't no callin' no police!" Evony didn't need to see the face she knew the voice. It was Drae, Tre's little brother.

Tre was one of Mel's little soldiers, he modeled himself after Mel. He always followed Mel everywhere he went like a little puppy or something. Tre had done eight months on Rikers Island for smoking weed in a cab and punching the driver when he asked him to put it out or get out. Hell bent on getting even with Mel who he felt left him for dolo in jail; here he and his little brother were robbing his crib. He was now an enemy where before he was a friend, a good one. He made every move Mel made. Him being up under Mel always had Evony feeling just a little uneasy and now she knew why. His grimey ass was out solely for a hit. All along he was a foe in friends clothing.

"Where is my baby!?" Evony asked after hearing E'monni's cries.

"Dat little bitch aight!" Drae yelled from behind her.

"Yo here go da bitch man!" Evony turned to face him wanting to slap the taste out of his mouth for his two remarks, but chose against it after feeling the gun in her side.

"Bring dat bitch here!" Tre yelled as Drae pushed

Evony towards the room. He didn't really feel it was necessary to hurt the chick and the baby, but he knew he'd have to. Tre was dead set against loose ends.

E'monni's screams echoed through the entire place. Once in the bedroom Evony came face to face with Mel who was bleeding. Evony was scared and confused. *Why wasn't he fighting back, he was only hit in the leg,* wondered Evony. The sight of the loaded gun at the head of her daughter made it obvious.

By the end of the ordeal Evony had been pistol whipped, Mel had been shot again, this time in his arm. And both were trying frantically to reach E'monni. The poor child was on the other side of the room in a pool of her own blood. She had a single gunshot wound to her almost two year old chest.

On May 16th, 2003 E'monni's two day fight for life was over. She was pronounced dead at 7:04a.m. This hit Evony and Mel like a ton of bricks.

E'monni's funeral was the hardest thing Evony ever had to endure. Her mother and aunt both showed up at the funeral high as kites and dirty as dogs.

Damn, thought Evony *she can't even get clean for her granddaughters funeral.* She was completely embarrassed by both crackheads, which is something she was learning to expect from those two. It was Cassie, her grandmother and Kyla who helped her keep it all together. The reality of the situation had set in that she was alone. E'monni and Mel were both gone.

Cassandra suggested that Evony come home with her, but Evony was a New York City girl and it would kill her to move down south. That was just something she couldn't do, not right now anyway. *Maybe when the time is right for me to slow down and grow old, then I'll think about moving* is what Evony told her grandmother.

Mel was arrested the night before E'monni's funeral. He was wanted in connection to the slaughter and dismemberment of Tre and his little brother Drae. He had murdered them the same night E'monni lost her life. Removing limbs from each body he dropped them into a trash bag together and delivered the bag with a note to the front door of their mother which read: *Now you childless too bitch!*

Here it was several months later and Evony was back living in Queens. She was back in her grandmother's apartment with her mother and her aunt. Before long she'd lost every thing of value. She went back to sleeping with one eye open. She vowed to get the fuck out of Forty again, but this time to stay. She couldn't take being a victim anymore to the two crackheads who had taken over the apartment.

Mel had been sentenced to double life and insisted that Evony move on with her life. Evony refused to just walk away and tried to still be a part of his life, but with no calls and her letters being returned unopened she got the hint and let him be. Mel was to serve every day with no parole and gave no cares; as long as the two niggas who killed his baby paid with their life he was content! He had avenged his baby's murder and that's what he would live with for double life.

Evony couldn't help but notice how beautiful her cousin was. She had always lived her life in Kyla's shadow. They both grew up poor with terrible mothers and invisible fathers. Somehow it was Kyla who always excelled. They ran the 'hood together, hustled niggas together and was on they grind together, but Evony despised the fact that Kyla always ended up with the better Vic. For one reason or another that perplexed Evony deeply, she just couldn't understand why she couldn't command the respect from guys that Kyla did. Although both ladies were stunningly beautiful, it was Kyla who stood out. She even had a livelier presence; Kyla was very warm and easy to talk to. She was a friend's friend. If you had a good friend after one meeting with Kyla they would be a good friend of hers also.

Evony thought like the rest of the hood; that Kyla's days as Tye's woman were numbered and would soon end. Evony starred at Kyla as her thoughts started to drift, *here she is stunting in all of his shit!* "Damn, she really has no idea," mumbled Evony to herself.

But, then again, *what if Kyla's days with Tye weren't numbered*, Evony began to wonder. *She does seem to be the exception to his one or two month rule.* Evony as well as the rest of 'hood was well aware that somehow Kyla had Tye eating out of the palm of her hands, this made Evony, the 'hood and every woman before her yearn to know how she'd done it.

Kyla having Tye open really didn't shock Evony. Kyla had always been able to get every Vic in her life to trick major doe, Tye would be no different. Evony couldn't get half as much from the men in her life as Kyla did. Then Mel came along and answered all of her prayers and in a lot of ways Evony had begun to think she and Kyla were on the same level. Then, like snatching candy from a baby, the only good thing that she had was taken away from her. Where Kyla got paid, Evony could only get laid. Some of Evony's men even went as far as trying to get at Kyla while they were still with Evony. Evony envied the life Kyla lived, it had been hers just months ago and now she wanted it again! She was determined to get that life back. In Evony's eyes Kyla had it all; the doe, the whips, the jewels and the ballingest nigga in the 'hood wifing her!

Evony appreciated the fact that Kyla looked out for her after all she had gone through, but it wasn't enough. She was already tired of being Kyla's underdog and was preparing for another come up. Evony felt she deserved to live this life too! *Why did Kyla deserve to be the only one happy*, thought Evony as she followed Kyla into the Prada store, watching her every move.

Tonight was an exclusive Babyborn party and everybody and their mama would be there. Jamaica Avenue was jam packed with people finding outfits for the club. It was hard to tell that it was 7:30pm, near the Aves' closing time and people were steady racing in and out of stores looking for footwear, an outfit or both. This was one reason Ev & Kyla went to the city to cop something uniquely official. Most chose to come to the club in Jamaica Ave. wear and got mad when they saw their outfit in the club on different backs in different shapes and colors. But in Jamaica Queens, the Ave. was the epitome of shopping. Everybody found a reason to come to the Ave. Some came by choice mostly to shop or pay bills, while others were forced to come via work or visiting their Parole Officer.

Today, Kyla and Evony only made an appearance on the Ave. to get their hair and nails done for Babyborn's party at club Mercedes tonight. Kyla only bought clothes from the Ave. when she was single; now that she was with Tye her money was long so she'd go a long way to look good, shit, why not? He was paying for it.

Evony was starting to get bothered by all the guys stopping Kyla, but as soon as they had a friend for her she'd forget all about it. Kyla and Evony had met so many different men on this day that Kyla had no idea what Evony was so upset about. The only thing Evony seemed to want to talk about was finding a man. Kyla didn't understand this at all, especially since both of them had just met some real official dudes with some real official cash. Kyla told some of the men they met to come to the party tonight, but this wasn't really necessary since mostly everyone knew about the party already.

Evony couldn't believe what Kyla was doing! She as well as Kyla knew the club was going to be off the hook and that Tye would go crazy if he caught any of these men in her face. Kyla laughed it off when Evony brought it up.

A few hours later they left the Ave, all shopped out and full on pizza, nothing was better than a slice from the Ave. The girls ended their afternoon and prepared to begin their night. Evony, driving Kyla's whip pulled out of the parking space singing and laughing, "Ain't no party like a B-dubb party 'cause a B-dubb party don't stop!"

STREET GLOREE

IN STORES SUMMER 2006!!!

"A BOOK BY EBANDTE GOTTA BE GOOD!"

ABOUT *STREET GLOREE*

Meet Kyla, a 'hood Cinderella who's no stranger to hard times. This bombshell beauty goes from ashy to classy in just a matter of months! She's the envy of all girls, the desire of all men, the love of Tye's life and the root to all evil!

Next up is Evony; Kyla's hard-luck cousin who just can't seem to get it together. Although Evony is just as beautiful as Kyla, she can't seem to get out of her cousin's shadow. Where Evony glittered Kyla shined. Where Kyla got paid Evony could only get laid. Fed up and sick of being Kyla's flunky, Ev prepares for a come up that will not only change her life but the lives of everyone involved.

Finally we have Tye; the tall, sexy and rich hustler who inherited his mother's take-no-shit attitude, his father's trust-no-one mentality, and his little brother, Nate. The life Tye lives is no holds barred and bullshit free. He lives by one motto; *trust no one and suspect everyone.* Knee deep in the game, Tye finds himself the target of a hit with no idea who ordered it. With the love of Kyla, the devotion of his soldiers and the anger of his brother, Nate. Follow Tye as he sorts through the good and the bad of his motto, all to find out who wants what's his.

"Street Gloree is a tale of Love, Lies & Betrayal at its best! If there were ever a book where the characters grabbed and held your attention from start to finish, this is it!!!"

-Ebony Stroman Bestselling author of
THE GAME CHOSE ME

EBANDTE INC. PUBLISHING
P.O. BOX 341147
JAMAICA, NY 11434
646/421/1710

ORDER FORM

ALL TITLES ARE $14.00 EACH. PLEASE ADD $4.05 FOR SHIPPING & HANDLING VIA PRIORITY MAIL

AVAILABLE NOW!!!

QUANITY

THE HOOD-by Ebony Stroman & Dante "Te-Shoota" Clarke

THE GAME CHOSE ME-by Ebony Stroman

UNFALLEN ROSES: PETALS & THORNS-by Anthony Walker

PRE-ORDER *STREET GLOREE*-by Lataica L. Thompson TODAY!!!
This title will be available in the summer of 2006

BOOK TITLE: $14.00 + $4.05 S&H TOTAL = $18.05

*PLEASE NOTE: Ebandte Inc. Publishing deducts 25% off of the sale price for orders being shipped directly to **colleges** and **correctional facilities**. Cost are as follows:

BOOK TITLE: $10.50 + $4.05 S&H TOTAL = $14.55

MAKE ALL PAYMENTS TO EBANDTE INC. FORMS OF ACCEPTED PAYMENTS ARE MONEY ORDERS & INSTITUTIONAL CHECKS.

"A BOOK BY EBANDTE GOTTA BE GOOD!"